PRAISE FOR *SHELL*

'An ambitious coming-of-a-country's-age novel . . .
evocative, learned and moving.'
Sunday Times

'A luminous look at a city at a time of change, a time when the
building of the Sydney Opera House was a reach for greatness.'
New York Times

'A shimmering love letter to Sydney, with the husk of the emerging
Opera House its beating heart . . . Required reading.'
Australian Women's Weekly

'Olsson's writing is beautiful, captivating, and is
enough in itself to recommend this book . . .
Her descriptions are vivid, evocative.'
New York Journal of Books

'Destined to become a classic due to the exquisite imagery
of [Olsson's] prose. If the test of contemporary fiction is
whether a second reading delivers fresh layers of insight
and meaning, the answer here is an unequivocal yes.'
Sydney Morning Herald, Best Books of 2018

'Imaginative and lyrically descriptive,
it's a beautifully written book.'
Choice

'War, architecture, guilt, salvation, politics –
this book has a little bit of it all . . . A fascinating look
at Australia during the Vietnam War, the creation of the
Sydney Opera House, and the ever-present battle between
the violence of war and the beauty of art. Recommended.'
Historical Novel Society

'Kristina Olsson is such a graceful, wise and perceptive writer.
The woman's massive heart is one big literary taproot feeding
all of us answers about the Australian condition.'
Trent Dalton, bestselling author of
Boy Swallows Universe

Shell

Kristina Olsson

SCRIBNER

LONDON NEW YORK SYDNEY TORONTO NEW DELHI

First published in Australia by Scribner Australia,
an imprint of Simon & Schuster (Australia) Pty Ltd, 2018

First published in Great Britain by Scribner,
an imprint of Simon & Schuster UK Ltd, 2018
This paperback edition published by Scribner, an imprint of
Simon & Schuster UK Ltd, 2019
A CBS COMPANY

Copyright © Kristina Olsson, 2018

SCRIBNER and design are registered trademarks of The Gale Group, Inc.,
used under licence by Simon & Schuster Inc.

The right of Kristina Olsson to be identified as author of this work has been asserted
in accordance with the Copyright, Designs and Patents Act, 1988.

3 5 7 9 10 8 6 4 2

Simon & Schuster UK Ltd
1st Floor
222 Gray's Inn Road
London WC1X 8HB

Simon & Schuster Australia, Sydney
Simon & Schuster India, New Delhi

www.simonandschuster.co.uk
www.simonandschuster.com.au
www.simonandschuster.co.in

A CIP catalogue record for this book is available from the British Library

Paperback ISBN: 978-1-4711-7265-6
eBook ISBN: 978-1-4711-7264-9
eAudio ISBN: 978-1-4711-8165-8

Printed and bound by CPI Group (UK) Ltd, Croydon CR0 4YY

MIX
Paper from
responsible sources
FSC® C020471

For Sharon Olsson

and for

Jill Rowbotham

Sandra Hogan

Marg O'Donnell

Kay Smith

Jo Clifford

Contents

November 1960	1
Autumn 1965	3
May 1965	121
Winter 1965	151
July 1965	165
August 1965	231
Spring 1965	253
Summer, January 1966	349
February 1966	361
Author's Note	366
Acknowledgements	373

Ideas come to us as the successors of griefs, and griefs, at the moment they turn into ideas, lose some part of their power to injure the heart.

Marcel Proust, *In Search of Lost Time*

Sydney, November 1960

The day the great man sang, heat blazed in haloes over Bennelong Point. This is what Pearl will remember, later, this is what she will say: that his voice turned the air holy. Men, sweat-slicked, stood with bowed heads or hung off scaffolds, swatting at flies and tears. Few looked at the singer; they needed all their senses to hear. Needed their whole bodies, skin and eyes and hearts, to absorb what they couldn't say: that sacredness had returned to this place. It flowed through them on a single human voice, through their bodies and the building that was rising beneath their hands.

Pearl stood with the other journalists, and watched the men grow luminous. Wept as she understood: that it wasn't just the building or the place Robeson had sanctified, but the labour. The valour of it. The modest hearts of workers. In his songs, in the faces of the men, was every story she had ever tried to write. This one too. She closed her eyes as the voice trailed away. Words formed and crumbled in her head, insubstantial. She gripped her notebook and forgot to write them down.

Autumn 1965

She walked towards the quay in opalescent light. The city closed down, prosaic, the horizon grubby with clouds and promising nothing. It was like this sometimes: as if Sydney was within her, an idea she carried around, vaporous, unexamined. Until, on evenings like this, it revealed her to herself. She was hollowed out, impervious. As torpid as the streets.

Usually, the city was enough: a scoop of bridge as she rounded a corner, the harbour shattered by sunset. Her friends in the back bar of Lorenzo's talking of protest, of marches, the poetics of action. She loved these nights, the conversation and argument, the taste of insurrection. They made her brave. From the *Telegraph* building to Hunter Street she would be optimistic, glad. The fight rising in her at the door of the bar, the defiance she was born to.

But tonight the air was precarious. All sandstone shadow, smudgy. She thought that time was like this too, a spongy edge, imprecise, as close and as far as memory.

Shell

As her dead mother's face. The world had turned her a year older in summer. In four years, she might die. Her mother had died at 36; the calendar led Pearl towards it like a dirge badly played, like this vagrant shadow she moved through, that moved through her. As if she was porous, as if there was no substance to her at all.

She recognised it now. Fear, familiar as a friend, precise as a knife. Not of death; though for years it was what she expected: to suffer as her mother had. This might be worse, this prospect of slightness, of falling short. She'd felt its weight since she was fourteen – there would be two lives to live, the one she was given and the one her mother lost. As if loss could be recouped somehow, her family restored. As if she could save them.

⁓

Her day had begun as they always did: with the smell of newsprint and the faces of boys. There, among bold headings and columns of type, they waited: serious, smiling, patient. She ignored them at first, skimming headlines and leads. Turned pages on the potential in their eyes. But each day one, at least, that forced her hand. A frantic calculation: how old, what suburb? An ache in her, whatever the answer; her brothers were there, in every young man who passed in the street, stepped off the ferry, gazed out from a page of the *Telegraph*.

Today it was footballers. Pre-season training, so they still looked coltish and soft, a bunch of local lads mucking around in the park. One reached for a pass with a thief's intent; she'd leaned in until the photograph blurred, until the face was no longer Jamie's as he swiped the milk money, or Will's as he eyed the twins' toast.

Six years. With each one, her fear grew: they wouldn't know her. She wouldn't know them. Boys changed, grew jawbones and beards. Their eyes: had they sharpened with their faces and their sorrows? Had the small soft bodies she'd helped feed and wash grown hard against the memory of her? Or would they still hold her shape in new muscles in their arms and their legs, in the hands they'd once placed against her cheek at bedtime: *Sing to us Pearlie?* They'd been two and three when their mother died, adolescents when she'd seen them last. Now they were men. Or nearly. Who may not want to see her at all.

She stepped up her pace towards the harbour. That morning, as she closed the sports pages, her contact had called. The phone shrilling in the early quiet of the news-room. Her heart flapped in her chest; it could only be one

5

person, though he usually called at midday, when the newsroom rang with noise and adrenalin. But when she lifted the
phone his voice was no different: soft, subterranean, as if it
flowed over pebbles. *There's a bus at six-thirty.* One sentence,
the call over before it began. She held the receiver hard
against her ear. Sometimes he paused before he rang off,
and in that gap she could see him, hunched at his desk, lips
parted over what was unspoken. His pale bureaucrat's face
flushed with the euphoria of risk.

A current of anticipation bolted through her, but she
lowered the receiver slowly. As if his breath was contained
there, all he had to tell. *What have you got?* she wanted to say.
Is it the date, the time? But back in its cradle the receiver was
mute, the Bakelite dull and indifferent. So was the fashion
feature unfinished in her typewriter. She glanced at its plain
sentences, its tedious tone. Lifted her fingers to the keys.
A cigarette burned down beside her.

Now she crossed Pitt Street in a pulse of office workers,
the last of the light in her eyes. Turned up the hill to Macquarie
Street for the pleasure of old buildings, the Mint, Sydney
Hospital, Parliament. Then the library. Below her the new
ribs of the Opera House reached up, bleached bones against
the paling sky. The building failed to lift her tonight; it looked

like something broken, too difficult to fix. Perhaps, as some said, it would never be finished. Her father might be pleased; a monument to politicians, he'd said, peering at the sketches in the *Herald* years before. But Pearl had looked at the artists' impressions and even then felt her heart shift. Look carefully, Da, she'd said quietly. Maybe it's a monument to us. But like some in the newsroom – *mating turtles,* they laughed, *a collapsed circus tent* – he wouldn't be swayed.

At the top of Bent Street she looked left and right. Sat at the bus stop until her man appeared, tie loosed, hands in pockets as arranged. A middle-aged public servant, his countenance dulled by routine. Expressionless. She stood then; as he came up beside her she tilted her face to the sky. Even so she knew his lips barely moved as he spoke, pressing lightly over brief syllables. *Melbourne,* he said. *Next Wednesday. Tenth of March.*

He took out a handkerchief, wiped his face as if to clear some residue, a letter or noun that might betray him. Glanced at his wristwatch, then turned and walked away. Pearl watched him go. His suit ancient and loose, the pants shiny with wear. Chifley wore his suits until they were threadbare, her father once told her. People loved him for it, the old prime minister: his humility, his insistence on staying with them. Unlike the new one. In this way Patrick Keogh expressed his hatred for Menzies without having to say his name. It was like a code of honour, an act of resistance, this un-naming. So Pearl had learned her politics by inversion, always the positive rather than the negative, the heroic rather than the bastard. It gave her an optimism that couldn't survive her childhood. In that moment at the bus stop, she hated Menzies more viciously than her father had.

A bus appeared on the other side of the road. It snorted and swallowed him, the man in Chifley's suit. Pearl stood in the vacuum and watched the bus disappear. The date ticked dangerously in her head. *Tenth of March.* Just over a week. In eight days the first marbles would roll, the first ballot for conscripts for Vietnam. Menzies claimed otherwise, but they all knew: it was a lottery, a deadly one, and if you were twenty and had the right birthday, the right number on a marble, you'd win a free ride to the war.

Jamie was twenty. And might have the right birthday. And next year, so might Will.

~

The harbour was a spill of darkening water. She sat on the grass at the end of the quay and watched the sky absorb its own colour. Tried to catch the precise moment when daylight switched off. An old challenge, and she never won; tonight she turned her gaze from a lumbering ferry to find the city already faded, shrinking into shadow. When she thought of her brothers this was just as she saw them, their shapes retreating, faded to grey. Their faces refused to be fixed.

At seven she pushed herself up and walked to a phone box on George Street. Dialled a number inked onto her hand. Ray. Her closest ally in the group. An hour later, in the dim light of the back bar, she listened to him announce the ballot date as if the leak was his own, as if he'd conjured it, as if he'd worked the contact himself. A seam of quiet triumph in his speech. It had to be like this, she knew, to protect her and the contact, but she hated Ray for whole minutes, for the fidelity of his voice, the conviction in his eyes, how plausible he was. She looked to the ceiling, sickly yellow with smoke, and then to the floor. Closed her eyes against what would follow: the murmurs and barks of outrage, the calls for placards and protests. It felt suddenly predictable. Empty.

Voices rose and fell. Disembodied, they took on a menacing quality, as if they'd emerged from the rough darkness she'd walked through, the grubby streets. A dog's warning growl, a tubercular cough. Then Brian's unmistakable snarl: *For fuck's sake, what did you all think? That they'd cancel because*

9

we didn't like it? She opened her eyes, turned to look in his direction, watched him lunge at a beer jug and refill his glass. *We all knew it was coming,* he said, accusing the room. *Now it has.*

The air fell momentarily still. Then, as if at some signal, it became fraught, the voices charged with adrenalin. Usually Pearl's voice would be with them; instead she glanced to the door, longing to leave. Tonight she could not feel what they felt: the charge of energy beneath the anger, the excitement. It was paradoxical, and familiar – they would all say the draft was criminal, a bastard act, but in truth the news enlivened them, validated them. She'd felt something similar in the newsroom when reports of a disaster broke. A crackling intensity, almost erotic in its heat and rush. And a collective sense of purpose, of responsibility: to translate a world confirmed again as incoherent, random, impersonal.

She inched sideways, dipping her head, making herself small. Tonight nothing felt impersonal or random. For Pearl, the news had assumed human faces: Jamie's, Will's. Standing there, she'd realised. That's what they wanted, everyone here: the human faces of conscription. If her comrades learned about her brothers, knew their names, they'd fall upon them as surely as a journalist would. The movement needed emblems. Examples. Real men, not numbers; flesh and blood.

But they didn't know about them. And wouldn't. The decision hardened in her: Jamie and Will would not be used. She was surprised by the strength of her own conviction. No one would know, not here, not at work. She had a sudden image of Henry at the news desk. Sleeves pushed up, eyes narrowed to a looming deadline. She would not tell him about the boys, and she would not give him the leaked ballot date. The decision sat heavy in her stomach, but there were old scores to settle. She looked away to the back wall now, as if her thoughts were traitorous and might be visible, might be read.

The temperature in the room had turned feverish. Plans were made, tasks allocated. She had to go before her face or her silence betrayed her. She skirted the discussions and made for the door. As she reached the back hallway a voice followed her, male, drunk: *Another leak, Lois Lane.* A cough or a laugh, she wasn't sure. *Baby, you keep screwing Superman.*

She was almost ready for him. Without turning she said calmly: *Keep screwing yourself.* But the coward was gone.

⌒

She stood at the rail of the ferry, pulled her hair into a band against the wind. Gulls shrieked in their wake: *too late, too late.* To one side of her a young man pressed a transistor to his ear and a woman slipped a foot from her shoe. Brian's words rang in her head: *Did you think they'd cancel because we didn't like it?* Yes, she'd wanted to say. Yes. A part of me thought it couldn't happen. But the gulls kept crying the truth: she'd known for months that it would, they'd all known. In the years since her mother's death she'd found a mechanism for forgetting, a lever that turned her blood cool. She felt it in her body: it switched one Pearl off and another on, a girl without history or conscience. A girl unencumbered, trying life on for size. But in three words, *Tenth of March,* her history had spoken back.

Darkness thickened as they passed Bennelong Point. In starlight the new structure was a strange oceanic creature mantling the land. Each head turned to it, a gravitational pull. *God help us,* said the man next to her. But now Pearl could see how its new curves pulled at the water. She'd heard the first thing Utzon had done, before he thought about design, before he began to draw, was to consult the sea charts for Sydney Harbour. It made sudden sense: the building was marine more than earthly. From this angle, in this light, it was not a structure but an eruption from the sea. An act of nature rather than man, a disturbance. She stared at its massive base, a plinth for a sculpture or a ceremony, and thought about surfaces, the familiar faces of earth and water, what lay beneath. About the architect's way of seeing.

The ferry moved them on. Mrs Macquarie's Chair, the finger wharves of Woolloomooloo. Garden Island. She counted them off, a prayer over worry beads, as the boat arced towards Manly. Then turned to see the last of the Harbour Bridge. As a child she'd thought some kind of magic resided there; that as her ferry slipped beneath the exact midpoint of the arching steel and concrete, she was at the fulcrum of a great mystery. In that very moment, caught, frozen, she might be altered. Might become *steely*. The grinning face of Luna Park soon told her otherwise: she and the world were no less ordinary, no less fragile. Still that vault of bridge and sky made it seem possible that her very cells might change.

Nearly thirty years later, she could pinpoint the day they did.

It was her first week at the *Telegraph*. She'd come to journalism late, after years of waitressing and night classes, the School Leaving Certificate she'd missed out on, courses in typing and shorthand. But her love for it was instant and profound. From the beginning she was obsessed by the process; the notion of a story, what it was, what it could do, the risk and potential of it. Ideas flared in her dreams.

She'd tried to explain it to Jamie and Will. *Work,* she'd shrug when she finally got to the orphanage at Croydon, and it was true. The people she'd met, or interviewed: the Lord Mayor, Dawn Fraser. They sat on the grass of the boys' playground and ate the Violet Crumbles she always brought, but their eyes were blank. *Kick the ball, Pearlie,* they'd say, and she didn't resent it. They were children; they couldn't know how it was. That walking into the newsroom was like an erotic encounter that made her forget everything else. Even them. In those early days, she couldn't wait to start each shift. Had met each story and interview like a lover. Each new day made her skin spark, swelled her sense of herself. This new Pearl, enlarged by confidence, surprised her too. What she was capable of. Steeliness.

They'd run away from St Joseph's before Jamie turned fifteen. As if they'd lashed out in their loneliness and confusion, the lengthening weeks between visits. Even then, they had suspected: her new life was bigger than they were. They must have known they couldn't compete. But couldn't understand. Now, ten years after she'd first walked into the newsroom, she couldn't account for it herself. Wasn't she their Pearlie? From the day their mother died, the love she'd spent on them. She'd emptied herself, hour by hour, so there'd be no room in them for suffering.

Before long they barely remembered their mother. A shadow figure, another baby at her breast. Then nothing. Only air stretched thin with crying, Pearl holding their father's head against her. Then their Da's ravaged face as he packed their singlets, their socks and coats into bags. And Pearl, her hands grasping theirs as they left the house, for the last time though they didn't know it then. Wave to Da, she said as they walked to the big black car, and they would never forget how shiny it was, how thrilling and terrifying to climb onto the back seat. Pearl between them, her mouth a straight line. Wave to the wood pile, the orange tree. And they did.

She'd had one phone call from them after they fled, their voices turned manly to stop her worrying, or to stop her chasing them. A friend's uncle ran cattle in Queensland, they said. They'd get work fencing or mustering, as labourers or roustabouts. You can't ride, she reminded them, gripping the phone, trying for calm. They'd never been outside Sydney. The closest they'd come to horses was the milko's mare, shovelling the steaming piles she left every morning into buckets for the vegetable garden. You'll kill yourselves, she said.

It'll be great Pearlie. Will laughed down the line. Jamie said, *I'll look after him.* But Pearl knew who was likely the scared one, the one who'd break his bones. *Look after yourself, Jamie*, she said. *We'll write to you*, they promised. *Write to your Da*, she said. But part of her − guilty, unexamined − was relieved.

They did write to their father. A year later a note in a grubby envelope, postmarked Bedourie. 'We are fine and brown as nuts,' Jamie wrote. 'We have learned to ride and fix fences. There is steak three times a week and jam tarts.' In Will's ragged hand: 'Da, there are ant hills big as houses. It is hot as blazes. I know how to cut balls off bulls.'

Then another year later, two? − she couldn't remember: a postcard from the coast. Somewhere north of Brisbane, all tinted blue sea and bathing beauties. It was hard to tell whose writing. But through the scrawl she could read she'd been wrong about Jamie; it was Will who was vulnerable after all, especially in a fight. A small misunderstanding with a ringer, the card said, Will's wrist in a cast. When it mended they might make for Victoria. They were living on mangoes and fish.

That was all. They didn't know about their father's accident, the stroke that had felled him, right there on the foundry floor. That she'd moved him to the care home and let the house go. If there'd been more cards or letters they would have gone to the dead letter office, she supposed, though for months she'd checked with the new tenants, collected notices and bills. When Menzies had brought in National Service, she'd begun to search in earnest: electoral rolls, telephone books. Queensland, Victoria. She couldn't find them in the phone books, and of course they weren't on the electoral roll. They were 18 and 19 then, not old enough to vote. To get a passport, buy a house or a beer. But they could be forced into army fatigues, she thought now, biting her lip. Given a gun to kill boys just like them, boys they didn't know, had never seen.

The ferry slowed. Voices rose and fell around her. Two men brought their palms to their hats, an orchestration of limbs. She looked up, and between half-heard words and phrases, in the shifting space between earth and sky, she saw it: the boys had been abandoned by them all. Mother, father, sister. Through death, grief, selfishness – in one way or another, they'd each disappeared, left them. Leaving was what her brothers knew. What they expected. She watched Manly materialise in the gloom. Of course they wouldn't bother coming home.

From the ferry terminal she walked quickly towards the beach and the rectangle of red brick flats on the hill. Sounds reached her through lace-curtained windows, thin walls:

muffled conversations, music from a tinny radio, a child's sudden cry. But when she turned the key in the back door of her flat there was silence. Just the clock in ticking darkness. She hurried from one light switch to another, as if brightness and colour might have their own sound, their own weight.

Fluorescent tubes revealed rooms unchanged by the past few hours: there was the brief shock of crockery still cupped on kitchen shelves, photographs safe in their frames, records in their rack. They did not reassure her. She pulled off shoes and stockings, poured a drink. Took it to the back step, sat in its time-worn curve and peered into darkness.

The night garden was thick with dreams. Beneath the earth, beneath the eyelids of birds, in the air that came like an exhalation from the sea. Pearl listened. It always felt closer at night, the slump and hiss of waves like an old man breathing. What did old men dream? Did they re-make the past, did they weep in the night? Did they dream old lives, angels, the faces of those still unborn? She knew what her father would see in his sleep. Not angels but the faces of his boys as they played in the garden, ate their porridge, waved to him from the welfare's black car. She'd watched him through the back window as he'd stood, staring, a hand extended as if the dusty tracks were a line he could pull to bring them back.

She leaned forearms on knees, sipped scotch. Her head reeled with the stars.

Where are you? She said it aloud to fix them in their flight, the galaxies of possibility. Looked to the Southern Cross: an old habit from childhood, her mother's finger tracing its shape in the night sky. *Alpha, beta.* In her own lonely year at the convent, sleepless in a narrow bed, she had sought out the blue blaze of its most southern and brightest star. *Acrux,* Sister Jeanne had told her, and the name and the star became an obsession. Whenever she found it she could hear her mother's voice.

The alignment of words and stars. She straightened. Pictured the dark stone of the convent, wooden floors that reeked of Phenyle. The pinched alabaster faces of nuns, their sour eyes. And Jeanne, the youngest, one of them but separate, as human and ordinary as the children. She read books, told stories, laughed like a drain. Covered for Pearl when she snuck off to see the boys. And then failed her when they ran.

She tilted her head to the Cross, burning bright. Closed her eyes, wished on Acrux. Or was it a prayer? For absolution, for mercy. That's really all we want, she'd read somewhere. Now it felt true. She opened her eyes to the merciless heavens, and saw there was no choice. She would have to start with Jeanne.

Shell

~

All night the shush and beat of the road. Axel lay in his bed and thought that maybe the human heart was pneumatic, a fist of rubber, no more fragile than the tyres squeezing bitumen outside his window. But daylight unfurled him like a flag. He stretched his limbs beneath the sheet, spread his palms across his chest, the beat there relentless. Ka-boom, ka-boom.

He rose early and walked to Circular Quay where he could sit with coffee and thick toast and watch birds wheel above the ferries. The water grey at that hour and splintered with memory, shifting in currents, dangerous. There were unguarded moments when he felt it in his body: the pull of dark water. Of immersion. Of nothing but a liquid embrace, a return, back, back.

He would emerge from these moments weightless. Lift his eyes, searching: a leaf would do, fine-veined. The press of air on his face. Or his hand on sandstone. Once, in the gardens, a ladybird, its miniature perfection. The tremble of the leaf beneath it brought him back to the world. His surviving self.

~

He had arrived in Sydney as summer was tipping over. Even then, everything he saw or touched felt warm: each place, each sweep of landscape or seascape was mediated by heat and light, and his body moving through it. In that way, he thought, he saw with his skin, felt his way with his pores, open or closed to the elements and this light. He had lived in the dark for months of every year, among shapes hunched in snow, made new by it, and strange. This, Axel knew, had made him different. He thought of these people whose lives clustered around the harbour, their houses with open windows and doors and balconies, everything flung wide so they took great gulps of the world. The new Opera House, even half-finished, expressed them perfectly, sails hoisted in currents of summer air.

When he left Sweden, winter was conceding slowly to spring. The horizon a frail line of possibility once more in the early mornings. It was a fine string that tautened his dreams; he would stand at the window not knowing if he was awake or asleep. Outside the world was more than it could be, bigger than the day to come and the night just gone. Brimming.

But he'd always loved autumn most, those days before the rain came and everything was drawn in crisp outline: slate on a roof, fronds on a pine tree, a woman's eyelashes. The detail of things. Before the obliteration of snow. His body felt like a child's then. Unafraid. Limbs loose, feet and fingers prickling with questions. He took long runs through forest and field, climbed trees before their leaves fell, high enough to see the village toy-like, miniature. Figures moved around as if they were singular, not part of this big pattern. He would feel a shiver of pleasure, watching.

On these adult excursions it was the child's eye that surveyed and recorded, was imprinted with form and detail, the intricate curves and lines of the world. Once, surprised by rain as he wandered out of the forest, he'd run to the bus shelter. Leaned against a post and watched fat raindrops smack onto bitumen. The realisation sudden and sure: the glass candleholders his uncle had made were the precise shape of a raindrop exploding on the road, a liquid coronet. Surely it was every child's desire to hold such a coronet in his hands, these two-second miracles splashed and strewn so extravagantly around him. To crouch and capture one, two, three in a curved palm before they died away. That, he saw then, was precisely what his uncle Lars had always done in glass: translated the shapes of nature, its sculptural language and form.

And so, in a different way, had Utzon. The thought leapt with the gulls from the rail of a ferry as he watched it tack a seam across the harbour. What more was this new structure than a lush shrub the architect was coaxing from the ground? Or shards of Copenhagen china? Like Utzon, Axel knew these shapes; he'd grown up with them, they were within him. Despite the newspapers, the grumblings in the street, the building had never seemed strange to him. Always it had reminded him of a bowl, newly shattered, and of birds. From the day he'd seen the model in Höganäs it had consumed him, beaten in his head like wings.

Now, though he had been working at the site for a month, though he'd walked the same path to it every day, it still took him by surprise: the tremor of emotion as he rounded the quay and saw the sails arcing out of chaos. As if he'd come upon a rare and beautiful animal in a stark landscape. There was no Swedish word to describe this, no English word that he knew; it wasn't as simple as 'awe' or even 'love'. It was the clutch at his heart as he lifted his eyes to its curves and lines. Its reach for beauty, a connection between the human and the sublime.

He left the crusts of his toast to the pigeons and raised a hand to Yanni wiping tables inside the café. As he moved down the quay he passed other faces, familiar but unnamed, behind milkshake machines or piles of newspapers or flowers bunched in buckets. A spill of voices, a swell of leaves and petals in the strengthening sun. And now, something else on the periphery of his vision. A beat, an energy. There, behind the news stand, words jagged into the air. They jerked sideways above a shifting sea of heads, placards held aloft to be read: 'No War', 'Out of Vietnam', 'Don't Register'. The bodies moving beneath them at once languid and urgent, the faces smiling and snarling and smiling again.

More placards appeared, more words. Loud voices bulged into the space in front of him. He dug his hands into his pockets and turned a shoulder to the looming crowd, pushed and edged through the noise rising around him like a tide. Grimaced as his foot crunched another – *Shit, man!* a girl yelled – but one more push and he was on their flank. He turned then, an apology half-spoken. *Förlåt*. But the girl was gone, already lost inside the march.

Axel stood still. Sweat leapt from his pores. *Jävlar!* The curse mouthed rather than spoken as he breathed out, trying for calm. He tipped his head back, looked at the sky, wide and empty of trouble. His heart slowed. The moment passed. He released another breath and resumed his pace towards the point. He was, he realised, thinking in his own language. Every day he struggled to find meaning in this local form of English he was expected to use. Even alone in his workshed he fought with it, with words. Drawing, blowing, ideas spooling through loops and funnels of molten glass.

It wasn't just a matter of mechanics, of alphabet and grammar, or even habit. There was something less tangible at play, something about the imagination, about feeling. He had grown into his craft as much through language as he had through tools; had learned it at sentence level, thinking in simile and metaphor, using image and emotion. He had begun to understand this at his uncle's side, this link between language and art.

But symbol and metaphor were lost down here beneath the heavy hand of heat and lethargy and a vastness of sky and ocean and air. Beneath a particular attitude, he saw suddenly, one the protesters with their placards might sense: a kind of huddling around sameness, a retreat from risk and – despite the openness of air and sky – from exposure. He saw it plainly in the derision of Utzon in the papers, the growing clamour of voices mocking his vision. As if they were ashamed of a building that might reveal them, the soaring shapes of their dreams, the true interior of their hearts. As if they were afraid of grandeur.

Now he stopped as he approached the security gate, and looked beyond it to the ridge that ran out to South Head. Listened. The sound of incalculable distance rang in his ears. It whipped around the rock of the headlands, to him the spine of some giant sea creature, its flesh flayed by wind. Everywhere he looked in this place he saw what Utzon saw. The drama of harbour and horizon, of cliff and ocean, and at night, the star-clotted sky. It held the shape of the possible, of a promise made and waiting to be kept.

How could such a place be named by this arid language then? The English he had studied at school had not prepared him for this country. Its sentences were without rhythm, flat, featureless. He understood well enough, the women especially, who spoke without guard. They were different to the women he knew at home. He wondered if it was a matter of sophistication or history or even weather, this difference. This leaning into or away from another's sentences, or into or away from landscape, or surroundings. The things you were willing to reveal, what you were willing to hear.

Sometimes he would stand on the quay and let the streams of people part around him like water, and he would listen. Words, phrases, perhaps a whole sentence – *and I said to her she'd be a bloody fool* – and he would try to hear what was there, what was in the words that made these people. Did their language make them feel a different way?

Once, standing still in afternoon sun that slanted across the water, the moving bodies, he closed his eyes. And opened them to a vision: the new building lifting its wings above the land, the water, above all these heads that didn't know, not yet, what it might say about them. How free they were to become who they were, or could be.

⁓

He picked his way around the site to his workshed on the eastern side of the podium. Out of habit he bent his head, looking for imaginary obstacles; he needed these few minutes to isolate his thoughts. His early work in the glass shed was solitary; for Axel this was essential. But the elements demanded it too; the mysteries of fire and water and minerals could not be roused if there was a crowd. This had been his first lesson in glass: the maker had to exclude the world, forget even himself, sometimes. *You have to be present but invisible, like your soul,* his uncle had told him. Axel was just a boy then; he thought the soul was a ghostly twin that lived inside people, in the heart or the head, a shadow person. Later he would understand that for Lars, for the best of them, perfect glasswork *was* the shadowy twin. They were constantly in search of the soul.

But that day, two decades before, the word fell into the dim air of the shed in Åfors and charged it, so that Axel felt as he did in an autumn field before a storm. Not afraid, but sensing its raw power, elementary, in the tips of his fingers and his feet. He looked for some clue in his uncle's face, but it was unaltered, already turned to the forge. Axel did as he'd been told and retreated to a corner to watch and learn. To be invisible too.

The shed had been assembled near the water, away from the routes taken by most workmen and the storage areas for roof components and steel. This pleased him. He'd rarely worked in close proximity to others, or under their scrutiny. That would come when the work had developed its form, when its physical requirements exceeded his own hands. Until then his needs were not extravagant, he'd told the site manager by telephone from Sweden those months before. Furnace and crucible pot to begin with, benches and tables and hooks. High quality sand. A maver.

Perhaps a desk and chair, he'd added after a moment.

There was a grunt at the end of the line. It'll be basic, the man said.

But Axel could already feel the Australian sun at his back. That's fine, he said, imagining light at the windows instead of darkness, glass pierced by the colours of the antipodes. He gathered his own favourite tools for luck, the clipping scissors and tongs he'd always used, and sent them ahead by ship.

Now he unlocked the door and went to the back of the shed, to a small table set away from the furnace. This was for thinking and reading as well as drawing; he did not believe this piece of glass could be properly designed on paper. Rather he would sit with coffee and write down words and phrases, or sketch a thought in lines and angles. There were various objects he had found as he walked to work – a piece of twine, a hair ribbon, a corner ripped from an old street map. As well as photographs of doorways, an advertisement for something called 'brick veneer'. The city in various lights.

He tacked all these to a sheet of ply beside the table, along with assorted press articles: a woman who quoted Shakespeare for a shilling outside the library, labourers in a tunnel at the Snowy Mountains Scheme, Jørn Utzon sailing at Pittwater. Someone on the engineering team – Jack Zunz? – had passed on various reference books: Australian art and topography; history, both terrestrial and maritime. Even novels. This pleased him. He had learned during his years of study in Stockholm, and his work at Åfors and Kosta, that design was rarely the result of one stream of thinking, one tool, one dimension.

Two years before, he had written Utzon a letter. Emboldened by praise for his own work in Stockholm and New York, Axel picked up his pen. *I am a glassmaker from Småland,* he wrote. *My people, like yours, know water* ... Then he took a breath and made his offer. Six months later, a reply: *I have seen some of your work*, the architect wrote. *Why don't you come to Sydney?* There was no concrete brief, but Axel knew what was required for the foyer of the major hall: the shape of an idea to match the opera house in its scale and its flight. A piece of art that might have its own presence or, like the building, transcend the possible, the partisan. Language itself.

Now, though he had been in Sydney for weeks, there was still no contract between them; he had not even met the great man. Other architects dropped by, engineers, various foremen. The commissioned glass was mentioned only in abstract terms, in queries about the adequacy of the shed and the information he had about Sydney, about Australia, about the building and its history. There was an understanding between them all, he soon saw, that the glass project would stand alone. That it would be an accretion of observation and reflection. That Axel would render thought and impression as surely as a builder rendered a house.

So at the furnace and the table, he experimented with shape and colour, with ovoids and rings, blue, white, some of them clear, some shadowed like ice. He read and watched and walked the site, walked the city. Listened. Drew. The lines like an embarkation, a glimpse at a landscape already receding, so he had to look hard to keep it in his head. And to gather the courage to see what the lines might reveal, not just about what was in front of him, but within.

He thought often of Lars as he worked, as he translated the delicate geometry of harbour and sky, the stream of light. As he tipped the pipe to his mouth and his breath inflated the bulb of glass, malleable as a lung. The memory of his uncle had entered his own glasswork like language, become intrinsic to it, a kind of conscience. He could hear it: *It's there in your hands: light and heat and depth.* And: *Wait for the shift. In you and in the glass. The connection between the two.* That, Axel knew, was where the secret of each piece was hidden, in this tension between man and glass.

Shell

Each day, when he looked up and saw that hours had passed, when he lifted his eyes to midday light at the windows, he would greet the others who, of course, had been in the room the whole morning. Not just Lars but his mother, his father. And Utzon. Always Utzon. He felt the architect's presence as a subtle weight in his wrists, in his shoulders, in the play of possibilities as the pipe emerged from the furnace, in the first push of breath in its throat. Then it was just he and the work, the small miracle of the gather, clear and clean from the fire. He had to be wholly present within it, lost to all else, for its secrets to be revealed. The world retreated to a bowl of light and possibility.

~

Pearl woke early in dream-tossed sheets. Children had been trapped on buses, passed through windows to gargoyle faces, carried off into darkness. Her twin sisters. Were they? The straw-coloured hair, inscrutable eyes. In the dream she had lost the use of her arms, watched on as they were taken, expressionless, looking back at her over the shoulders of strangers. No sound. They'd never made much noise, hadn't even cried much as babies. But she'd wanted them to cry in the dream, to claw, scream out, fight. Instead they'd complied with their captors, or so it seemed. Her own arms stuck to her sides.

She pushed herself upright and reached for pouch and papers. The ritual of tobacco – pinch, order, roll, her tongue against thin paper – dislodged the dream pictures. They were never literal, she knew that. For days she'd been thinking about the Freedom Rides through western New South Wales. The activist Charles Perkins, the protests at Kempsey and Moree. She'd tried to interest the women's editor in a story about Perkins leading Aboriginal children through the gates of Moree's swimming pool, where they had been banned. Was that it? She leaned back against her pillows and inhaled. Turned her face to the long sash window, where shapes emerged slowly from shadow. The nicotine did its work.

The burr of the telephone brought her back to the room. She levered herself upright, shrugged an arm through a shirt on her way down the hall.

Trouble is, the men in this country. Ray's drawl, his lazy diction. He'd grown up poor in Marrickville and didn't try to disguise it. His vowels remained broad and flattened, he seemed incapable of saying *your* or *and,* but beneath his street sweeper's speech was one of the sharpest minds Pearl knew. She balanced the receiver between shoulder and chin, pushed an arm through the other sleeve. Pictured him, the crease of skin between his eyebrows, one hand raking his hair.

The army'll make their sons into men, eh? That's what they'll say. Sort 'em out. Something, fabric or skin, rubbed against the receiver, then the snap of a struck match. *Menzies is counting on it.*

Pearl glanced up the hallway. Had she put out her own cigarette? Distracted, she said: *Menzies is a fool.* Outside, a kingfisher dropped one pure note through the cool air. She shivered, pulled the shirt close. *Everyone knows.*

An' half the sons'll think the same. He went on as if she hadn't spoken. *War's a great lark. Adventure, women.* She heard him exhale. *They'll be queuin' up for their bloody ballot papers, you watch.*

She wanted to say, not my father, not my brothers. But the lugubrious voice rolled on. *Fuck these pansy protests, they won't change nothin'.* There was the grumble of an electric jug. *We wanna harden up.* Then he muttered something about work, and was gone. As usual, no hello and no goodbye.

She filled her own jug and put it to boil. His words in her head: *They won't change nothin'.* It was true: the protests went almost unnoticed. The phrase 'National Service' rang nostalgic in this country, with its images of clean-cut boys and bright metamorphosis: from untidy youth to uniformed men, bronzed, strong, responsible. Ready to fight for freedom. Who would reject it? In the factories and sheds, in Pitt Street? Her father, of course, she knew that. Patrick would see right through it.

Light pressed at the window. She opened the kitchen blind. First week of autumn, the sun hesitant, shy as a bride at five a.m. her father would say. As a child she'd imagined a girl in a dew-damp dress, white as the morning, its hem grubby against the grass she fled over. Later she understood better, but on those mornings when she'd willed herself to wake and sit in the early chill with him, it was part of a fairytale in which there was only the two of them, she and her father. She leaned close to smell his work shirt, shivering in her thin nightie. Shared his weak tea, watched the smoke from his durrie float across the backyard.

Her own rollies had never tasted as sweet as she'd imagined. She'd thought they'd be just like those mornings, which held the deep flinty smell of her father's breath and skin, like the embers of old kindling. She'd searched for years for precisely the right tobacco, settling recently for a blend of plum and spice she found consoling, if not sweet. Those hours with her father re-enacted in the rhythm of the match striking, the tobacco catching, the shape of thumb and forefinger around the smoke.

He could still manage one with his left hand. Every week, in a parlour wheezing with old men, she would slot a smoke between his fingers and wait as he raised it to his lips. The match lit an unalloyed pleasure in him, flushed the sorrow from his face, and on that first deep draught he would turn his head to her and smile. Crooked, fleeting. It didn't matter. She would fill two hours with talk and politics, at least half of it on the scoundrel prime minister, all the while rolling and rolling, filling his tin with smokes to last a week. Filling the air with banter, anything but the obvious: the appalling absences, his wretched loneliness. For whole minutes, she did not have to look into his eyes.

No matter that Patrick rarely spoke now, that the stroke had taken his voice and his strength and half his memory. His eyes held everything, all that he'd lost. Spoke for him: where are my boys? Even the twins visited, bringing husbands and grandchildren and flicking the blonde plaits they both still wore. They swept in and kissed their father and sat babies on his knee, then left again in a bubble of their own self-sufficiency. Pearl had never quite forgiven them their luck. To have one another, a mirror image, physical proof they were not alone. Patrick would smile his half-smile, his good arm around a baby, his gaze just over their heads. As if his sons might arrive at any moment.

She sipped tea. Re-lit her cigarette, brushed tobacco from her blouse, scattering the shreds of memory: her father's voice, clear as a bell and as sure, at the kitchen table before her mother got sick, before Jane was born. Uncle Kevin was dead of the malaria he'd got in New Guinea, the stinking war still killing a year after it finished. His voice like crushed glass as he told them. He wiped a handkerchief across his face, looked around at their faces. And swore to her mother, to the boys themselves, even as they waved their baby fists: there will be no wars for my sons.

⌒

She walked into the *Telegraph* building at a quarter to ten. It was her habit to be punctual; she'd learned it as a teenager, keeping chaos at bay for the others and for herself. She'd found routine and order comforting then, a way to negotiate the days. A cushion against grief, against the appalling and sudden recognition, as she washed a bowl or pushed a broom into corners, that her mother was gone. She might cry then, hands pressed to her face, but the soft clack of the clock, the minute hand relentless, pulled her back to the room. The lump of mutton stewing, the sting of onion in the air.

In the partitioned cubicle off the main newsroom she collected the day's edition and sat at her desk. She'd laughed when they'd told her: the women's pages. The punishment so transparent, and all for one unguarded moment, her face caught and snapped at a protest. She didn't regret it, even now, months after Menzies brought his midnight bill to parliament. There were few in the chamber that night to object, to hear him talk about 'National Service' or 'aggressive communism', and it was too late for the papers. So they'd cobbled together a rally in Hyde Park the next day. On their placards: 'It's not National Service, it's the draft!' And: 'Out of Vietnam!' A week later she was summoned before the news chief.

It's too obvious, Pearl, he'd told her. *You're too obvious. You've forgotten the rules.*

She'd sat opposite him in his glass-walled office. Screwed up her face. *What rules?*

Henry's desk was littered with papers and notes and a dummy layout for the front page. He played with three paperclips, pulling their ends apart. *Without fear or favour, all that. Remember?*

She held his eye. *I have no fear,* she said calmly, and shrugged. *And I don't favour anyone.*

He cocked an eyebrow. *Depends on who's reading.* A hand in the air to cut her off. *The protest was the last straw, Pearl. Heart on your sleeve, for all to see.* He let a second tick by, a beat. *Including the boss.*

Come off it Henry. The effort to contain her voice. *That rally was in my own time. Are you saying I can't have a private life?* She tipped her face to the ceiling to hide her smirk. *So much for democracy,* she said.

So much for objectivity. He leaned forward. *You're a reporter, Pearl. You report the news, not make it.*

She tried not to blink. *Don't patronise me Henry.* Her voice a low growl. *We go back too far.*

He had the decency to blush. Five, six seconds ticked by on the newsroom clock.

Finally: *Look,* he said, quieter now, pursing his lips. *You know Bob won't fire you. Just lie low in women's for a while. All right?*

She stood then but kept her eyes on him. Anger flamed in her throat. *No promises, Henry.* Then turned for the door. Over her shoulder: *Remember that line?* She didn't wait to hear his reply.

That had been November. She'd measured the time by the stories she'd missed, could have no part of: the Wanda Beach murders, the ban on Dawn Fraser, Churchill's death and funeral. The Rolling Stones. The Freedom Ride just a week before: what she'd have given to cover that. Some days were worse than others. A kind of grief possessed her: every few hours she would leave her cloister for yet more coffee from the cafeteria at the end of the corridor, but really to inhale the smell and feel of real news. Smoke and ink, the clash and banter of fifty typewriters, human voices rising and falling and always the air of some impending drama, a kind of lull that was the newsroom waiting, holding its breath, even as its engines churned and composed, deciding the news of the day.

An unlucky error of timing: she looked up from the page to meet her editor's eye. Pressed the stub of her cigarette into the ashtray, once, twice, taking her time. Pushed back her chair. Betrayed nothing as Judith briefed her: a preview of the Royal Easter Show, a chat with a charity matron, the weekly fashion piece. And – Judith was all apology – they'd forgotten the Recipe of the Week. Could Pearl dredge one from the files?

The banality of it all – skirt lengths, hats at Randwick, the call to conformity – was like a dead hand on her shoulder every morning as she walked through the door. And there was the certainty that, as she returned to her desk, as she searched old editions in the library for Rhubarb Crumble or Shepherd's Pie, her colleagues in the newsroom were watching. The news editor himself probably, waiting for her to cross another line.

She typed up a recipe, grimacing over the ingredients for Spicy Meat Loaf, and finished a trite piece about fearful young women on shadowy beaches. She hated these stories. It wasn't just the subject matter but their flattening effect, the way they turned real lives two-dimensional, like the paper itself. Objectified them, made them items to be read and turned away from, unlike the social columns, the display ads for frocks and appliances. Capitalist press, her father would say, it's what they do, and lately she'd begun to understand what he was saying. That the newspaper barons were heartless, manipulative. Like puppeteers, pulling invisible strings.

~

At lunch she dropped a notebook into her bag and left the building. Wandered down to Pitt Street. The windows of Grace Brothers were all new autumn fashion; she wrote: 'stilettos, pencil skirts, denim. Pillbox hats, rolled collars, Jackie Kennedy. Shrimpton, goddess of Carnaby Street'. It was a bit like thinking and writing in a foreign language. Pillbox hats? Her eyes went instinctively to her own knee-length skirt, the collared print blouse from her mother's cupboard. She ran her hand over gabardine, firm across her thigh, a reassurance. She couldn't bear couture.

In a phone box nearby she pushed a coin into the slot. The convent's number carved into memory. She left a message for Sister Jeanne.

Back at work she filed her fashion story, then pulled out a folder labelled 'Affront'. In the first weeks of her exile from the newsroom, she'd concocted a series on forgotten women writers. Good series were popular with editors – the regular guarantee of filled space on the page. A guarantee for Pearl too: they might protect her from some of Judith's more vacuous story ideas. Already she had enough names to string it out for months: Kylie Tennant, Katharine Susannah Prichard, Jean Devanny. Eleanor Dark, Christina Stead. *Write one up*, Judith had said, *and I'll see if it fits*.

But Pearl had been delayed by the pleasures and disappointments of research. As she read, it became clear how interconnected the women were, how different their lives to those of their male counterparts. It was all too familiar: they'd all lived in captivity, caught in the prescribed role of caring too much: for husbands, children, parents. Into this crowded cage they still managed to squeeze writing. Good writing: in the thirties, she realised, they'd published more quality fiction than men had. While washing nappies, feeding elderly aunts, playing helpmeet to husbands. Pearl looked at her folder and then around the room. 'Affront.' At the mid-point of the sixties, what had changed? She pulled out her notes on Jean Devanny and Kylie Tennant and began a tentative draft.

Time was sluggish. As the clock dragged to five, she gathered the files spilled across her desk. In the library she dropped them on the wide wooden counter next to someone else's returns, plain manila folders tagged with subjects and dates. Then turned and walked back through the newsroom, listening to snatches of phone calls, conversations. Stopped near the news desk to eavesdrop. Something about the Works Minister, incomplete drawings, contractors. Tom, one of the boys on the political round, was trying not to shout at the chief of staff. *This is the real story,* she heard him say, as if he alone knew, *not the blackfellas in Walgett, or Borneo or the bloody election. It's that fool Ryan.*

Tom stalked away, still talking over his shoulder to those on the news desk. He raised his brows as he walked past

Pearl. *You watch,* he said, to her and to the room. *Utzon doesn't stand a chance.*

—

There must be records. If they've had jobs, paid rent. She sat opposite Jeanne in the plain convent library, her thoughts derailed by the nun's bare head. Or nearly bare. The heavy black and white wimple was gone. In its place a plain white band that exposed dark hair. It made her look a different creature to the one she'd known as a teenager. A woman with a woman's feelings and thoughts. A woman's body. Pearl's own thoughts skittered away as she spoke. She tried to focus but was distracted by the nun, the way her eyes looked now, her skin, the movement of her head. Fluid, unrestrained. But somehow, less certain.

She found herself speaking in a different way. Felt a shift in the power differential; she was no longer the child, impressionable, naïve. May not even be, she realised with a start, much younger than Jeanne at all. She sat back in her chair, tucked her own hair behind her ear. Straightened her spine.

Jeanne frowned. *You'd have to know what kind of jobs. The sort of work they'd done. Victoria's a big place.*

No idea. Pearl shrugged. *They did station work in Queensland, years ago. Horses, fencing.*

So they could still be in the bush.

I don't know. Possibly. Pearl felt an old defence tighten in her chest. It gave her voice an edge she hadn't intended.

Jeanne stood and moved to the sofa. Patted the cushion beside her, the familiar gold band on her wedding finger. *They're two needles in a big haystack. You could look up the names of some stations and ring them, I suppose.*

Pearl ignored the implied invitation. She thought, not yet. *For some reason I thought the church could help.* She looked directly into Jeanne's eyes.

The nun raised her eyebrows. *Only if they were going to church.*

I thought you lot had ways to find missing children. Networks. Files.

There was a two-second beat before Jeanne replied, two seconds that spoke what they couldn't say. That they'd both been angry after the boys left, each blaming the other. The two telephone conversations they'd had at the time made it worse. Finally: *Jamie was nearly fifteen, Pearl,* Jeanne said levelly. *That's not a child.*

Nearly fifteen means he was fourteen. And Will was a year younger.

And now they're young men. Jeanne lifted her face to the ceiling. The crucifix against her pale throat the same one she'd always worn. She said: *Pearl. I suppose there was an assumption, back then. That they'd be with you.*

Pearl felt the colour rise in her cheeks but she held Jeanne's gaze. *Well, they weren't. And I had problems of my own then, Sister.* The title a punishment they let hang in the air between them.

Until Jeanne spoke again. *All those months, Pearl, and you didn't come. They watched that gate down there every Saturday. They waited for you.*

Late sun through the high leadlight window: it turned the air in the room crimson, yellow, green, and there was the smell of scrubbed floors, meat stewing. Children's voices rose and fell, the plink of an untuned piano. Her stomach hollowed. For two seconds she was that girl again, crying in the dorm downstairs, missing her mother. Jeanne the one who came to her. *Will's nearly nineteen now. And Jamie's twenty. It's an unlucky year to be twenty.* She paused, then spoke the nun's name. *Jeanne* – Her voice cracking. *Don't you get it? Jamie could be drafted. And not just for the army. It would be bloody Vietnam.*

A light flared in Jeanne's eyes. The air broke open. *Christ,* she said. And pursed her lips, looked to the walls, the ceiling. As if Jesus was there, as if her saviour could hear her and might intervene.

Pearl allowed a half-smile. *Not sure about Him. I need concrete help now.* She looked down to the floor, the dull boards, then up to the nun's eyes. *I lost them once already, Jeanne. I won't lose them twice.*

~

They walked together beneath an arching cloister. Pearl felt Jeanne's hand slip into the crook of her arm, and looked down at the pale skin of the nun's fingers, the scrubbed nails. There was something artificial about the clean surfaces, the smooth fabric of blouse, her unmarked hands. Why had she not noticed that before? As they reached the door Jeanne stopped, raised one eyebrow and smiled. *We'll find them,* she said. *We've done harder things.* She glanced at Pearl. *Like arithmetic. Like spelling.*

Something in Pearl subsided. She turned and, straight-faced, rattled out a string of letters. *O-r-n-i-t-h-o-r-h-y-n-c-u-s.* The rhythm still locked in her throat. It was the way Jeanne had taught the infant class to spell, almost singing. Pearl, stuck in the convent that year, had been her assistant, collecting composition books, checking times tables. She hadn't suspected that Jeanne was cramming her head with everything a motherless girl might need in the world outside. Spelling, grammar, a way of speaking. Lessons in applying lipstick. *Blot ten times.*

She smiled, self-conscious. As she began to move away Jeanne spoke again. *You should try the Salvation Army,* she said softly, as if she didn't want to be heard. *The Red Cross. They're better than us with missing persons.*

⌒

Fifteen years. She had gone from girl to woman and, in the space of half an hour, back again. Pearl walked down the curved stairway, through a sandstone arch and into a garden. The roses were in their autumn flush. Pearl's senses reeled; her eyes heard colour, her tongue tasted fragrance. At fifteen it was her consolation, to sit between beds of soft-cheeked flowers, rubbing fallen petals between fingers and thumb. Even then she'd felt it: a mild erotic charge. Now she stood still among head-high rose bushes and realised she'd been a bit in love with Jeanne back then. It wasn't surprising: her adolescent heart had nowhere else to go.

She followed the path down the hill and past St Joseph's to the playing fields. Somewhere a clock chimed the half hour, folding through the air, metallic. And with it, Jeanne's words again: *missing persons.* When did the boys become *missing*? What did it really mean? Without. Deprived of. Deficient. Aching for. Or: disappeared. Unaccountably not present. The words had a sinister edge, implied foul play.

She shook her head. The boys were somewhere. They were not missing.

Perhaps it's me. The realisation like a bolt from the invisible saviour Jeanne had invoked and believed in. She, Pearl, was the one who was missing: that other Pearl, the one the boys had loved, who'd washed their grubby limbs, adored them. That girl was gone, had been unaccountably absent. Had acquired a veneer to protect herself, a shell she could slip beneath, to hide from the predatory world. And it had prevented others from looking in. She hadn't known until now that it had also stopped her from seeing out.

⌒

On some days, like today, Axel had to will himself to stop, to walk out and join the groups of men crouched with their sandwiches and cigarettes in mottled shade. Tea in thermoses, enamel mugs. Carpenters, labourers, steelworkers. They were still strangers to him; their informality and their ease with each other intensified his newness, his separateness. In his first days he had been introduced to many in the perfunctory way of the locals – a name and a nod – but their work beneath the podium or high in the air above his workshop distanced him. Though they were of dozens of different nationalities, in Axel's head they constituted their own culture and breed, stronger, braver, freer than he was. Part of him wanted to be more like them; this was one of the things that kept him away.

He had met two Danes on Bennelong Point; they'd exchanged curt greetings in both tongues. Like the others they were not shy. They drank each evening with the other carpenters at hotels around the quay; he'd seen them in the bar below his room. And though he longed to use his language, to speak without doubleness, he wouldn't with them. He already knew that with them he could not open his mouth and feel like himself. Could not utter words and sentences that would return him to the person he was. Beneath their accents they were as different to him as anyone else, and he'd invented himself as readily with them in Swedish as he did with others.

These two had been witness to Axel's early humiliation on the building site – a ritual, but he hadn't known it then. He'd been crouched at the edge of their group at smoko, drinking the sweet black tea a young labourer had offered him. He caught pieces of sentences: *Fuckin' commos ... I'm not goin' they can all kill each other.* A pause and then: *Where the hell is Vietnam anyway?* Someone mentioned Singapore, New Guinea, names from the Second World War. Battles their fathers had seen, unknown and foreign to him. Axel turned a chip of concrete over in his palm, half listening, his thoughts elsewhere. Until a hovering awareness of eyes turned towards him, and a question repeated.

What did your father do in the war?

The tone mocking and familiar. He glanced towards it. Some current of aggression ran out from the man, looking for earth, and he felt it in the seconds before he replied. *Milked cows.* Surprising himself with irony. His voice even, the concrete turning in his hand.

Silence ticked in the air, two telling seconds. *That's great.* The man's eyes narrow, his lips hard. *When someone asks he can say, I squeezed tits for my country.*

Throaty laughter. Axel held his gaze. Long enough to see the Danes smirking nearby. Then he stood, threw the dregs of his tea on the ground as he had seen the others do, gave a short nod and walked away.

In his shed he slumped in a chair and out of habit rubbed a thumb over his wrist, the grey estuary of veins. He'd been a child in that war; he had milked cows. So had his mother. His grandparents' farm had fed them while his father was away, doing the work that was classified, even now. Still, that wasn't it. It was the tone of the man's voice, what it implied. That his father, like all Swedes, had done nothing.

He'd heard it before. First as a teenager, when he and his mother had taken a short holiday in Norway, years after the war's end. They'd been accosted by a drunk in Oslo and a woman further north. His mother had shielded him from the man, but he would never forget the woman's face as she took their kronor at a railway kiosk somewhere outside Tromsø. The Norwegian countryside was still marked by the Nazi occupation, fields and houses scarred by fire. *Swedes!* the woman spat, when she heard their accent. *I should charge you double. We paid for you in the war.*

He'd watched his mother's face darken. Her eyes. He was sixteen by then, with long legs and the voice of a man, but the woman's words made him mute. Even after his mother had steered him away, leaving their *våfflor* and coffee steaming on the counter, he felt curiously emptied of words. *Don't worry, Axel,* his mother said when they were back on the train. *She's right, they paid dearly.*

The whistle screamed and the train began to move. She spoke softly then. *She just doesn't know what it cost us.* She squeezed his hand and smiled. *But I'm sorry about your våfflor.*

The carpenter's insult came back to him now as he emerged into splintering sun, and saw the Danes at work in the forecourt, making timber moulds for concrete. Axel had heard about the architect's demand: the concrete finish had to be perfect, nothing less. The exposed surfaces, Utzon had said, would express the building as much as its sails did. By habit Axel swerved to avoid the two Danes, though in truth he would have liked to watch their careful labour. Each man bent to the task, oblivious to the day, to their own tensed bodies, the entirety of the effort around them.

As he wandered around he felt the energy of the work in full swing. Sometimes he saw the site as an enormous compass, from which infinite readings could be taken. He need only take a step away from his previous position and a new line of sight would emerge, a new reading of the place. So each day he chose a different vantage point. In this way he gradually came to understand not just the shape of the land and the job, but the interaction between all the spheres of work.

He paused in the casting yard. Men in hard hats and shorts bent to the acres of concrete, sculpting. Rib segments, ridge beams: they assumed the shapes of animals or their carcasses, hides bleached by the sun. Some pieces colossal, bigger than three men, others boned with steel and delicate as a corset. Weeks before, he'd stood beside one of the men who worked in the air, or so it seemed, installing rib sections and riding the hook. *Jago*, he said, offering his hand. They both stared at the scene before them, until Jago surprised him with tenderness. *They look like the future,* he'd said, arms folded. Axel glanced sideways: the face was soft, serious. This man had his hands on these giants daily, and still they were not so familiar as to be ordinary to him. They agreed they were already beautiful; their forms, what they suggested. And grinned, each recognising something in the other. The interchange dislodged Axel's guard, and an invisible barrier slid away, at least with Jago. A tentative friendship was born.

Axel took his cue from these shapes and forms, seen through Jago's eyes; it was in this way he might organise his own work. It might be sculptural in the same way the building was, the thinking as well as the form. This was what Utzon wanted, something alive to the eye. In the gloom beneath the concourse Axel could see what the architect meant: what had begun as a mundane assembly of materials – sand and lime and pebble – was now a thing of beauty, a ceiling of ships. Sitting here was like being underwater, looking up at the hulls of twenty boats floating side by side. Or the corrugations in mudflats left by a departing tide.

Until then he had thought concrete brutal. Used internally it was a material of expedience, easy and cheap. But here it was tactile as fabric, evocative as wood. He spread his palms wide on the surface beside him and wished he could reach up and touch the ceiling, absorbing its calm energy, what it spoke of: strength, beauty. Workmanship. In this way the building emphasised its materials but also its surroundings, made them more themselves.

Everywhere he looked, this is what he saw. Even the men, shirtless, their helmets tipped back from faces as open as the sky. They bent to their work, or spidered over the giant ribs, and in all of it – their sweat and argument and their deep attention – they were transformed too. Beautiful, authentic, precisely themselves.

⌐

He bought a sandwich from the kiosk near the car park and sat with Jago and the other riggers in the shade. The day was hot. *Too hot for March*, said one of the locals, *could melt your insides*. As he spoke he fanned his face with a discarded newspaper. *Not* your *insides,* said another, nodding at the expanse of stomach exposed by a blue singlet. The man with the paper ignored the barb. The others chewed their sandwiches and pies. Then: *What's wrong with these people?* Pages skittered across the ground and the man turned his head, spat. *Drover's dog knows what the problem is – bloody architect's never here.*

Axel looked down and away. As if the man's voice was a solid thing, its aggression wounding: *Never bloody here,* the man repeated, perhaps fearing they hadn't heard. *And he gets paid a fuck-load more than we do.*

The paper had fallen open on a story about some plywood mockups, the Minister's refusal to pay 'exorbitant' bills from the local manufacturer. It was the third story in as many days about the blowout in costs and the lengthening projections for the building's completion. Axel felt a tightening in his stomach, beneath his ribs. Even the men, he thought. Or some of them.

Hang on Clarrie. It was a young rigger who worked high in the air, manouvering rib sections into place. A precarious job, and the men did it without harnesses, their bodies moving like extensions of the cranes. *Have you ever* looked *at the place from up there?* He spoke in a low drawl, leaning back on his elbow, a smoke burning down between his fingers. His grubby hard hat beside him, marked in felt pen: Johnno. *It's bloody beautiful mate. I tell you, it's like* – he shrugged – *I dunno. Like some other power dreamed it up. Someone* – the cigarette traced an orange arc above his head – *up there.* He glanced around. *You know?* The others blinked gravely, avoided his eye. *It's fuckin' genius mate. Genius. That's what we're paying him for.*

Silence, like the tail of a bright comet. It stung Axel's eyes. He wiped them, hoping no one saw. To disguise his emotion he picked at the slices of bread in his hand, the odd contents of his sandwich. There was something yellow and viscous on the cheese that didn't look or smell right. Jago leaned towards him. *Corn relish,* he said quietly. *It makes me cry also.*

A general shuffling then, soft moans as men stood and stretched, balled up sandwich paper and wandered off into their afternoon. Axel bent to retrieve the discarded newspaper and the young man's voice lifted over their heads once more as they dispersed: *But it's time we all got a pay rise. Eh Clarrie? We're fuckin' geniuses too.*

~

The tenth of March dawned an ordinary day. No different. The heedless world: it could still take Pearl by surprise, that daily suffering and triumph left no visible trace. Mothers died, children disappeared, and still the world turned, the moon rose and slid away. In the newsroom the relentless hum of story, as if each edition brought that world into being every day. But today the preoccupations of the women's section were shadowed by the weight of her own.

She sat with an atlas, open on Indo-China. Burma, Malaya, Korea. The final *a* and its upward lift. It made the names delicate, feminine. Vietnam was an arthritic finger pointing south; no musical *a,* but still she could see a girl, oval-eyed beneath a wide bamboo hat. Rice fields feathered behind her. Pearl ran her palm over the map: the bone of the eastern mountains, forest green to the border, flecked with villages, unpronounceable. Did that make it easier for pilots to drop their bombs? If you couldn't name a place, if its letters refused your attempts. She'd seen anger flare in people when they couldn't spell a word. Couldn't find their way to meaning. Perhaps war was a failure of imagination, she thought. And nerve.

She closed the atlas and returned it to its shelf in the newsroom. Stopped to hear the midday bulletin on the police roundsman's radio. Standing there, staring at grey carpet, she felt the air thicken. Some inner gravity tipped and wavered. She kept her feet planted. But the bulletin reported only the spin of wooden marbles in a barrel used for lotteries, for games of chance. Loud protests on the footpath, chanting and yelling. She imagined the demure façade of the government building made sombre and furious by the lack of decorum.

There would be no announcement about the numbers, she knew that. Still the day had fallen heavy around her, expectant, like the day of an execution. She shivered as she subsided into her seat, and put her hand to her forehead as she would to a child's, testing for fever. A wave of nausea rolled through her. Years before, she'd sat in the newsroom and felt this roiling apprehension when a young boy was kidnapped from a street in Bondi. His father had recently won the Opera House Lottery. She'd stared at the boy's photograph, the gap-toothed smile that was also Will's. At the time she hadn't understood her reaction; she'd waited obsessively for news of him, cried when the police reporter told her Graeme Thorne was dead. He was just a boy, an innocent, younger than her brothers.

She picked up the phone now, asked for a line. While she waited she ran her fingers over typewriter keys, searching for meaning in the familiar: *a s d f / ; l k j.* These days she barely glanced at the keys, could type blind and fast, rarely faltering. Now the pads of her fingers traced over the letters as if they were code. The faint indent in the vowels, *a e i o u,* and in *t,* in *s.* If she closed her eyes and waited, perhaps they'd spell out names, the numbers of those chosen. As if the machine was a Ouija board. As if some evil or sorcery was at work.

News? Suze didn't bother with hello.

No, nothing. Her voice toneless. *Maybe,* she said, *it's not really happening. Maybe they're making it all up.* That was exactly how it seemed: as if somewhere in Melbourne, in an anonymous room, a group of men was playing with magic. One press photograph had been allowed, but one photograph meant nothing – she knew how subjective photographs were, how malleable. No more truthful than drawing, than writing. They might have taken it yesterday. And who knew what happened after the one photo was taken? Or before? No one was there to see. No witnesses.

Yes, they might just sit down with a beer and decide which numbers they want. Or don't want. Suze struck a match at the other end, exhaled. *Maybe they won't pull them from the barrel at all.*

Pearl was silent, imagining.

If you can't see something – if you don't believe in it – is it real? Suze laughed softly. It was an old joke between them, a line from a children's story, used to excuse one or the other for bad behaviour, or to deal with hard things.

Pearl stroked the black keys, stared at her own fingers. Magicians pulling numbers from a hat, pulling cards from a loaded stack. Waving a wand to make people appear or disappear, as if it was all a cruel trick. *Maybe that's what they want, a kind of fake innocence around it. As if they're not responsible, just following orders, as if it's out of their hands.*

They both fell silent. At last Suze said: *What about the protests?*

Who cares? Pearl meant it. In her whole body she could find no interest in the politics of the day, the machinations of dissent. She told Suze she'd let her know what she heard and hung up, then stood and went straight to Judith. Anger boiled beneath her skin, flushing away the nausea. *I'm not well,* she told her, and it felt true; she'd been lamed by the day and its potential. Judith examined her face over cat's eye glasses. *You do look off,* she said. And went back to her list. *It's nearly five. Go home if you've filed.* Pearl threw a cover over her typewriter and left the building.

~

The rule was, she would not call. If there was urgent reason, she knew where to find him: from Monday to Wednesday he caught the 5.30 train from Central; the bus at six from Macquarie Street on Thursday and Friday. He would always, he said, be five minutes early.

She found him standing behind a pillar on the main platform. Anonymous in brown suit and narrow tie. She wound her way through the waiting crowd towards him, stood as close as she dared. Not a flicker of response in his body or his face. After a minute: *The numbers,* she said, looking at her shoes. The heels were scuffed. *It's personal.* Then looked up and straight ahead.

He turned his head away. Perused a poster for carpet shampoo on the pillar. *The month?* The words dissipating in the air like mist.

Her own voice a whisper: *February.*

No sign that he'd heard her, no twitch or nod. His face as blank as every other. She became aware of bodies moving, proprietorial, towards an approaching train; he joined the queue for the door and was gone.

⁓

Two days that stretched to nothingness, in which every worst scenario was probable. She ghosted through them, alive only in the depths of research for Eleanor Dark or Kylie Tennant. Their extraordinary fortitude, their *guts.* Their open criticism of men and society, its treatment of women. At night she drank enough to ensure deep sleep, the sleep of the dead, her mother would say. Shrugging off headaches in the morning.

Late on the third day she packed her files and checked with the wires reporter once again. Nothing. The phone rang as she approached her desk and she answered it in her peremptory way: *Pearl Keogh.* No embellishments.

A vacuum that wasn't quite silence. She didn't realise she was holding her breath. The world shrivelled to a bubble of air around the receiver, her hand gripping its curve, the ragged edge of a manila folder on her desk. *Yes?*

His voice down the line then, reciting numbers. For the seconds it took she did not breathe. She knew this because when the phone clicked and buzzed she could feel only an ache in her chest, a pressure that released itself on the breath she finally drew. Sounds returned to her then, the hum of traffic, tack and ping of typewriters, the rush and pump of footfall all through the working building. She bent her head, smiled without knowing, ran her hand over thighs and knees. As if she'd left her body for whole minutes and just returned. She breathed in again, out. Dialled Suze. There was no number for Jamie.

⌒

Axel leaned on his elbow, his eye skimming the shed floor. Everything he had done to date seemed not irrelevant, perhaps, but out of place, out of time. The glass shapes he had toyed with did not speak to him, not in a language that resonated with thought and feeling. Not with this building, its place here, nor with its designer's intentions as he knew them. It was early days but still, he had hoped for more.

Shell

He began to think it was he who had lost his way, his awareness of necessary context and connection. There were days when he felt unmoored, without history; even without skill. He looked over the medley of experimental pieces in which he had tried to evoke the sky and the sea, the dreamlike freedom and limitation of horizons, and struggled with blueness, with light. He was, he knew, second-guessing the architect, terrified of his potential to fail. There was so much he didn't know.

The street map of Sydney was spread on the table at the back of his workshop. Axel folded it, pressing fore-fingers along creases, meticulous. The way to know a place, his mother had said, was with your feet, your legs. Even in winter. He could see her still, striding out where the snow was solid, skiing cross-country to drink coffee with a friend. Miles: she thought nothing of them. You should really taste that air, Anders, she'd say when she came back, as she shook her hair free of her woollen cap, took off her jacket. His father, in the corner chair with a book, would say nothing, but there would be the trace of a smile behind his pipe.

It was late morning. He locked his workshop, the map in his hand. In his mind's eye he could see his path: through the gardens, down to Woolloomooloo, up through Potts Point and around the bays – Elizabeth, Rushcutters, Double, Rose.

Imagined shadows deepening through gardens and parks, the slant of sun on calm water. But as he pocketed his key and wandered through the site, stepping around steel and concrete, he was surprised by an almost empty forecourt, an odd absence of noise, and remembered the stop-work meeting. *The draft,* he'd been told the day before. To Axel's blank face the labourer added, *National Service. To get recruits for the army.* He'd explained then: compulsory registration, the ballot for 20-year-olds. Wooden marbles and birth dates. Vietnam. That word again.

He wandered half-heartedly towards the Botanic Gardens gate and the gravelly sound of a loudspeaker. Part of him wanted to skirt around the men and keep walking, to breathe calmer air. But the ballot, the idea that a man's fate could spin and drop in the hands of another: this made him pause. It wasn't the notion of National Service; he had done his own, like every Swedish boy, unworried by the spectre of war. This was different. He thought of the marbles he had played with as a child, the rough glass rolled between forefingers and thumb. A boys' game but they came to it like colonels, each intent on a win. Each strike planned with precision.

He slipped into the crowded circle of men. Their eyes were turned to a makeshift stage and the voice of a union organiser, his words made brittle by amplification. *Not our war.* Axel listened and tried to follow, glanced briefly around. Something in the tone of the meeting made him anxious. He tried but couldn't locate its source; the sea of faces was alive with something he couldn't catch, couldn't access. He turned and began to edge his way out, murmuring an apology, his head down. At the crowd's perimeter odd phrases rang out, a word, a low whistle. As he made open ground he briefly heard the union man more clearly. *Reds under the beds* – and a gravelly roar in reply. It lodged in his ears, like the sound of an injured animal, frightened. He didn't want to hear any more, but still words and phrases came to him, partial. *We have no fight with … Any member who resists … It falls to us …*

The world around him shrank and concentrated. He stopped. *It falls to us.* More words came to him then, nearly twenty years old but clear enough. *The task falls to us. All of us here.* His father's voice, singular among many, not in volume but in authenticity; he knew that even then. Even then, crouching in the attic where he wasn't meant to be, looking for hidden Christmas presents. It filled his boy's heart with dread.

The same dark feeling churned in his chest now. Such words could be dangerous. The weight of them, the responsibility. He hurried on into the gardens, shutting out all but the vault of sky and trees, his eyes searching out one perfect shape to calm him, one thing of beauty. The harbour intricate behind thatched branches. The line of a hill, consoling as a breast or hip against his own. He loved these gardens, the sweep of grass, the great knotted figs. Paths between plants so wild he might have dreamed them. Bird of Paradise, Dragon Tree, Cabbage Tree Palm.

More than once the shape of a shrub, an alignment of leaves, returned him to infancy; he wanted to crawl beneath them, look out at the world from their safe harbour. All his life, this allure of enclosed spaces. He'd tacked clumsy shelters into trees, into corners of the garden, the space between his dresser and his bed. Had emptied his wardrobe once, folding himself into it to read. He'd heard his father telling a friend it wasn't so odd, not at all. Didn't we all want the womb again? Invisibility, secrecy. The watery echo of our own heartbeat, unassailable.

Axel remembered these words too: spoken lightly, so that no one could guess their true weight. Six months after, his father was gone. Had disappeared, turned invisible, become his own secret. But not to Axel. These years later, he still sifted the clues in his head, all the stones his father had dropped for him. Water, the letter *A*. Anders, Axel, America,

Argentina, Australia. The whole arc of the world. He would lie on the beach at Manly, the thud of surf in his ears, knowing the same sounds were felt by someone on the west coast of America. So that the great Pacific Ocean linked rather than separated them. He imagined the figure of a man, his feet in the sand, one hand raised to shade his eyes, backlit by the glow of California.

When he came back to himself there was an urgency in him, in the wind through the great fig trees and the percussive flap of leaves. He knew he would have to change his plans. He checked his wristwatch, strode down to Macquarie Street and into the city; was on a bus within ten minutes. He spread his map across the empty seat beside him. The coast around Sydney: its multiple points and headlands like fingers of seaweed floating out into the water. North of the harbour, there were roads that ribboned between beaches, the villages like loose beads. He leaned in close: as if the boatshed he sought might be marked, as a town hall might be, or a cathedral. A place of importance. But of course there was nothing to be seen.

The first time he'd made this journey he'd had to ask the most basic questions: bus routes, directions, times. He made inquiries at work, his face composed, unaffected, about places to swim, points of local interest, proximities. In the end it had taken hours from the time he'd left the Mercantile. He'd finally reached Palm Beach in the middle of the afternoon, too late. He'd stopped at a snack bar at the edge of the sand and was met with wide smiles and shrugs when he asked about Utzon.

Now the bus ducked and weaved through the streets of the northern beaches. He ticked them off on his map: Queenscliff, Harbord, Curl Curl, Dee Why, Collaroy, Narrabeen, Mona Vale. As the bus emptied he kept his finger firm on the wave-like pattern, moving it carefully: Bungan, Newport, Bilgola. Nearly there. He lifted his eyes to the horizon now, assembling a picture in his head. Avalon. Whale Beach. This horizon, these trees: this is what Utzon saw, what Utzon heard, what he smelled every day. The bus lurched, stopped. Palm Beach.

He walked about in dazzling sunlight. The air was granular, salt and sea spray. The usual cafés, a fruit shop, a window of bikinis and floppy hats. Nearer to the beach the smell of pies, hamburgers frying, suntan oil; a mix peculiar to him but not offensive. It seemed to belong to the shining young bodies queuing for food and milkshakes, or lounging on the sand, watching the surf.

The beach itself was a long crescent, curved to a rocky headland, its lighthouse a white smudge against blue. Houses clung to the hill directly behind the beach. But there were no boathouses. How could there be? The sea was like a hungry monster here, clawing at the shore to fill its empty belly. He stopped a sea-slicked young man with a surfboard under his arm. Again, the smile, the shrug. Sorry.

The sun was fierce; his scalp pricked with heat, his feet tender on blazing sand. He bought soft drink in a green bottle at the beach snack bar and wandered up and down. Looking for hidden inlets where a boatshed might be, tucked out of sight, out of the public eye. There were many tall palms that might conceal something, but on close inspection didn't. Perhaps it wasn't a boatshed after all: how could a group of architects work in one of those? Finally he went back into the village and asked: Mr Utzon, his office. He'd been working there for months. Blank faces, one after the other. He sat on the grass near the beach. Watched low waves slump to shore.

In Hellebæk he could feel the man, at least. He'd gone looking for Utzon's home in the tiny Danish village, again without directions or address, knowing only it had been built near a forest and a lake. That the house lay low against the earth, sat lightly, hovering. White paint and glass. He would know the architect's house when he saw it, he was sure of that. He already understood its shape, its lines.

That whole area was so much like the countryside at home in Sweden. The forests of birch and old pine, the tides of leaves. Low wooden houses, birds circling. The sound of wind and water, water everywhere, the land a thin skin over an invisible sea. And in the end it didn't matter that he didn't find the man there. He saw him everywhere, walking in the woods, by the bulrushes edging the lakes, at his drawing desk. Drinking coffee, playing with his children.

It was the same in Helsingør, a short train ride away. From the waterfront Axel had stared at Kronborg Castle, the way it seemed to float above the water of the promontory, clouds roiling over its bulk. He'd tried to see it as Utzon had, imagining his opera house. As Shakespeare had, imagining Elsinore. The sombre stone and turrets were solid, immutable, but when they were softened by clouds its scale became more human. He'd shrugged, as Utzon might have. Hamlet, after all, was just a man.

When he'd finally seen the plans for Sydney's Opera House, the early photographs of the building in construction, the shape of the harbour and Bennelong Point, he had thought: of course. He is the only architect for this project, this place.

Home from Åfors for a weekend after the results of the competition were announced, he told his mother about it, about the extraordinary design, that the winning designer was Danish. He was in the kitchen, brewing coffee, slicing cheese.

What is his name? she asked from the sitting room, reading before the fire she had lit that morning. Outside the world was muffled and thick with snow. *I haven't heard the news for days.*

Utzon, he said, lowering a tray onto the small table and settling down beside her. *Jørn Utzon.* He bit into an open sandwich, dropped a sugar cube into his cup.

His mother looked over at him, frowning. *Utzon?* She sipped coffee. *I wonder if it's the same one.*

Axel raised his brows. Held a piece of salami out for Aldous.

But she was staring at him, saying, *Are you sure it's Jørn Utzon? Is he young, still in his thirties?* When he nodded she smiled and picked up her coffee. *Then it must be. Your father and I knew him. Briefly.*

When? The question like a cry, so that Aldous lifted his head. Something in Axel's voice had galvanised him, but he settled to sleep again. Axel cleared his throat noisily, coughed, his hand to his mouth. *Bones in the cheese.* He smiled. *I meant, did you meet him here?*

She laid her hand on his shoulder. *It's a long time ago, Axel.
Jørn did some work with the Danish Brigade. They were smuggling
Jewish people out of Denmark. You won't remember.* She paused,
thinking. *He was working in Stockholm then, in an architectural
office. Copenhagen was occupied, he couldn't practise there.*

He looked at her over his coffee, trying for calm. She
said: *We didn't work with him directly, not Anders and me at any
rate. But we liaised with the group. He was very young, in his early
twenties. We met him only a couple of times. But I remember the
intelligence in his eyes, in his face.* She held the cup in the fingers
of both hands. *And so now he's going to be famous?*

They had settled to their afternoon then, the books
and newspapers he'd brought. Occasionally one would read
something aloud to the other, make a comment on this
or that, the light silence lifting and falling in the room like a
curtain billowing from a window. His mother looked forward
to these times more than anything, he knew; these weekends
in his company, the conversation, books, the comfortable
quiet. It was a mutual joy.

But gradually, as he sat there, he was seized by an anxious
energy. His head alive with an insect buzz. It alarmed him
at first; he tried hard to disguise it, finding more snippets
to amuse her from the newspaper, teasing out her reactions

so he didn't need to talk. He didn't much trust his voice. When the coffee pot was empty he fell upon it gratefully, went to the kitchen for more. *None for me, älskling,* his mother called, so he filled his own cup and added a measure of akvavit.

In the sitting room he picked up a book of poetry in German from a pile on the table. Rilke. Within ten minutes the words and the akvavit had taken effect, and the urge to flee the house, to find Jørn Utzon, had gone. But in the following months, in the years of his apprenticeship, he sought out every project Utzon had drawn, read everything he could find about the man. When he discovered the architect was immigrating to Australia with his family for the years of the Opera House project, he knew what he had to do.

⌒

But now he couldn't imagine Utzon on Palm Beach. There was no correlation; it wasn't the same. Gulls strutted and cried, the air crisped over water that was constantly changing. The shore shifted, slid away with the tide. He linked his fingers around his knees. He might never find the place Utzon worked in. But he knew the architect well enough; he would prefer to be out, by the sea, walking on the headland, noting every curl and fist of foliage, bending to new shapes in leaf and flower, looking not at the ocean itself but through frames of branches and boughs at the splintered blue. He saw the whole through the partial. Everything mediated by its frame, leaving imagination to do its work. He loved him for that.

In the late afternoon he stood and brushed sand from his trousers. Walked to the bus stop and was not unhappy.

On the journey back a man sat across from him, bent his head politely, went back to his newspaper. Axel leaned across the narrow aisle. *I hear the architect of the Opera House has a boatshed out here,* he said, *a kind of working office.*

The man lowered his paper. *Yes,* he said. *Not at Palm Beach itself. It would have to be the around the other side, at Pittwater. Lots of boatsheds around there.*

Axel nodded and smiled. Turned to the window. So, he thought. Yes. It made complete sense.

⁓

How much had she drunk? Days later, Pearl would remember the dizzying mix of beer and something sparkly, thrown down fast in joy and relief while they sat in the ladies' lounge at the Federal. Two hours later, the surprise of unsteadiness, an unfocused walk to the bar, where she ordered a jug of water to stave off embarrassment and the stupefying tears that threatened, sudden, unforeseen.

There's another ballot in six months. As relief gave way to an old pessimism. She tipped back water, refilled the glass.

He won't be in it. Suze was serene in booze, sure of herself, infuriating.

While Pearl began to leak at the edges, emotions fragile as wet paper. She was determined to be bleak. *And next year both of them, Will too.*

It won't happen. Suze looked her in the eye, or tried to. *He's only up for one ballot, Pearl.* She emptied her own water glass, lowered it. *Quit this shit, sweetheart. You've had good news.*

Pearl squinted across the table. *Well. You know me,* she said. *Hell, since I was ten.* A grimacing smile. *Old catastrophe thinking.*

Suze leaned in, whispered. *There was a catastrophe, love. No wonder you feel like that.* She swallowed more water. *You were still a child when your mother died. We'd only just put away our dolls. Remember?*

That one with the weird hair. I used to dream she came to life.

We were starting to outgrow things, toys, skipping. Even our mothers. Their old-fogey ways.

Pearl said nothing, so Suze went on. *We wanted different lives to theirs. We used to sit around at school and tell each other how much we* hated *them.* She leaned forward. *Pearl, are you listening to me? It was a terrible time to lose your mother.*

~

It was after seven. Axel slipped quickly through the Mercantile's public bar, hoping to avoid Mrs Jarratt — *call me Olive* — and make the bathroom before the other men. The various moods of Olive Jarratt were hard to predict. In the days after he arrived she'd stood back from him, regarding him as she would a wild creature that had wandered into her bar. Watched him from a distance, kept her conversation to a minimum.

You'll get your tea every night, she snapped out the first time they met. Axel was diverted by her nostrils, which flared after every few words. *Full board, except for lunch.*

He'd been in the country just four hours. Tried for courtesy. *Full board,* he repeated.

Yep, she said levelly. *All found.*

He gave a twitch of a smile, a half nod, and didn't move from the patch of swirling orange and brown carpet inside the front door.

Mrs Jarratt sighed. *You get your breakfast and your dinner here,* she said loudly, as if he was deaf, indicating behind her to a room with plastic-covered tables and a sideboard stacked with white cups. *Your room cleaned once a week and your sheets. The rest* — she looked him up and down — *you do yourself.*

He dropped his eyes to his shirt and khaki pants, to check all was in order. But Mrs Jarratt had already turned away. He watched her haul her bad leg towards the bar. *Plenty of caffs in town to buy your lunch,* she said, chin to her right shoulder. *Probably a canteen down there at the Point.*

But after several weeks he realised he'd passed some unspoken test. She relinquished her customary abruptness and began to speak to him in a monologue, comfortable with his silence. Would materialise beside him at any hour and resume a conversation of her own invention, on various subjects he rarely understood. Out of politeness he would nod, attempt an expression of interest and after five minutes feign an appointment or a headache. Now he took the stairs two at a time, praying they wouldn't squeak.

He saw the letter as he unlocked his door. Blue airmail envelope, King Gustav Adolf on the stamp. On the back, *Mor,* in her plain hand. Nothing else. He placed the letter on the table; made himself wait until he'd showered, pulled a razor around his jaw and upper lip. As if she could see him. As if she was physically here, looking him over to make sure he was all right.

His room was plain: single bed, iron-framed, beneath a window that looked out over George Street. A small table and chair, a cupboard of dark wood, rough mat on the floor. Someone, a previous tenant he assumed, had left a wooden crate in the corner and two postcards tacked to the tongue-and-groove: Hong Kong harbour jostling with sampans, the Empire State Building. He would stand in front of these, smoothing back lifted corners, seeing his father between the sails of the boats, or walking up 104th Street. Hands in his pockets, whistling perhaps.

———

Suze leaned across the narrow table. *Listen to me, Pearl. This isn't your fault. You didn't start the war in Vietnam and you didn't invent bloody conscription.* She grabbed her hand. *And you can't save them from everything.*

Pearl blinked and swallowed the sob rising in her throat. Only Suze could do this, pull tears from a well she thought was dry. She was sober now, or close enough. She pressed her lips together, bent her head. Then dragged a sleeve across her cheeks. *I owe them,* she said.

You owe yourself, Suze said. Plucked up her bag and tapped Pearl's shoulder. *Let's go.*

They walked through rain-slicked streets towards Lorenzo's. Suze's choice, and it took Pearl by surprise. Suze hadn't been to a meeting in months. *I like the cause but not the people,* she'd shrugged when Pearl pressed her. They linked arms and walked without speaking.

—

Axel pulled a comb through his hair. Not wanting to sit in his room or force down the bitter brew that was the price of conversation with other men downstairs, he tucked the letter into his shirt pocket and walked to Lorenzo's. The consolation of real coffee. He'd discovered it within days of arriving: Italian, too strong, but amid the accents and faces of Lorenzo's Bar on Saturdays he cared less and less. He began to dream the aroma, beans in a grinder, the smell rather than the taste in his mouth. It had been like this at home: the smell of coffee had seeped into the curtains and rugs, baked into the walls by a fire that, in his memory, was always lit. Though it wasn't, not in summer, he knew that.

At night the bar was noisy and alive in a way it never was in the mornings. The barman ground beans and tipped his head towards a door at the back. *Meeting,* he said.

Axel sat at a low table with coffee and schnapps, stirred sugar around in the cup. Picked up a *Herald* discarded on a chair. Yesterday's, but no matter. He challenged himself to read to the end of a whole page without stopping at a word. But there he was again: snagged on a phrase, the letters impossible, his lips moving soundlessly over and around shapes that sat on the page like sharp stones in his path. 'Thespian.' He ran his fingers over the letters, his tongue refusing the 'th'. Eye and mouth conspired: he couldn't pronounce it so he couldn't understand it. Stupid. He gave up on the word, took a mouthful of schnapps. Browsed photographs instead. Then pulled out his letter.

Min älskling – always the same beginning. The one he used too: my darling. *Each day Aldous lies by the stove and mourns. His tail lifts and drops when I come into the room, his eyes follow me but his head doesn't move. Until the clock sounds three, the chimes soft as his paws on wood, and he is up and nudging my knee for the walk we take each afternoon. Can he count? Those chimes like a finger pressing, one, two, three.*

Axel lowered the airmail sheets onto the open news-paper. Tipped his head back, eyes to the ceiling, where Aldous and his mother moved against planes of deep colour, green, yellow, and then abruptly into white. What might have been fields and snow was just this, a background to the fine detail of his mother's coat, her skirt and boots, the hairs of Aldous's tail stiff with alertness and joy.

Of course, he misses you too. So we walk. Last week there were snödroppar beneath our feet, but they are all of spring so far. Fresh snow yesterday, and it stayed into the day, on branches and paths and chairs so we couldn't sit out, Aldous and me, and I wanted to, even in the weak sun. I wanted to sit and breathe in brand new air, feel the seasons change.

I imagine you there, Axel, in air that must be just like this. New. A place where surely change is daily, unremarkable. Is it? All that sun and warmth, it must make people brave. Make them kind.

His eyes went to the dark rectangle of the window. An old conversation: when he first went to study in Stockholm, at Konstfack, he and his mother had talked about art and change, how the best artists, the way they thought, could impact on the smallest thing, on every part of life. *When you go into a place*, his mother said one day, *look closely at the buildings, their windows and doors, look for paths along a river, or the seafront. So that people can walk by the water. So they can look out. And in the woods, so they can look in. Seats beneath trees. Places for children to play. Do the doorways have overhangs, shelter from the rain, the snow? Or for your old mother* — she raised her brows, mocking — *to rest on her way up the street?* She'd turned to stoke the fire. *These things make people kind, Axel. They lift their spirits.*

Axel didn't need to be told. He'd sought out all these things early here, as he looked for the form his glasswork might take. He looked at what was there, but mostly he looked for what was not there. For the missing or the denied, at what might be hidden. This habit, he knew, was born in him. He came from a place where shapes and contours had more than one meaning, and where the language of myth was the language of every day. In places all over Sweden, in Norway and Denmark too, the line of a hill might be the ceiling of the underworld, graves dug deeper than memory and ordinary to the eye. They were not hidden but ingrained in perception and outlook. No hill was just a hill.

At first he'd looked for shapes as Utzon had. In nature and in the structures built for families, for communities, for deities. Kronborg, the Mayan temples and their stepped platforms, their sculpted levels linked to make a meeting place between heaven and earth. So Utzon said, at any rate, and Axel had understood at once. It was not about religions so much as narrative and sacredness, the ways the earth was inscribed. The Mayans had their own way of communicating this, ways of passing their myths one to the next through ceremony and story and the grandeur of stone.

He thought of his mother treading her own stories through the forest, and knew those ways were missing here. Australians appeared to have no myths of their own, no stories to pass down. He'd read about the myths of indigenous people, the notion of a Dreaming and the intricate stories it comprised. He wondered if Utzon knew these legends, their history in this place. Had he known anything of Aboriginal people when he designed his building? As he sat down and drew shapes that could turn a place sacred? Turn its people poetic: their eyes to a harbour newly revealed by the building, its depths and colours new to them, and surprising. Perhaps that was what the architect was doing here: creating a kind of Dreaming, a shape and structure that would explain these people to themselves. Perhaps the building was just that: a secular bible, a Rosetta stone, a treaty. A story to be handed down.

If people would bother to look. If they'd bother to see.

From the room at the back came shouting and laughter, words shuttling back and forth. The language of debate, earnest, blasphemous; sentences ran together in waves over his head so he had no hope of comprehending. Only the occasional *bullshit/fuck that* or volleys of hooting laughter. It all made him queasy. He turned the pages of the paper, ignoring the 'th' word but wishing once more for someone

Kristina Olsson

beside him, prompting him as his mother had, her hand on his face, turning it towards hers and sounding the word, her mouth careful, particular over a *j* or a *z* or an *a*. She would smell of whey, cardamom, snow.

⁓

The streets were suddenly cool after days of heat. They walked down Broadway towards the city, heels hard on the cooling pavement, pulling cardigans to their chests. The early dark lapped at buildings and faces, deepened the layers of sky. Pearl felt the occasional rub of her friend's shoulder against hers, caught the wheaty scent of her hair, consoling as summer grass. *You can't save them:* she didn't believe her. Suze was an only child, with the insouciance of someone who'd been the sole focus of family worry or care. Their friendship had been made solid by this difference; they'd never had to compete.

Suze was the day to Pearl's night, a child of wind and air. She'd walked through her days with an absence that drove teachers wild; fey, untroubled, bright. She flourished beneath the benign neglect of parents who loved her but largely ignored her. Pearl had fallen in love with their American accents, the calm of their household against the chaos of her own. The exotic smell of their kitchen – goulash

and Welsh rarebit, curry and shortcake – became the smell of them. Suze was born exactly nine months after they'd landed in Sydney; there was no hint of America about her. *She's an Uzzie,* her father would say fondly whenever Suze uttered anything about America. *McCarthy can't get her.* A wide smile beneath his beard. She'd grown up without the obligation of worrying, or caring too much. Pearl knew it made their friendship all the more miraculous.

Outside Town Hall station a man crouched in a ragged blanket, his hat upturned before him. *Evening ladies.* The voice battered but his eyes were bright, mad, the gaze out beyond their faces and into the dark. They were caught in a funnel of people around the entrance, moving them forward. It didn't matter. Pearl stopped, spun around, shuffled back. Dug in her pockets and bent to him, wrapped his fingers around a pound note.

Suze was quiet as they fell back into step. *What?* Pearl glanced towards her.

Seconds ticked by. There was the click and scuff of their heels on bitumen. Finally: *That old man,* Suze said. *What did he say to you?*

They slowed their pace towards the corner. *He said, thanks sweetheart. Will you marry me?* Pearl laughed softly in the air between them. But Suze was blinking, her lips pursed.

He's all right, you know. The headlights of cars caught and released them, tyres pressed over the wet road. Pearl turned. *Suzy? People look out for him.*

Suze moved her head from side to side. Slowly, as if there was something she didn't believe, or couldn't understand. *It's not him,* she said, *it's you. You shame me sometimes, girl.* She sniffed, threw her arm around Pearl's shoulder. They walked wordlessly through the light gauzy air of the town.

⁓

There were more people in the back room than Pearl could ever remember. It was almost wall to wall. *The ballot's spooked everyone.* Bridget shrugged when Pearl found her. *And there's talk Renshaw will call the election.*

They fought their way to the bar. Male eyes on Suze, her long unruly hair, angelic eyes. Pearl handed her a scotch and leaned in close: *Don't mention Jamie.* Suze frowned. *Just don't.* She smiled and steered her back towards the group of women.

They came in halfway through Bridget's sentence … *the ones who get investigated? Those girls at Wanda Beach. Like it was their fault.* Eyes wide above her glass. *Like it matters what sort of girls they were, what school they went to. They bloody well had a right to be on the beach, whatever time it was.*

Della shook her head slowly. *Yeah, well I'd love to be able to walk around the harbour or down the beach at night, but no way.* She waved her glass around. *It pisses me off but I'm scared.* She shrugged. *I admit it.*

See? Bridget barked. *We move through the world in a different way. Men don't think twice about walking in the dark or leaving a door unlocked, a window open. It's fucked.*

Pearl thought about her solitary walks home from the ferry, often late. The bodies of those girls in the dunes, the sand claiming them. If you never went anywhere alone, was that acquiescence? If you relied on one man for company, for protection, for sex?

So weird, she said. *You take responsibility for yourself and you're suddenly culpable, asking for it.*

In the lull that followed they could hear pieces of conversations from the bar, from the back of the room. There was, Pearl knew, a wellspring of intention, a thousand plans for action. But even here, even tonight: the ennui she'd felt in the days before the ballot. It crept along her veins, made her blood sluggish. The mere mention of another demonstration made her tired.

Therese came to stand beside her. *Personally,* she grinned, indicating a loose group of men inventing slogans nearby, *I don't go anywhere without my hat pin.*

Then Suze spoke, quiet, even. Something in her tone made them all turn. *There are parts of a man,* she said, *that will shrink at the sight of this.* Pulling a bright red pen-knife from her jeans pocket.

Sputtering laughter. The women dispersed then to join other knots of conversation; Suze kissed Pearl's cheek and left to catch a cab.

Within an hour, the room felt too moody, its jokes and spats exaggerated, edgy. Pearl slipped out, needing food – peanuts, anything. Moved through the crowded front bar, scanning the room, nodding at familiar faces. Special Branch hadn't bothered with Lorenzo's yet, though she'd seen them weeks before, skulking behind trees during a gathering at the Domain. But there, in the corner, someone new, alone with his newspaper. Wire-rimmed glasses and the face of a boy. Thatched blond and intense, bent to his reading as if his life depended on it. Or as if he didn't have one.

From the back room came a general shuffling towards the street. Therese suddenly beside her: *Coming?* she said. *Party in Darlo.*

Shell

Meet you outside. Her eyes on the blond boy. He was older than Jamie, younger than she was. There was something in the tilt of his head, the line of his back.

She moved towards him, doubling around behind his chair. Dipped her head to his neck — *Are you hiding, comrade?* — and he raised his head without turning. But when he stammered an answer she felt it immediately — his voice, the smell of his skin, and moments later, his eyes — the bolt of pleasure, the kick in the belly, the flush of heat that came with wanting.

~

It had taken only a minute, two. The door behind him opened to a spill of men and women and noise. Words and phrases barrelled into the air, shattered around him, so that Axel, trying to listen, felt partial too. An old fragmentation. He dropped his head to his newspaper, the consolation of still pictures, sentences in print.

Later it would be her voice he remembered, and her eyes. Or rather, a sense of being seen. They'd spoken but they hadn't met. Their few words might fit into a palm, rubbed with a thumb, tossed up to feel their weight. Why then did he feel a transaction had been done, a proposal made and agreed to?

She said: *Why are you hiding?* Or some such. The voice low and sudden in his ear, conspiring; his skin pricked as if dipped in cold water. Then a woman's cheek against his. Breath clammy with alcohol. A phrase of his father's came first: *I beg your pardon?*

She was crouched behind him. An arm over his shoulder; he registered orange and brown on a sleeve, a marcasite watch.

Nothing to be afraid of here, she'd said.

He still hadn't seen her face.

She squeezed his arm then, and leaned away. Gone. He let newsprint swim up from the page for two, three, four seconds before he lifted his eyes towards the door. Flecks of orange flashed like low flames among the figures moving out into the night. Which one? A pale head turned to his question – did he say it out loud? – the face serious and open as a friend's. She held his eyes until the dark engulfed her. He sat staring for whole minutes as if she was still there. As if *she* had asked the question: *Which one?* Me, he wanted to say. It's me. He swallowed the last of his schnapps, and the bolt of warmth might have been the drink or it might have been the joy and fear of recognition. Of being seen.

Shell

He'd returned to Lorenzo's every night for weeks after that, a tremor of hope in his chest. But though the meeting room filled and tilted with sound and emptied again in the late hours, she wasn't there.

⌒

On Saturdays Axel would walk the early morning streets, greet men sweeping the pavements or wandering home with stunned eyes after night shifts at the wharf. The sky the colour of new milk in the pail. At the market he bought his scant supplies: fruit, soap, hard biscuits. Looked in vain for something resembling the cheese he loved at home. The old Greek women would smile and offer him discs of Cyprus bread. No cheese. Only the feta they made themselves, bitter to his tongue.

The sun was still low in the eastern sky, the day open. He was at once repulsed and drawn by the idea of the city and its watery edges: harbour and river and sea. Felt an obligation to know them, to see them in all weather, as if he was earning the right to be here. As if the right to create this glasswork demanded something in return. A concession, perhaps, to the people and the place, all that went before here, everything he didn't yet know. To pay attention: like a kind of tithe or tax on his presence. It was, he thought, a small price for the return. He set off towards the harbour.

Down at Woolloomooloo, he stood to watch the activity around the old wharf. An air of dereliction attended the men and the buildings; even the water appeared faded and dull and, like the men, overworked. He looked closely: here, among the sheds and decaying warehouses, there might be a building suitable for the next phase of the glasswork, when a bigger space was required. When there would be a team of glassmakers, furnaces, annealing ovens. The glasswork itself. And Woolloomooloo Bay was not so far from Bennelong Point.

At Rushcutters Bay the air had turned silver, and the sun struck lozenges of light across the surface, more lovely than he had imagined. It was, he thought, as if the harbour had split into two different bodies of water, such was the change over the two miles he'd walked. Rushcutters itself was a different colour: parks of rich green, trees that threw shadow and shade. He thought of the Mercantile and the scabrous streets it stood in. This place had once been no lovelier, he knew, the bay shallow and dull and swamped with rushes.

Before he'd left Sweden he had tried, unsuccessfully, to learn about the city he was coming to. He had been working in Malmö, making a piece for the town hall, but he could find little to help him in the library, or even at the university in Lund. So he'd caught the ferry to Copenhagen: if Utzon could see the sea charts for Sydney at the Australian Embassy there, then surely there would be maps and photographs of the place, press articles, general information.

Yes, of course, said an attractive young woman in a room hung with photographs of the Sydney Harbour Bridge and kangaroos in grassy fields. She had a charming accent, more formal than the Australian men he'd spoken to by telephone, more British. But still the flattened vowels, the *twang,* she called it. And blushed. He was offered pamphlets about weather and industry and beaches, and finally books that looked to Axel like school history texts. They were by and large a recitation of facts; convicts, explorers, wheat and wool. One-dimensional.

He thought then he would have to walk in this place, as his mother said, and wait for the country to reveal itself. But then from the sombre pages of a book passed to him by one of the architects, he learned something of Sydney's early history. This felt important in a place so content with itself, so disinterested in *how* and *why.* He'd begun to read about the first days of the British colony. ('Colony' he'd had to ask what it meant.) Here at last were scattered references to indigenous people, the groups who had first lived here, had hunted and fished and sung and danced here. On the very land, he realised, he worked and lived and walked on.

Now, at Rushcutters Bay, a startling story came back to him about the punishment of two convicts in the earliest days of New South Wales. The men were 'flogged' – whipped or beaten, he understood – for stealing fishing hooks and lines from the local Aboriginal people here in this bay. But the beating was so severe that the natives, watching nearby, wept loudly, and a woman had rushed forward to attack the man with the lash.

Axel's eyes flickered over the park and buildings, the gothic trees he'd come to know as Moreton Bay Figs. Did their great roots mingle with past times, now layered beneath this one? What was in this soil he walked on, beneath the polite paths and grass? At home in Småland he might have known, from his parents' and his uncles' stories, from listening and watching: a Viking grave, a buried village. But even though he looked for signs, as he trod the neat streets around Darling Point to Double Bay, he could see nothing but surfaces. The bright veneer of the place.

When he reached Point Piper he took a laneway past the yacht club. Stood on a miniature beach as the sun began to strengthen. Wished he could see through the earth he stood on, to find traces of the people who were here first. He wanted to see how they lived, hear them speak, hear them sing. He wanted to look into their eyes. To meet the woman who could not bear to watch a man flayed for taking a curved hook fashioned from a shell, a fibrous line. Even if they were her own.

~

Pearl could smell the place as she went through the gate, within minutes of getting off the bus: a pall of deteriorating flesh, of talcum powder and disinfectant and yesterday's roast. The staleness settled on her as she walked the corridors; it took a long soapy bath, whenever she got home, to scrub it from her skin. The funereal scent of lilies on tables and sideboards deepened the offence. She hurried past them, trying not to breathe.

In the common room a radio was tuned to the races. She stood momentarily in the doorway, readying herself. It was hard to tell if anyone was listening; the dozen or so faces were blank, unmoved by the race caller whose cries ricocheted around and evaporated among the crochet and antimacassars and the thick, listless air.

Patrick Keogh was in his usual chair, close to a French door that opened to the garden. She wondered if, in the world he inhabited, this was part of his escape plan. Through the door before anyone noticed, across the lawn, over the high brick wall meant to deter patients like him. Who might regard the wall as a minor obstacle; who might measure its height against the depth of their own misery, and run for it. She watched Patrick's still profile as she crossed the room; from this angle he might still be young, his mind and body strong, untouched by demons. Sadness balled in her chest, sudden and hard.

Sometimes he did not recognise her immediately. She had tried to get used to it but each time he turned a blank gaze to her a piece of her shrank. It was made worse by his eyes, as blue and fierce as they ever were. *Hello Dadda*, she said now, softly, fingers light on his shoulder. The race caller's voice trailed away to winner, favourite, odds.

Now Patrick twisted his torso, a mechanical man on low batteries. Regarded her. Seconds ticked on the black and white institutional clock. Clack, clack. Recognition crept to his eyes like a slow dawn. A twitch, a crease at the side of his lips, the closest he came now to a smile. She bent to him, kissing his forehead, relief flushing through her. The world tilted back into place.

Pearl pulled a chair close and took his hand in hers. Their familiar routine: they sat together as the last races were called, her father's gaze fixed on the radio as if he could see the track, the hooves and whips and silk. Maybe he could; she hoped so. In between she made small talk, the weather, the garden, football scores. Labor's chances at the election. As she spoke her eyes flicked over his clothes, his shoes, checking that his lovely, spade-shaped fingernails were trimmed and clean. She pulled a tube of moisturiser from her shoulder bag and smoothed it over the dry skin on his hands and his forearms, continuing her prattle.

She'd always known she wasn't his. What she'd have given, when she was younger, to be his flesh and blood. It meant nothing now; she was so utterly his daughter in every other way. He'd made sure of it, making no difference between her and the ones who followed. And he'd named her. Though she was three when she met him and had been Shirley forever. The story of her re-naming became part of her personal mythology: six months after Amy met Patrick, as soon as she was sure of him, she had introduced him to her daughter. And Patrick, bending to take her hand, had said simply, *Shirley, is it? Well. Shirl the Pearl.* Frowning gently at her, and at her mother. Then: *Amy, that's who she is. Just look at her. That's her true name.* He smiled like a priest, baptising. *Pearl.* It was the moment, she knew, when he became her true father.

Now from the corner a ragged cry went up, the words harsh, unknowable. It was Billy, no older than her father, his face anguished, hands gripping the arms of his chair. He cried again. One or two faces turned to his and away again. Billy blinked at them, subsided, and was quiet. The rattle and chink of the tea trolley sounded in the corridor.

Pearl looked to her father, but his eyes were untroubled. Then: *Where's Amy?* he said. *Where's your mother?* This happened sometimes, his voice resuming the strength it once had and his forehead creasing. *Is it onions she's gone for?* He swung around to her. *We've onions in the garden!*

Pearl squeezed his hand. *She'll be along soon, Da,* she said. *Don't worry yourself. She'll be here soon.*

A woman in white appeared at their side with clay-coloured tea in a thick white cup. Pearl watched her father's fingers curl around the handle. Once it was the chains and hooks and ropes of wharf or foundry, a beer glass, fiddle strings. Now his hands around a teacup, this slight tremble, was enough to make her weep. She looked away. A magpie crept from the lawn to the patio, tipped back its head and carolled. *Just look at this visitor now,* she laughed, and Patrick turned his ear to its song. The remnant of a smile crossed his face. His dear face. Pearl swallowed hard. Amid all that had been taken from him – wife, family, memory – this remained. Just he and the bird, watching each other. She heard the low push of air as her father tried to whistle.

She stood behind his chair and wrapped her arms around him. *The boys will be along, Da.* The voice of a fourteen-year-old. She came out of nowhere, still needing approval. Did he hear her? It didn't matter. The words had been spoken aloud now; he might remember what she said, he might not.

As she left she looked over her shoulder. His face was still turned to the magpie.

~

The bus ploughed the ordinary streets back to the city. She thought about her parents, what love was. Their marriage had been like any other, she guessed, up and down, happy and besieged by turns. She had always seen her father as the hero in it, circling her mother and her moods, her wounded sense of herself. Amy's face: the twist of her lips, the way they pressed over a joke or some displeasure; the lack of emotion in it sometimes, though that usually meant fury. It soon showed up. She'd skin spuds as if they were alive. Pull weeds from the garden, vicious, indiscriminate. Back inside her hands snapped dry washing into folds. But much worse than that: the thunderous silences that rolled around a room, collided with everyone, bruising.

At these times her father would busy himself at the wood pile, or walk to the shop for a paper or a pouch. If she was quick enough Pearl would slip through the gate and walk with him, quiet at his side. After a few moments: *She's got a fine temper, your mother,* he'd say, hands in his pockets, looking straight ahead. She would feel – briefly, softly – his palm on her head. At the shop he'd buy barley sugar twists.

But she saw now they had understood each other. As if the things that had passed between them had brought them acceptance, and a restraint – at least from Patrick – that meant there were few arguments. Only the kind of questioning Pearl loved, a kind of storytelling between her father and her twelve-year-old self, a way of winkling out his take on the world.

But why would the government hate the workers? What's the sense of it Da?

They think we're below them, girl. Down there with foxes, with dogs.

But foxes and dogs are clever.

They are. But still treated badly, still at the mercy of men.

Why?

Maybe they're scared of their cleverness. Their teeth.

You're making fun.

I am not, Pearl.

The workers do the work.

They do.

You're a worker, Dadda. Do they hate you?

It's not personal, girl. They don't know me.

And if they did – said her mother, clearing plates.

Her father frowned. *Maybe hate is the wrong word. They need us, but they don't much like us. They need us to keep in our place so they can keep in theirs.*

Where?

All the rich houses. The swanky hotels now, the silver service. If they keep us beneath them they can stay on top. See? On the table he made a triangle with three matchboxes on the bottom, two on top, then one more. *There's always got to be someone at the bottom.*

Pearl would keep that image for the rest of her life. The triangular shape of the world. What it was that pushed and pulled and held its fine point. It was there in her father's fingers, the line of grease he could never scrub from his nails.

～

Axel's Saturday walks settled him, endowed a kind of possession that driving never could. And afterwards, footsore, thirsty, there was coffee. Each week he sat at the same low table, the Saturday *Herald* on his knee, or a letter from home, or his history book. Today it was the paper; a habit, now, to check for stories of Utzon. Nothing. He turned the pages over again, making sure. Then a presence on the seat beside him. He turned. Early afternoon sun slanted through glass and settled on her face, in her eyes, so her skin was infused with light. She said: *Pearl Keogh*. And offered a hand. The name no surprise: she was luminescent. *Axel Lindquist*, he said, trying for calm. Grasping the hand, the strong fingers. On her wrist, a marcasite watch. She said, *Shall we have coffee*, though it wasn't a question, and turned her head to a waiter.

He folded the newspaper and pushed it to the side. Then: *You Swedes*, she said. *Meant to be good lovers, aren't you?*

Axel glanced past her to the street. They'd known each other precisely ninety seconds. But now her smile widened, opening up the still space between them. *Is that so?* he said, returning it.

⌒

They caught a late afternoon ferry and sat outside. The lowering sun washed over them, along the deck and the passengers leaning at the rails. In that mild air they spoke without wariness, words and thoughts considered and offered as evidence of who they were, or might be. Something in the light, in the roll of water beneath them – in the very decision to catch the ferry – made them brave. Or perhaps, Axel thought later, it was the physical spark of their first sentences – *Meant to be good lovers, aren't you / Is that so?* – that fired the air around them, took them beyond that to reckless.

A journalist. The reply to his question casual, the words snatched by wind. But he thought: of course. Her easy questions, the veneer of toughness she'd need in that world. Now she waved his own questions away, and asked him about his home, his work. So he told her about Småland as a way of answering both. About lakes strewn across the land like shards of glass. His province, he said, was merely paths between water, as if the earth was a veneer too. As he spoke he had a clear picture behind his eyes. The certainty he'd had as a boy: even when the sun shone uninterrupted from a clear sky, the land held a memory of water.

He'd felt a shock of elation when he realised the connection, the inevitability: that glass would be made in this liquid place. *But of course I had known it all along, even as a child,* he said, *watching my uncle at the forge. Like a dragon, I thought then, breathing smoke and fire.* This kinship of glass and water. So water itself became a substance, something to look through, and outwards to the world.

Pearl asked: *What was your first piece? The first things you made.*

He smiled a boy's smile. *Trolls,* he said. *With strange heads and large noses. And a jar for flowers.* He felt colour rise in his cheeks. *My mother still has it.* There it was before him, clear and unsettling as a dream: uneven, misshapen, the bubbled glass tinged green from iron in the sand. His mother coming through the door with flowers from the fields, setting them in the jar where their fragrance mingled with coffee, with cardamom. And another smell, sweet, acrid. Because, at the edge of the picture, his father, the tobacco tin open by his side.

He would roll the papers with exactitude, pass his tongue along the edges, tucking, tapering. Always one for his mother first. If it was summer they would go outside in the sun and crouch together like thieves. His mother tipping her head back and exhaling, his father twisting his lips to send the smoke sideways. Axel would kick a ball half-heartedly around the garden, pretend not to watch. But the intimacy of this ritual would stay with him, the casual arrangement of their bodies, the unison of breath, inhale, exhale, cigarette between thumb and forefinger, elbows on knees. He saw that they barely glanced at each other. It wasn't necessary.

Shell

He turned to Pearl. Fine strands of hair, straw-coloured, whipped around her face. *There was so much I didn't know. Don't know. Still.*

She shrugged. *I know less with every year.*

He squinted at the setting sun. *For a long time I wanted everything to be perfect. I thought it was just about effort, and skill.* He stopped, afraid of saying too much. Of what he couldn't say in English, not properly. How his glasswork had flowered into complexity, a way of shaping his yearning, of what he saw – the lakes, the shore and its paths, rain, snow. His liquid world. The terrible strength of water and of glass. Their fragility and beauty. *I was just a child then,* he shrugged.

~

Later, in her bed in a room that held the sound of the sea, he woke to find her eyes on him. Lying on her side, head propped on her hand. They looked at each other until she said, quietly: *Nothing can come of it, Axel. Just this. Skin. Amnesia.* She let her head fall to the pillow. *It's nice. That's all.*

He was dulled by sex and sleep. *Amnesia?* The word out of context, dragging at his brain. Then: *You mean – a way of forgetting?*

Yes. She yawned, her hand on her mouth and then on his chest. They spoke gently, as if there was a child in the room they did not want to wake.

Axel looked up at the ceiling, closing a hand over hers. *For me*, he said, *it's the opposite. With you my body remembered itself. As if it was –* He turned his head to her. *Fully conscious. Even my hip bones. My eyelids.*

She frowned. *Aren't you conscious at your work?* She thought of his fingers and hands, their delicate negotiation of her body and of the materials and tools of his trade.

Yes, of course. But only of the work, what it asks, what it demands. He paused. *It's different.*

She thought about this. The thin curtain lifted and fell, an echo of his accent; the words settled on her skin. On the weight of her legs and shoulders against the sheets. She closed her eyes and turned to him. They slept.

$\sim$

In the morning they drank tea at a table by the kitchen window. Pearl tipped a matchbox end to end, looked out to the garden through narrowed eyes. She wore a permanent squint, Axel thought, wore it even in her sleep. At first he had taken it for interrogation, or an analytical attitude to everything from a government policy to a blade of grass. But perhaps it was not aggression so much as uncertainty. It gave her a fierceness she might need in a newsroom, but some men, he knew, would look her in the eye and see a challenge there, a glove thrown down. Jonas in the casting yard, for instance, would want to take her down a peg before she even said hello.

He smiled to himself: the local slang he'd absorbed.

What?

He shrugged. *Odd expressions. Your language. Sometimes I think you have to learn it twice. English, and Australian.*

But she was blank, quiet, a child pulled too early from sleep. So he kept his voice low. *When I was very young,* he said, *I used to dream in words. No pictures. In the mornings I would tell my mother: älva, bil, ljusstake. Elf, car, candlestick. If she asked what they did I couldn't say. Instead I would spell them out.* His finger moved on the table, making word shapes. He watched her, followed her gaze. She didn't speak. *Tell me your earliest memory,* he said.

Her eyes on the wood of the table top, as if his words were inscribed there. *First memory.* Her fingers on the matchbox. Tip, tip. Then she looked at him. *Or first sense? Not sure they're the same.*

Seconds of silence as Axel sought the difference. But before he could answer: *The smell of urine, mine, some other child's. A sheet with a diamond pattern. A late storm* – she glanced to the window – *and the sky, split with light.*

The word *light* held by the ticking air between them. Then: *My father,* she said. Her voice trance-like, removed. *Leading me away from the smell and the crying.*

Axel looked down, unsure he was meant to hear. It was as if she had told an old secret, or pulled something hidden from beneath the bed, so old she barely recognised it. He stilled the urge to touch her. Looked past her to the hallway, to roses on old wallpaper, faded, pale. There among them, his own father's face.

For a long time I thought I'd dreamed that. The sheet, my father.

He waited.

It took ages to find the right questions. Eventually I asked him about that place, that smell. Had I made it up? He hesitated, my father, and then he told me. You had another life for a while, he said, you and your mother. Before I met you. Before you chose me.

Axel looked quickly around him, imagining the conversation in this kitchen, the child, the man. The shadows of other children.

There was only one answer I wanted. It was the only one he gave. He said, you are mine, as much as the twins are, Jane, the boys. My Pearl. Haven't you always been?

He waited. Then: *Where are your sisters now, your brothers?*

Pearl lit a cigarette and exhaled, waving away the smoke and the question. So he was startled by what came next. *Lost them all.* Her eyes, her voice once more her own as she told him.

Six children and a mother dead from blood poisoning. A father drunk on grief. Pearl the eldest at fourteen, unable to stop the disintegration, the scattering to homes and orphanages. The baby taken by her mother's youngest sister and the twins, even at eight, had each other. It was the middle ones who suffered. She told the story as if reciting from a school text. The words cold stones in her mouth.

She kept repeating two words, 'the welfare', as if they were obscene. This confused him. In his mind 'welfare' translated to benevolence. Food for every child, warmth, medicine. Dignity. *I don't understand,* he said, his hands in his lap.

She raised her eyebrows. *No,* she said, *it's different where you come from. Here it's the people who take your children away. For being poor.*

Homes, he heard. That were not like homes at all. Her brothers had fled the beatings and the loneliness. *But I've got to find them now,* she said flatly, *before the army does.*

More questions flared in him but he kept them to himself. They sat in silence. Then she pulled the empty cups towards her. Without looking up she said: *And you, Axel. What's your wound?*

He blinked at her, tilted his head.

The thing that hurt you.

His face was a shutter that opened and then closed. *I'm not sure —*

My mother died when I was fourteen. She ran a finger over her forehead. *See? You can read it on my face. That's how it's always felt.*

His hands cupped together in his lap. *Oh. Fourteen.* He paused. *You need her then.*

There was the raw blue of sky and one bird, crying. She said, *Yes, I did.*

He let her words settle. The weight of them. Then: *My father is missing,* he said.

He told her about the work his parents had done in the war. Bringing Jewish people out of Europe. The White Bus movement, the Danish Brigade. Some vague and forgotten member of the Swedish royal family, doing deals with Hitler to free Jews from the camps. Clandestine meetings and voices he could hear from his bedroom, someone in the spare bed for a night and then gone. His father away for a week, a few days, and then, after Axel's tenth birthday, not coming home at all.

I've never heard of the White Buses. She eyed him as if he'd made it up.

He didn't flinch. *No one — how do you say it? — made a song and dance. How could they? There were so many who were not saved.*

Pearl plucked the cups from the table and pushed back her chair. *Yes,* she said. He heard her behind him at the sink, refilling the electric jug. He might have imagined it, but he felt the air turn raw, jagged.

Sweden was neutral in the war, she said. He could hear the click as she plugged in the jug, turned it on.

Her voice came to him as a soft echo, bouncing off the wall she faced and the familiar innuendo of others. He let it remain there between them, let the seconds tick away. Then: *Neutral, yes. Which was not as easy as you might think,* he said. *And not as straightforward.*

He laced his fingers together on the table, turned his face to the window. A bird hung there, its angle improbable, as it sought the syrup of crimson flowers bunched along a branch. The tree burned with colour. Axel didn't know its name. He was still disarmed by the notion that flowers grew on trees here rather than in the ground. He walked home some evenings beneath galaxies of red and yellow and ivory, navigating his way by them, cluster and constellation.

What is this tree? He turned as she spooned instant coffee into mugs. The odd brew another new experience, not wholly pleasant.

A cursory glance over her shoulder. *Callistemon,* she said tartly. *Common bottlebrush.*

But Axel found their spiky plainness beautiful, the messy flowers steadfast in the wind and sun.

Pearl put the coffee in front of him and turned away. *Got a meeting this morning,* she said. *I have to make a call.*

⌒

Later, this is how she will remember it. The telephone on the hall table, her hand along its curve. The wind stilled, bringing the rush of traffic closer, a dog's bark. So she might have imagined the click when she pressed the phone to her ear, a noise she will recall as one brief pipe of a cicada and the ear's expectation of more. It was that expectation, an absence of sound rather than a silence, that turned her stomach. She was barely aware of returning the receiver to its cradle. Stared at it, and at her own hand, as if they might be contaminated. She turned to Axel and said: *My phone's been tapped.*

⌒

No one could be trusted. Pearl knew this in her body. But it had bloomed into consciousness with her mother's death, when a cleft opened up between her and safety. Suspicion calcified in her limbs. It had taken a long time for them to unclench, for any optimism to return. *Loosen up,* one boyfriend had said when she was nineteen, *we're not all bad.* She wasn't convinced, but something in his tone had nudged at her. It was, she saw too late, his unencumbered childhood; he had no reason to be fearful, no reason to distrust. He anticipated only safety and goodness, expected it in the world and in others.

She sat on a bus and looked at faces sliding by on the street. Her lips pursed over her own naïveté. Why hadn't she seen it coming? All these people on the footpath, on the bus: they would vote for a government without rigour or compassion, applaud when young men were sent away to war. Or when spies were turned on neighbours, shadow people who dealt in secret dossiers and threats. They were all cheats and liars, and worse: they had turned her fearful again, paranoid even, terrified of what might be next.

Part of her, she knew, would be forever stuck at that moment in the flat. The shock that had registered in her body, as if the dull carpet she stood on had been alive, electrified.

Now she shrank against the window with her forehead to the glass and saw the city flicker past, reduced to scenes, each one unknowable now, a façade. The women with their shopping bags, the men in doorways. She hated them for it, all of them, for what she'd felt as she stood there, gripping the telephone. The cleft re-opening, her whole body sliding towards it.

⌒

She got off the bus near Central. It was early, so she wandered into the station. She loved the open canopy of the vaulted roofs, the benign light. And there was safety in the air of the country and interstate platforms. They were consoling in their intimation of distance, of elsewhere. The threshold between here and there. She sat down on an empty seat on an almost empty platform and let other places and other lives ghost along the tracks in front of her, around the ornate steel above.

Three children slumped resentful on a nearby bench. Crumpled shirts and too-big shorts on the boys but below her plain skirt the girl wore patent leather shoes. Red. Her legs stuck out straight from the seat and she stared down at the shoes, the miracle of them. The boys shoved and shouldered without conviction, their faces pale and tired. But something in the girl had been wakened in the shine of the patent leather. Pearl watched her and knew: the little girl was seeing herself there, some bright potential, for joy or beauty or something larger than what she had or what she was.

The knowledge caught in Pearl's throat, stung her eyes. She watched this girl but saw another, years older but the look was the same, staring into a window at Mark Foy's, where dummies wore dresses a mother might wear, or that a daughter might ask to, and expressions that might tell her what she most needed to know. What a woman might be.

At twelve she'd watched Amy for ways to be a woman a man would love. Sideways looks at the cut of a skirt, the colours in blouse and ribbon. Her hair tied this way or that. The way she arranged her features as she pressed pastry on the table – the thinness of that pastry, the movement of floury forearms. The shape of her lips when she sang to the baby. Or gathered the washing in.

Pearl listened, and saw. Even then, there was something in Amy that repelled and frightened her. She couldn't acknowledge or name the thing; it lived alongside the love that burned in her as she watched her mother at the treadle machine or bending to kiss the boys. She grew to fear the love she saw reflected in her, a love that could relinquish volition and accept servitude, daily. The *dailiness* of it. Her mother's anger, simmering, subcutaneous, hinted at where it might lead.

At twelve Pearl had resisted the surrogate role she was meant to assume as the eldest. Though it was hard with Jamie and Will who, at one and two, had been displaced by the new baby at their mother's breast. Could find nothing to compensate, unlike the twins. Then, or later. It was for them that she'd made her decision. That was how it felt. A week after the funeral, when the gulf of grief, kept shut by the flurry of arrangements and visitors, had opened at their feet. One day she was at school writing a composition on the Commonwealth, aware that no one in class could bear to look her in the eye, and the next she was tying her mother's apron around her waist, hooking marbles out of Jamie's mouth, the baby howling on her hip.

A note was sent to her father: was there no alternative to Pearl's leaving school? The girl was bright. She might go far.

But even if Pearl had passed on the note, Patrick Keogh was beyond replying. It wasn't just the grog, not then. For a while he simply lost the capacity to translate the world around him. He knew his girl was clever; he loved her quickness, the way that, even at twelve or thirteen, she'd known how things stood. The inequities of life. But his own loss had blinded him to hers; he could not see that her world had collapsed into itself, vanished in a day: her mother, her schooling. But Pearl was not blind to her father. She saw him diminish, shrink before her eyes.

He'd never been much of a drinker. A glass of beer before his dinner at night, two on Fridays. A skinful at parties, yes, for the courage to sing 'Molly Malone' and 'The Black Velvet Band'. His face tipped up like a choirboy. But the voice in his throat had the longing and loss of Limerick ground up in it, a fine slurry, her mother would say, kissing his eyes when he'd finished. Pearl, in a corner with the babies, watched the other women wanting to.

That face again, just weeks after the funeral. Some nights he would look at her with the eyes of a child who wants something but is afraid to ask. Or hasn't the words. But she was too tired, too needy herself. If she'd still had her religion she might have named it, spoken it for him: mercy. Might have found it in herself, and gone to stand behind him in his seat at the table's head, put her arms about his neck. Consoled him with stories, with songs.

But by nine o'clock she was all used up. *Goodnight Da,* she'd say, throwing a tea towel over the clean dishes in the rack and plucking the last empty bottle from his hands. *Go to bed now.* This turning herself into someone else each day.

This fight, as she spooned the porridge, pulled singlets over small heads, stirred the copper, to be what she had to be: immune to her previous self. To her plain, untroubled girlhood.

Still, even without the drink, Patrick would have been unable to respond to the teacher's note. Pearl knew it, and understood that despite his pride, his plans for her future, her father was grateful for her decision. And that his gratitude was as big as his shame.

When her mother's sister offered to care for the baby, she looked at Jane asleep in her cot and wept for the first time.

Sitting at the station now she could only look back at herself with pity. Because it was whimsy, she'd only played at being a woman. Imagined it, dreamed it. Even at 32 she was still dreaming it, still trying on womanhood as she had her mother's hairbands, regarding herself in the mirror. As if the glass was regarding her, and might speak, saying *yes, yes.* Or perhaps, *not yet.* Despite the clever blond boy she'd taken home the previous night and just abandoned, without ceremony, outside her flat.

She glanced again towards the children nearby. Beyond their heads the row of clocks moved on. The boys found the energy to argue and the girl cried out, her head tipped back. *Mum!* And a woman at the magazine stand turned. Pearl stood, pulled at her skirt and walked from the platform. Stepped into the current of people moving towards the station entrance.

Ray was lounging against a stone pillar. He fell into step beside her. *They've bugged my phone,* she said into the arched sunlight. It was particled with shadow. Out of the corner of her eye she saw his head jerk sideways and then back. *Let's get a drink,* he said. Dug his hands in his pockets as they walked. Autumn sun slid over awnings and paths. He steered her towards Elizabeth Street, and as they approached the bar he said, *Timing's interesting.*

She stopped on the footpath in a drift of fallen leaves. Aware only of the sound of her voice, a low hiss in the air. *Why?* She swallowed. *What do you mean?* A breeze picked up, leaves flipped around her feet. There was nothing else, just the bladed edge of the world, tipping.

He turned his face towards her. *Just heard. Troops to Vietnam. Conscripts too.*

Blood avalanched through her veins, taking voice and words. The air stilled. Finally: *When?* An undertone, ice sliding through water. She stepped across the leaves and waited, her back to him, so when the answer came it might have been from anyone. *Soon,* he said.

May 1965

The *Sydney* and its cargo had slipped silently out of the harbour just after midnight. No crowd to farewell them, no wives or girlfriends. No official salutation, no music or flags. Just the southern stars to steer by, its own navigation lights. But as the ship met the mouth of the harbour, a banner, the length of five men end to end, whispered from the shimmering cliffs: 'You Go to an Unjust War!' A silent battle cry from the powerless, the mothers and sisters and aunts. But the ship ghosted past, eyeless, blind, nosing the Pacific Ocean, grinding its passengers north.

There was fury at the cowardice of it, the lack of honour. *What they'll do,* Della said, reading the reports in her kitchen, *to avoid a few protesters.* Pearl folded leaflets, pressing hard on the creases. She knew where the rage began; it had boiled in her for months. They were all powerless before the old men of Australia, their cynicism and lies. The collusion of her newspaper colleagues, joining the troop ship secretly as it cowered in the shadows of the harbour. And Menzies, making plans to do what he swore he wouldn't: send conscripts to war. They *knew* he would. It was another announcement in a midnight parliament, no one to object. The man was scurrilous, a coward. The stealthy departure, Pearl saw, symbolised it all. Made the rest of them powerless, mute.

A demonstration, even a placard, at least felt like volition, felt like a voice. Would have given them a sense of agency. *How do you think I feel?* she said, not meeting Della's eye. She pulled the last from a cigarette and ground its end into the ashtray, savage. The betrayal: her own editor had known, and Henry. It had suited them to keep the government's secret this time. And not just for the front-page accounts, the interviews with soldiers. It became their secret too. It made the mindless work of the women's section more galling than ever. She felt more powerless than she ever had, her hands tied.

Still, part of her wondered about the boys on that ship, their own volition. They might have volunteered to be soldiers, but how many knew what it entailed? They might be as ignorant as she was. How much choice did they really have, the sons of the poor and the naïve? Had they been on deck to see the banner, did they know what it meant? And the furtiveness of their departure: like sly dogs rather than heroes, slinking off in the dark. She felt the shame of it for them, the suspicion they must have: that there was something wrong in all this. It was not the way their fathers went to war.

In the days after, the newsroom rang with pro-war rhetoric. There was, Pearl felt, barely a dissenting voice. Only one newspaper – not her own – editorialised against it, and Arthur Calwell led the opposition in protest. From her desk she watched as each edition rolled out, scaring up the national fear of 'Communist China' and the return of the 'Anzac spirit'. Australia, it seemed, had conjured a war for itself out of nowhere, out of nothing, a war that wasn't a war and an enemy no one had heard of. When she stopped a cadet reporter outside the clippings library one day, he could not tell her where Vietnam was.

How could the whole country support this war? That was how it seemed. The losses and terror of World War II were just twenty years behind them, Korea only twelve. We followed Britain into the first, she thought bitterly, and America into the second, and now, compliant children, we were following them to Vietnam. And Menzies – she wanted to shout it to the newsroom – Menzies had led them into all three.

Shell

The full team was now at work in a dilapidated warehouse at Woolloomooloo Bay. It was near the site of the old swimming baths, and a pleasant walk back through the Botanic Gardens to the Opera House. At first a few of the youngsters had frowned at the shabbiness, of tenements and streets, the air of decay in the area nearby, but Axel saw other particularities. This was the place, he was sure, that could locate and hold his thinking, contain his anxiety, anchor him. The shabby wharf and crumbling houses, the naval yards. And the rusted sheds like the old hot shops of his childhood, where his uncle still made his glass.

But more than all that: here near the water he could still feel the presence of Utzon, the boy he had been, growing up around the shipyards where his father had worked. Aage Utzon, he told the students. A naval architect; his sons had spent their boyhoods in boats. The coastal village of Aalborg was not like Woolloomooloo; its red-roofed houses and churches were centuries old, its air mild. But the colour of its harbour was uncannily like Sydney's; its blue as deep, a pure cerulean, and singular. The town clustered around it so that, like the workers at the Opera House, the villagers could go fishing right in the middle of town.

He had assembled the team of local craftsmen and students early. Insisted they should be involved as soon as possible to ensure that, as his drawings progressed, his small experiments, they understood the work at a cellular level. And that they understood him. This was paramount. At this stage the glassmaking was essentially a collaborative affair. It required not just craftsmanship but generosity, loyalty, trust in each other. They would be working with volcanic heat, with high risk. They would each depend on one another, not least Axel, who would entrust each man and woman with his vision and his heart, the translation of complex idea to tangible object.

The necessary equipment for the project had also been installed: the big furnace and crucible pot, annealing oven and mavers, welding equipment and steel. Sand. The enormous old benches were soon covered in tools: scoops and ladles, tongs, clipping scissors, grinders. At the back, an office and lunchroom had been divided off from the 'factory floor'. He and the senior men would gather in this space for discussions, to wring solutions from problems as they worked towards the final form. It was far from final now, but for Axel the real triumph lay in these fraught weeks, in the solving of difficulties, one try after another, until the piece held together in his mind and in space. Until his thinking matched the physical presence of the glass.

He had asked the students to consider some smaller pieces that might accompany the main one. Had them walk around the Opera House, examine its plans, and read the Red Book, a dossier of plans and sketches and reports Utzon had produced just after winning the competition. Axel was pushing them away from material value and pure technique. *You have the knowledge, all of you. So go beyond function, beyond order,* he told the group one day after they'd suggested clear crystal pieces, classic shapes all sheer or transparent. *The Opera House is not a classic shape. Have you noticed? What does it make you feel? What are your emotions?*

Of course, he said, *there is a place for pure skill. You must achieve it but then go beyond it. Beyond bland perfection, beyond mere things.* These young Australians, individually chosen for their potential, had not initially understood. They had blinked at him, nodding courteously, but in their eyes he could see it: they were constricted by convention. By the pursuit of technical purity at the expense of freedom. Was it their isolation here, their island mentality, that pushed them towards the utilitarian and prevented free flight? Surely, he thought, it should be the opposite. It wasn't that they didn't understand beauty. But there was a sense of being embarrassed by it, that it was an indulgence. The practical was held in such esteem. It made them too polite.

He thought about his own student days with Per at Konstfack. They had gone there together to study ceramics, and they too had been like these students; locked into presumptions about form and function, adopting a kind of toned-down simplicity their own country was obsessed with then. Axel had quickly become uneasy with the approach: *It's the downside to the welfare state,* he said to Per. *I can't bear it. It's not all about usefulness.* But his new teachers soon opened their eyes to the intellectual force in art, its expressive potential. They began to find their own style.

There'd been a letter from Per a month before, from Åfors. He was writing poetry at night, making glass by day. Experimenting with new types of moulds and colouring methods, running with the avant-garde, in a group of young people from various glass houses who challenged each other in the glass room and outside it.

He wrote about the 'Nobel Club' they'd recently formed. The name an ironic reference to the great man but really to their explosive meetings. *We had fun at the club last week,*

Axel read. *The press is reporting naked games in the fields and rockets fired at midnight, parties, homemade schnapps ... and some of it might be true. But you know how it is Axel, because we push each other in every way, and if we go beyond certain lines at the club then it works for us in the glass room too. We compete with each other, we go beyond what we thought we might, or could. We are all producing our best work, and the energy and sense of camaraderie is higher than ever.*

Axel smiled to himself now, as he thought of telling these young locals to just relax and take their clothes off, to enjoy some naked dancing on Bondi Beach. Perhaps that might produce some startling work in the glass shed, something beyond expectation. A piece to defy the great Australian complacency, a piece that was more than a scoop of bowl, or a perfect cup.

But Per was right. There were some shapes drawn in his notebook that slipped alongside conscious thought, shapes Axel did not know or recognise until he drew them. At times monumental, archaic, from the heads of the old kings, runic in their promise and mystery. Or miniature, frantic with detail, whole worlds through a window, or cupped and held like a ball. He would follow their lines on the page, trying for less, to eliminate falsity or sham. Tried to keep the form pure, free of rhetoric and sentiment. Occasionally he would take those thoughts to the furnace, would invite a local art student to assist him. And find himself speaking as Lars had, using language to shape the piece as much as his hands did.

That is the tension, in what the light suggests, where it falls or bulges, disappears. Or *Look into the deep, the heat fading to ice —.* If a student turned blank eyes to him, he was careful, but plain: *The pipe is an extension of you, the air from your chest. Do you see? The glass will reveal itself but will also reveal you.* That, he knew, was precisely what frightened them, what sometimes frightened him.

Now in the red-rusted shed near the water, there were two large prototypes and a gallery of pieces on floor and shelf and table. He stepped from one to the next, gauging colour and line, a finger to edge and roundness. One surface sandblown and ancient, another imprinted with wire net. Urgency tapped at his shoulders. And fear: the underbelly of art. The thought reverberated in his head: if the final piece revealed anything of this place, of these people, it would reveal just as much of its maker. He stood in the middle of the room, encircled. Felt a pulse, a current beneath his skin. It fizzed and faded. But he knew what it was: an intimation of the story here, of chaos shuffling its reptile feet towards order.

He sank to his haunches to properly see, let the hemispheric, the grooved blue, settle into themselves. The rheumy grey of the arcs and spheres. Let his body find its place with them.

~

What do they mean by the 'Country Party'? Do they mean they are a party for the whole country?' When the men began filing into the warehouse, Axel was reading the morning paper. *'And what is meant here by 'Liberal'?'*

There was the sound of muffled laughter and low hoots of derision. Axel looked up from the pages spread over his knees. Smiled. *I didn't realise I'd made a joke.*

The men fanned out to gather their gloves and tools. *They're the joke,* one of them said. *That's the meaning of Country Party. They're clowns, all of them.*

The senior man, Barry, looked over Axel's shoulder at the *Herald's* front page. *The Liberals are conservative. They joined up with the Country Party and they won the election this month,* he said. *And no, the Country Party is about people in the bush, the provinces.* He grimaced at an image of the new Minister for Public Works, Davis Hughes, who would now be in charge of the building – and of Utzon, who was smiling up from the page. *Don't know that they care much for opera.*

By lunchtime preparations for the next experimental casts were done. Axel sent the men home early and slumped in a chair, his legs thrust out before him. Took the deep breath he had withheld for the past hour, felt adrenalin seep from his body. The work was not perfect, just as he'd expected; the depth of curve had made it static and the colour had been guesswork, though the brown still pleased him. Not perfect, but still enough of the idea was alive in the work to take it to the next stage. This would be crucial, would make demands on him he had never before allowed. His head, his heart. He felt the fear of it pool in his belly. Utzon might talk about the edge of the possible, but Axel knew that in this new glasswork he was working at the edge of the known self. It was, he could hear Lars say, what all artists do.

When he glanced at his watch it was mid-afternoon; he tucked his swimming trunks into a pack and ran up through the Domain for the ferry.

Pearl had fought and cheated for time on her writers' series; it allowed the slip of consciousness that kept her demons at bay. Prevented her from saying too much, thinking too much. The lives of Devanny and Tennant and Dark fixed her mind on determination rather than despair, reminded her of the standard required:

Shell

In 1932, when she was 20, Kylie Tennant walked 600 miles from Sydney to Coonabarabran to record the lives of destitute families who had taken to the roads of New South Wales to save themselves. The Great Depression had exposed the injustice and inequality endemic in Australia's social and political systems. Her long walk also informed her furious lifelong fight for the sexual and professional freedom of women.

The next sentence began to form in her head. Something about that sexual and professional freedom, and its costs, its demands. The things Tennant and others had done to win it, or just to survive it in the thirties and forties. But her fingers stilled on the typewriter. She was still unborn in 1932, when Tennant had done her long walk. Her mother had been twenty-one; Tennant a year younger. At the end of that walk the young writer would marry the man she seduced on the banks of the Castlereagh, and embark on the most productive years of her writing life. She'd had two risky abortions to ensure it.

Her mother's face swam up before her, as it always did when she met or read about a woman of that time. The same hard fact of her life, of her mother's and her own, implicit in the expression she always wore. A year after Tennant's long walk, Amy too had been pregnant. Had she actively chosen to have her baby, or been too afraid to seek out an alternative? Pearl had never considered the fine line of it. Had assumed that for Amy, there was no line at all. There had been none for her either, when it came to it.

Her mother would be 55 now, if she'd lived. The tragedy of it, and the irony, Pearl could see, was that she hadn't survived her own innocence, in a way, the innocence of her choices. Had died in the aftermath of another pregnancy. She should have lived. As always she wondered what her mother would look like now. For Pearl she was frozen in her mid-thirties, still lovely, still angry. Would she have mellowed with age? Pearl tried to imagine her as a grandmother and couldn't. The only certainty was that she'd be raging against this government, penning letters to members of parliament against the war. Unleashing her formidable temper on local representatives, the system, on anyone who thought her boys should fight.

The telephone shrilled; she propped it against her head and kept typing.

There's a record of James and William Keogh at St Vincent de Paul's in Melbourne just over two years ago. Jeanne's voice was steady, promising nothing. *The right ages. They were there for three nights.*

Pearl stopped typing, held the phone hard against her ear. *And?*

And nothing. I'm sorry. Jeanne breathed out. *But it narrows things a bit.*

Pearl's first impulse was to say: *it's not enough.* She leaned back in her chair and breathed out, let it go. *It does,* she said, *thank you. Don't suppose there was a forwarding address, or work records?*

No, nothing. I spoke to the director, he wasn't in the job then. I left my name and number.

She replaced the receiver. Her chest empty and taut as a drum. This was how it was some days: this hollowing, her body a brittle shell. At these times her mind was not her own. At work she imagined silent enemies, at home she imagined shapes behind curtains or under the bed. She would check each room when she walked in at night, open cupboards, stare at the arrangement of items on shelves. Dark thoughts rushed in: she would never escape the women's section, and she would never find the boys, never know where they'd gone. She threw equations around in her head – what might be worse, their permanent absence, or telling her father? The weight of each in the air she walked through.

But in her head, her mother's words. All those years before, but written large in front of her, daily. *If they ever try to send them to war* – she'd eyed the boys, still babies dribbling their food – *I'll hide them in an attic somewhere. I'll get a gun and shoot off one of their toes.* Her fierce mother, who couldn't squash a spider or a snail. Who would never strike a child for punishment, not even when the twins accidentally burned down the woodshed.

Her mother would never have lost them.

⁓

Late that afternoon she sat opposite Suze in a back alcove of a city café. *Do you think they might target the boys? Because of me.* As if speaking the words might burn up the fear, the anxiety that stalked her. *They're capable of that. They could work the numbers so they both get called up.*

Suze frowned. *I don't think so, love. They're not clever enough for it.*

They're corrupt enough for it. She was sure it was not beneath them, whoever they were.

They tapped your phone, Pearl. They've tapped lots of phones.

In her rational heart, she knew this was true. But it was all right for Suze, painting in her garret. *I'm a reporter, Suze. And I go to protests. I march. Or used to. They'll have a file on me as thick as your arm.* She stared hard at her friend. *If they got enough they could jail me. I'd lose my job. My home.*

They ordered tea. As the girl left Suze straightened her back, hands clasped around a salt shaker. *Now, listen to me.* Then leaned in towards Pearl, her voice mocking, theatrical. *Have you heard of Mrs Booth's Investigations Department?* She smiled, her eyes wide.

Pearl levered her shoes off under the table. Her whole body felt tight, constrained. Now she allowed the muscles in her back and neck to loosen, and with them something childish. Petulance. *This a joke?* She pulled off her cardigan and dropped it on the seat. Her voice sullen, her eyes.

But Suze was practised with her friend's moods, immune. *No,* she said. *It's deadly serious.* She leaned further across the pink tablecloth, its embroidered freesias and leaves. *Mrs Booth was the wife of the Salvation Army boss, somewhere around the turn of the century.*

Pearl narrowed her eyes. She wanted to complain about Askin, the new premier, the direness of Tory governments in both Sydney and Canberra. *And?* She shook her head. *The country's going down the sewer. We all are, Suze. And you want to talk about ladies in bonnets.*

Come on sweetie, I'm trying to help. I know things are hard.

Can't even call anyone . . . She was furious but her voice caught, surprising her. Tears gathered behind her eyes and she blinked them back.

A tray arrived with teapot and cups, milk jug and strainer. Suze waited until the girl had emptied it and she and her green starched apron had gone. Then she grasped the teapot. *And.* The word louder than she'd meant it to be. She moved the teapot in a circle, once, twice. *Our Mrs Booth set up an office for locating missing people. All ages. Lots of people got lost in those days, apparently. Domestic servants, factory workers, abandoned children.*

Never heard of her.

Suze tipped the teapot back and then forward. Back and forward. *Now it's called 'The Salvation Army Family Tracing Service'.*

The ritual of tea. It calmed Pearl, usually. But the day had turned her contrary. She poured milk into cups. Silent.

For Christ's sake Pearl, listen. They look *for people. A lot of the time, they find them.*

⁓

Axel sat on warm sand. There was the sound of the sea splintering, and children. On the ferry over the water had been quiet, marbled. He'd thought of Stockholm and its islands, the boats skimming between them. Gamla Stan and its copper roofs. Grey skies that lowered and shrank the city and the harbour, closed everything in. *It's why I write,* Per had told him, years before. *To break through it, see around it.*

Axel had frowned at him. In Stockholm they spoke differently, vowels clipped and sculpted and fast. So he had to listen hard and follow the shapes of the words. Sometimes the end of someone's sentence arrived while he was still in the middle of it.

Per's sentence came back to him now on Manly beach, the wide sweep of the Pacific like a kinked cloth before him. He wished Per was with him, so he could say no, that's not why you write at all. If it was, why would anyone write in Sydney? Surely this endless equatorial light broke through everything. Poetry couldn't be possible here; the air was too thin for it, the sun too hot. How could poetry be made and survive in such brutal clarity? This wasn't a place of poets but of the body. He'd written as much to his mother on the back of a postcard – some forgotten beach, its surfers and bikinis, the shimmer of tanned flesh dulling the sky and the ocean behind them.

But today he wished he could join the surfboard riders. Be more like them. Their ease in the ocean reassuring against the figures that rose and sank in the waves breaking closer to shore, heads and shoulders appearing and disappearing in a way that could still unnerve him, though his early terror had gone.

In the past few weeks he had begun to learn about waves. Their shape and temper, their speed and velocity. Their behaviour at high tide and low, in southerlies and north-easterlies. The first few times he'd waited: he watched others and he watched the sea. Hesitated before a lurching rise of water, trying to time it, to lift himself a little in the way he'd seen others do, letting the wave buoy him up and over. But then – like today – he'd take a second too long and the wave would break and suck at him, tumbling his limbs, stinging his eyes. You had to grow up with it, he thought, this wild water. To feel anything like at home inside it.

Still, even in his tentativeness he preferred a decent swell, to feel the muscle of the water holding him, or nudging and shoving, lifting and dropping him. It gave him something to fight. Today, in waist deep water, he'd stood waiting for fear to leave him, for his body to absorb rhythm, until his blood pushed and pulled with it and his body stopped resisting. Until he knew he could win.

On the ferry back, he sat outside to feel the spray and rush of sea air. Inside, men read newspapers and couples leaned together, faces flushed with warmth. They didn't even look through the windows. But the ride towards the city felt to Axel like a homecoming. A cautious happiness crept through him as if it had been thieved. How could these others turn their backs to it? The Heads, the houses. The Opera House unfurling like a flower, like one of their waratahs. The wild and beautiful native that symbolised their state.

He already loved this sandstone city. At some angles on some days, it looked to him like a painted set, a picture from a child's schoolbook, every feature reduced to its classic shape. Oddly, only the bridge and the towering shells on the point made it real, their daring outlines pulling the scene into the present. The irony of perception. To him, even now, the Opera House rose up like an idea as the ferry approached the quay, something he'd dreamed and was slowly remembering. He didn't want to lose that sense of the place, wanted never to feel it as so familiar that he would sit on a ferry and look away.

At Circular Quay he walked past the queues and swung down towards the passenger ship terminal. The same route he still took some days: a left turn at Cadman's Cottage and up the stone stairs that served as old in this place, wide treads worn concave by the weight of 180 years. Above the wharves, and among the crumbling terrace houses, there were still one or two places like this. The Mercantile sat between them all, but it was weeks before he realised why he'd chosen the faded hotel: the steps, the old cottages, all stone and wood and shrinking as humans do, reminded him of home. The low, slate-roofed farm houses of Småland.

Now he pressed his boots into the curve of the steps, pleased by the notion of all the feet that preceded his here. Turned up George Street, past pubs and tenements towards the Mercantile. Home, yes, though it had taken time to accept it. Some days the hotel still felt like a small foreign country within another. The bar especially. Its smell: stale, as if the sweat of a thousand men had soaked into the planks of the floor. An acrid smell that went with the beer, strong and crude. No women. This didn't surprise him. He imagined his mother standing at the door, the shock of the sounds, the odour, the wild-eyed bravado. Then turning away.

My young Swiss friend. Mrs Jarratt came limping out of the kitchen with a tray of washed glasses, blocking his way. He stood back. Had no one heard of Sweden? His landlady let the tray down behind the bar, pulled a cloth from her shoulder and plucked up a glass to dry. He might have moved off then, the way cleared, but the air around her was expectant, loaded. He waited for whatever it held.

Troubles down there then. Her hand inside the glass, a bird's claw. *All over the papers.* She frowned, peering at the glass for smears. *It's the bloody election if you ask me. They need a sacrifice eh? That young architect, what's his name? Made his own bloody altar.*

Axel pursed his lips. *Utzon,* he said.

Yeah. Mr Unpronounceable. They'll skewer 'im, that's what I reckon. She stopped polishing and stared at a point on the wall, above the picture rail with its single framed photograph of the young Queen Elizabeth. *Foreign, that's the trouble. They don't like foreign.*

Axel winced.

Olive's voice dropped a notch. *I go down there, you know. Look through the fence. I'll admit, it's grown on me.* She glanced away toward the window. A whole minute ticked past, or so it seemed. Then: *Got a postcard, years ago, some customer.* She shrugged. *The Eiffel Tower — is it? Pinned it up in the bar.* Her voice almost wistful, and in profile her face had the dignity of a dowager, down on her luck. But then a sound like a bird caught in a trap. She was chortling: *Probably still there!*

A pause, or a subsidence. Axel frowned. Tilted his head, trying to make sense. The worn carpet made it worse, its faded whorls, circling on themselves.

Your building down there, she said, resuming her polishing. Colour swarmed in her cheeks. *God knows why, it's a bloody mess — but it brings that postcard to mind.*

A split second, a glancing light, and Axel was there in Paris, on the Champs-Elysées, his eyes newly open. The miracle of steel arcing skywards, leaping towards heaven. He looked at her. *Perhaps* — he put his hand to his throat, the tight hum of emotion. *Perhaps they both wake us up. These structures. Or wake up our dreams.* A weak smile on his lips: had he said that aloud? Did Olive hear him?

She looked at him as if she too had just been woken. As if the bar was full of men, listening. Her bony shoulders lifted and dropped. *Anyway,* she said. *We'll see. No use complaining.* And sniffed. *But people will.* She shoved the cloth into a glass and twisted it savagely. *Look back fifty years. Same thing, different complaint. And fifty years before that, and on back to bejesus.* A vein in her hand swelled and flexed as she worked.

He had no idea what she meant.

Fifty years is no time, Axel. Believe me. People say, 'It'll take a lifetime', as if that's forever. But I can tell you, a lifetime goes bloody fast. It's no time at all. She coughed, sudden, phlegmy. Crossed one leg over the other. Then held out her hands, touched finger to finger, counting. *Two thousand and fifteen,* she said. *That's fifty years. Hope your foreign mate gets it finished by then.*

Axel nodded. Recognising the cantankerous old barmaid as an ally. *He'll finish it,* he said. *If they let him.*

Olive tipped her head towards the front bar. *You hear a lot of bullshit in here.*

He smiled at her. Something like fondness in his eyes.

Yes, she said. *You know.* She picked up another glass and moved away down the bar.

———

Pearl woke with the biliousness of failure, of impotence. She rose and made tea in a blue enamel pot and left it to draw. Stepped outside. The air needled with new light, sharp points on which fear swivelled. The world had dawned resentful, half-hearted. She pressed her feet into calf-length grass, still damp. Raised her face to the sky to feel what the air held: the breath of small creatures, salt. The residue of night. The earth particulate at this hour, its edges blurred, its lines inexact. She opened her arms to it, the whole trembling world.

That's when she saw the bird. Or heard something bird-shaped. In those crystal seconds, that's how it seemed, that she'd seen the sound, her eyes forming the bird around it.

Tawny Frogmouth? Some species of owl? She saw it as a blur of edges, foliage, bark. Its plumage, even the part-closed eyes, were of the tree, grown from it or grafted, a small branch flaking bark. She stood still, hugging herself. An owl in the garden, her mother once said, was like a blessing. Beneath the clothes hoist, handing up pegs, Pearl had thought of raffles and chocolate wheels, a florin found on the footpath. *Like good luck?* she'd asked, eyes skimming thin limbs on a loquat tree. *A reason to hope,* her mother replied, pulling work shirts from the line.

Now as the light thickened she let a fledgling hope rise in her, feathering up and over her limbs. A rare optimism, and it warmed her as the world reassembled itself in colours tinted like old photos. Or in faces imagined in the night. She looked back to the tree, to the bird. Old questions leapt in her throat: was the child she'd been still in her? Guileless, soft, open to the world, in a way she had not felt for years. Which version of her was real? What was true to the self? She looked up. *Well?* The bird was inscrutable, as still as stone, but Pearl knew it saw everything, more than every-thing; it saw more than she did or ever would.

Sunlight lapped at the grass as she turned, took the back steps two at a time. Plucked up pencil and drawing paper and began to sketch the bird, the branch. Her brothers would love to see that owl. Minutes later she lowered the pencil and surveyed the ordinary walls, the ill-matched chairs, plain curtains that concealed nothing. The phone book was under a pile of newspapers on the table, and she idled through it to *S*. The Salvation Army.

She was already halfway down the hall before it hit her. She stopped, mid-stride. The habit so ingrained she'd already envisaged her finger in the dial, the numbers spinning. Her hand already cupped, anticipating the pleasing curve of the receiver. Its shape, its innocent pale green: ordinary and unassuming as a ticking bomb.

She dropped to her knees before the telephone, gripped the cord and pulled it from the wall. *Fucking morons!* The curse helped. She fell backwards with the effort and lay there, staring at the yellowing plaster of the ceiling, the cord still in her hands. It had made a satisfying crack as the connection severed. She hoped someone, somewhere, heard the sound, the snap of the line breaking, hoped it was loud enough to hurt his ears. His filthy eavesdropping ears.

～

She went back to various meetings, back to Lorenzo's, to the Newcastle. Everywhere there was talk of action. Her body leaned into it. She wanted, despite Henry – perhaps to spite him – to be physically involved, to add her body to the thrust of anger and distress. But it was worse than ever. The men had taken control; they dominated discussion of ideology and action, their voices loud and brutish or worse, calm and dismissive, arrogant. On her first night at the Newcastle she'd been surprised at the low numbers of women; now she knew why. In her short absence the group had changed its face. The women made tea and were handed the typing. The men turned a paternal eye to them if they spoke; nodded or smiled, and went back to their plans. Even Ray exuded a proprietorial air.

She listened to the ideas and schemes: demonstrations, fundraisers, midday marches to catch the lunchtime crowd. Someone had a contact in the Postmaster-General's. They might intercept draft papers, disrupt the recruitment cycle, alert brothers, sons, boyfriends before their letter arrived. But that wasn't enough to save Will from the next ballot. She would have to know where they were.

At work she half-heartedly read the first accounts from the field. Wrote about mini skirts, Mary Quant, anything that Judith threw at her. On the day she finished her piece on Kylie Tennant she sat back to re-read it, wishing she could summon Tennant's fortitude, her clear intention. Her own words mocked her. She rolled the last page from the typewriter and shuffled the pages into place on her desk. As she clipped them together, her phone. *The Federal.* Brian's reptile drawl. *Come for a drink. The revolution is nigh.* And was gone.

~

A small crowd had gathered in the beer garden. Ray was propped on a stool at a round silver table with two beers in front of him. He pushed one towards her and blew smoke into the air. She frowned at him. *Thought you didn't drink on week nights?* She dropped her satchel at her feet.

It's Wednesday, he said, *I make allowances for Wednesday.*

A few women from Sydney Uni were arguing with a boy about pacifism. He was spectacularly drunk. *You're an idiot,* Pearl heard. A long-haired girl in overalls was trying not to shout. *All you white males, you sexist pigs, you won't last. You'll die out like the dinosaurs.* But Brian was calm, moving amongst them all, speaking quietly.

Did you tell him to call me? Pearl cocked her head towards Brian. Ran a finger through the condensation on her glass. *I'm not high on his list.*

Nope. Not me.

Then Brian was next to them, smiling, sober despite the drink in his hand. *Lois Lane.* He lifted his glass. *How's Superman?*

He didn't wait for an answer, but lowered his voice: *Reckon he'd know about the next ballot or troop ships? With his X-ray vision and all.*

For a moment – her hands on the table – she felt out of time and place. The bar noise receded; there were just the words, reverberating. Because of course she'd got the first ballot date but nothing about the second, or about the first ship. And she hadn't heard from her contact in weeks, not since the state election. *No idea what you mean.* She looked away, unnerved by this new Brian. Calm, sober. More or less. *You're talking to the wrong girl.*

Well. Brian looked from Pearl to Ray and back again. *If you happen to hear anything.*

She grimaced a smile as he moved away.

Ray stubbed out his cigarette. *Nothin' to do with me.* He took his time grinding it into the plastic ashtray.

Maybe your man will know. Whoever gave you that leak about chockos. She tried to keep the sourness out of her voice, unsuccessfully.

But Ray's face was emotionless, as always. *Before you snap, mate, it came through Trev, in the office. Tell you the truth I nearly didn't tell ya, Trev's a bit of a loose cannon. Into conspiracies, sees 'em everywhere.*

She was poised to ask the obvious questions but he went on: *It was a one-off. He'd been at a wedding, cousin or somethin'. One of the groomsmen works for the Feds, right, and he's pissed, reckons he knows the prime minister, how the poofy little conscripts will wet their pants when they realise where they're goin' ...*

Pearl gulped beer. Her heart had slowed; it was so like Ray, the convoluted story, its provenance. But there was, she supposed, an outside chance it was true. *Trev's cousin,* she said.

Trev's cousin's groomsman.

Christ. She laughed and swore at the same time. *Well my bloke's disappeared so Trev might be our only hope. You better keep him sweet.*

Nah, Trev's resigned. Ray stood, pocketed his cigarettes. *Movin' to Brisbane. Reckons they need him more than we do.*

They both looked around when they heard Brian raise his voice nearby. He'd done the rounds of the room; now he was giving Della his full attention. *You understand eh, you know about this,* he was saying. *It's called direct action. If we can stop a ship they'll know we're serious.*

Winter 1965

The days had run quickly into weeks, and still he could not find the courage to contact her. As they'd left the flat that first morning, Pearl in one direction, he in another, she had called out: *You can ring me at work. Use a nom-de-plume.* But he had been barely able to think past the words, her face as she spoke them: *my phone's been tapped.* An old darkness rushed in, one he was unable and unwilling to fight. He noticed the sun but not its warmth; acknowledged the world but not its colour. The days passed, muted, empty. He was a sleepwalker with no past, no memory.

On his way to work the harbour glittered, a lazy malevolence. On days like this, in winter light, something pushed up beneath his skin and he shivered, as if the harbour itself had risen in him like a tide. On good days he could turn away, obliterate it; other days he felt his throat fill with it, his nostrils. At these times he spent hours alone in the shed at Bennelong Point. Poked and prodded at the forge without intention. Only in sleep could he lose the odd texture of his thoughts, the fear that rippled through them.

Since the election, he had begun to read the newspapers assiduously, hunting out stories about the Opera House. And to gauge the temperament of the city, its mood. At home there had always been newspapers, and even as a youth he'd learned that it wasn't just the stories and how they were written, or the headlines, but the placement of them, how photographs were used, advertisements. The weight given to each. There was a texture to the pages, a sense that you were in good hands, or not, and it translated to the texture of the city. A kind of beat. But here during the election campaign and ever since, the papers had become vehicles of fear.

The men he'd heard on the site reflected it. People who had never met the architect or examined his work had these opinions, outlandish, unrestrained. Through the papers – one or two especially – politicians on both sides invited the whole country to be pessimists. They outdid each other daily in their claims: the costs have blown out, we will slash them; it is taking too long, we will make it faster; the project requires scrutiny, we will investigate. The unions are out of control; we will control them. And worst, the architect has lost touch.

He is overpaid, an elitist who can't solve the building's problems. We will change that.

Every day, this fight for the worst.

For consolation, he went to the Botanic Gardens every lunchtime and lay on the grass, looked to the sky. He missed his mother. Her face above the steam of the soup pot when he came in from school. Or reading to him in milky light. As a boy he would sit close to her and run his finger down her thick yellow plait, tracing the weft of hair, in and under, over and under. Her calm. No, more: something he couldn't articulate and would not, in any event, admit. He had not yet loved a woman as he loved her. It was simple enough and had not disturbed him until now that he was far from her, and unsure when they would meet again. He tried to wipe the picture of her, the tears she'd almost choked on as he left, not crying. She'd held him hard and pulled away, her hands fluttering at his cheeks, one moment, two. Then she was gone. He thought of her life, the shape of it, without him. An unfinished square, perhaps, grief rushing in through the gap.

In his memory, she always smelled of snow. Would walk out in all weather. But in spring they would take their bikes and ride for days. In their panniers just one change of clothes and the cinnamon buns she made for her brothers.

There would be berries along the way, and water, a friend's cottage; he was never hungry. They pedalled the quiet roads of the flat country, beside meadows of clover and rape, and he was only surprised by hills the first time. After that he would wait for them, for the joy of breaching the top behind her and waiting, watching his mother's hair stream out as she flew down the other side. She would stand up on the pedals as she reached the bottom, laughing into the air. Something about that sight, her straight back, her shirt like a sail, made his child's stomach tumble. He kept watching her as his own bike leapt forward and his face met the spring wind. But he didn't need to. For Axel that moment she tipped back her head would go on forever. He could replay it at will for the rest of his life.

⁓

When his deep bleakness finally lifted the season had turned. Along with his work schedule: he was weeks behind. In the mornings he blinked into amber light. Rain cleared the quay, and a cool wind surprised him, slipping under his shirtsleeves and goosing his skin. Leaves crisped beneath his feet. Every day at Woolloomooloo and at Bennelong Point, he hoped for a sighting of the architect. A meeting, a discussion, even the coincidence of being in the same vicinity.

I'm afraid it's not likely, said Jago, pouring coffee from a thermos in the lunch shed. *There's been a falling out with the engineer.* Axel frowned. *They have argued, my friend. Disagreed. Some say it is fatal for the project.*

They said that about the election, Axel offered. *But we go on.*

Jago shrugged and pushed out his bottom lip. *At any rate,* he said, *the architects and engineers no longer pass freely through each other's spaces. The door has been bricked up. It's like a very painful divorce.*

Axel felt nausea burrowing in his stomach. *Surely he won't stay away. This is his building.*

Yes of course he will be here. Mondays and Thursdays, as he's been doing. But you can see why he keeps to Pittwater — there are no distractions there. No one demanding, complaining. Not even a telephone. He held out his hands, palms up. *I can understand it.*

As they walked out into the sun, Axel remembered the question he had come with. *What is a nondy plumber?* The impossible word felt like jelly on his tongue. Jago made a face; he was as mystified as Axel himself. They stood near the old glass shed and turned the word over, testing it for variations. It consumed the rest of the lunch break. In the end they went to Armand, who always kept a pocket-sized dictionary with his tools. The three men frowned over the small print as Armand's finger traced the entries for *n*. Finally: *nom-de-plume!* Jago's heels left the ground. *Nom-de-plume,* he said again, pleased with the sound. *An alias. A false name.*

Later Axel dialled the *Telegraph* from a phone box near the quay. When the telephonist asked for his name he said carefully: *Mister Jansson.*

⌒

That evening, eating fish and chips in her kitchen – Pearl rarely cooked, he soon realised, and there was no privacy at the Mercantile – she asked him about his choice of name. Laughing through greasy lips. *Why that one? You can't even say it.* The sounds and letters his tongue refused, like *th*. His *j* was like a soft *y*.

Jansson? It's a common name at home. Pronounced the same as your version, except for the first letter. He peeled a strip of thick yellow batter from his fish. *And it was a name my father used, sometimes.*

In his job?

Yes. Because it was ordinary, like Olsson, or Persson. And easy for people to remember. He changed the subject then cleared his throat. *Mr Jansson called to apologise. Not for his name. Because it took him so long.* Axel chewed fish, slipped a sliver of bone from his tongue. *He supposed things were a bit, well, difficult for you. Because of the phone.* He looked at her. *He thought you might need some time.*

They were sitting side by side, but still he could see the cloud that passed across her eyes, a visible trace. Then it was gone. She licked her fingers. *Only to settle my fury,* she said. *Not much you can do about Special Branch.* To his blank face: *Police who spy, fabricate evidence, tell lies.*

He coughed. *Were you afraid.* Like so many of his questions it sounded flat, like a statement.

Not afraid. She ran a finger over the rim of her glass. *No, that's a lie. Of course I'm afraid – they're thugs. But I'm more angry than scared. And a bit jumpy. I catch myself looking over my shoulder on the ferry, or walking home.*

As if you are being followed, or watched. He smiled at her. *You must be a very dangerous person.*

They sat quietly, drinking the beer he had brought, wrapped in newspaper like oversized sweets. Next door a door banged shut, and minutes later, music. The Rolling Stones. Pearl's foot tapped out the rhythm. She said, *Have you made any progress?*

He frowned, inclined his head.

Your glasswork.

Oh. Were her words oblique? He decided not. *Yes,* he

said. He tunnelled into language, trying for the right expressions. When they came he spoke them slowly, his tongue feeling for truth. *But I find it hard to read this place. Sometimes I want to turn it upside down, shake it. Or get a shovel and dig.*

She turned her glass in her hand, ran a finger through condensation. *To look for what?* She glanced sideways at him, but his eyes were on the wall, as if something might reveal itself there.

I'm not sure. So much is surface here, even people. Perhaps it's the sun. Perhaps – he shook his head. *What I want to know is: what is beneath it all, beneath the skin, beneath the city.* He took a mouthful of beer. *It's strange to me. More questions than answers. But then, it's always like that.*

It was difficult to explain. These cool days in Sydney, the occasional fog, were like Sweden in early spring. At this time of year, more than any other, history shuffled closer, a ragged old man in the cold, telling your fortune for a krona. The melting snow left fields tender and exposed, before the first flowers and spring grasses. A thin crust between this season and those long passed. Between this world and the last. Or the next. Stones and rocks glowed with damp, and it was easy to see his ancestors moving among them.

The bare, cold ground also revealed once more the mounds and clefts of ancient villages and lives. In the still cool air, their lines clear and sharp as if drawn by a blade. Sometimes the spade or plough turned time with the earth, striking metal in primitive shapes, rock hewn to weapons. The shape of a hull. Once, Axel had come upon a long, curved notch in new grasses, the land dipping and rising as if it were merely another place to play. He sat down in it, feeling the dimensions of its life and of those it carried. His own. A boat spearing through waves. He saw the hollow it made in still water, the paths it carved in the sea, and felt time melt like late snow, the pull of the past, a confusion of hours.

He had carried that memory with him into adulthood, its possibilities across oceans and hemispheres. This is what he wanted to tell her: that he looked at what was there, but mostly he looked for what was not there. If only he could express it. This search for the missing or the erased, at what might be hidden.

There is a word, he said, struggling for it. *The residue? Yes. What people leave behind. Their traces.*

He turned his face to her; she nodded. *Yes.*

You have an ancient culture here too. I'm trying to learn something of it. It isn't easy.

I'm afraid, she said, *that we've nearly destroyed it.*

He was quiet for a moment. *Yes,* he said finally. *Where is the Aboriginal in Sydney? It's like a picture you've painted over.*

She cocked her head, thinking. *We* have *painted over it. Layers and layers, obliterating them. I've never thought of it like that before. As if it's all still there, those old lives and ways. Under these, under ours.*

He shrugged. *A whole picture. There must be. A city under the city. And we walk over it every day.*

They finished their fish in silence. Axel was aware of her eyes on him. As if he wasn't who she thought he was. He yawned. Apologised. Then: *Let's go to bed,* she said, plucking fatty paper and cold chips from the table, wiping trails of salt.

In her bedroom he pulled off his shirt and singlet. Stood at the window, waiting. Outside, the ocean breathed its spiced air; in, out. There was no horizon; the stars were lit vessels, fishing boats, yachts, container ships, tacking across the dark. No sound. Only the waves, the low growl as they gathered, heaved to shore, heaved again.

He felt her arms slip around him, her face pressed to his back. Closed his eyes, turned to her, his hands finding her face. Her shoulders, her hips. She was already naked, her own hands busy with his belt, unbuttoning him. Undoing him. He shuddered as she sank to her knees.

Winter unnerved her. She shrank beneath it, small and child-like; her flesh absorbed the cold, her bones ached. At bus stops or waiting for the ferry, she stood stiff, arms wound about herself, chin tucked into a scarf. Her whole body charged with resentment.

All through her childhood, it had been like this. She was never warm enough. The others hadn't complained, not the twins, nor the little boys running barelegged in shorts. Still, in that first winter at the convent, the old bricks breathing frost, she'd taken thin rugs from a storeroom and hidden them beneath their beds in the boys' dorm. *Don't tell*, she'd warned them, feeling bad for the other boys. But not bad enough. *Wrap them around you under your blanket at night. Don't let them show.* If they were cold, she knew, she'd feel even more exposed.

It was a bit the same now. The wind and their absence made her feel skinless and crazed. She saw them everywhere: on trams, in doorways. On the street she searched the faces of men, their colouring, their hair. There were days when she saw them, was sure of it. Her skin sparked with anxiety and fear as she followed a glimpsed profile, pursued a face in a queue or a crowd. She wanted to approach strangers and say: *Have you seen my brothers? No I don't know how tall, how thin. I don't know what they weigh. They're just boys who look like me.*

She walked quickly through the public bars she passed, full of hope and dread. What kind of men would they be in these places? One late afternoon, a man leaned in the sticky light of the doorway, a child tugging at his sleeve. *Come* on *Dad, please.* Tears smeared her face. But the man's voice was gravelled with drink. *Soon,* he said, looking straight ahead. *Get home now.* A pause, then: *Now, I said!* It was a growl. *Before I belt ya.*

It took Pearl three seconds to pass them and only one to recognise the look in the girl's eyes. The love and hate of all daughters of drunks. She'd never considered herself one of them, even in the lost year after her mother's funeral, when Patrick sat at the kitchen table every night and drank and cried. It was the younger ones who needed him then; they had no idea how to behave. He was silent at times, angry at others. Mostly, he ignored them all.

But he had never raised a hand to them; they had never been smacked. Patrick abhorred the idea of an adult striking a child. Even in that terrible year, as he doused his pain with booze, he had got himself to the school and lashed the headmaster with his tongue. Jamie had wet his pants in prep class, had come home with the marks from a nun's ruler. *You think a belting will stop him missing his mother?* Patrick had brought the headmaster's own ruler down hard on his desk. *Thwack!* He'd laughed as he told Pearl later: how the man's *fat arse* had lifted off the chair, how he'd *farted in fright.*

No one, he'd told the man, watching his forehead bead with sweat, *do you hear? No one touches my sons.*

But he'd softened about the nuns. Sitting there at the night table, the young ones asleep in their beds. *Truth is Pearlie,* he'd said, prising the cap from a beer bottle, *they're just passing on the pain. Most of 'em. It's a cruel life for those young things.* Pearl, plucking toys from the floor, remembered sour faces in black and white, stern in the schoolroom, throwing dusters at misspelling or chatter. Were they missing their mothers in Ireland or Perth? Did they cry in the night, as she did? Did they dream of boys, those young nuns, imagine their kisses, the feel of a man's hand on their back as they danced? The drift of chiffon on their shoulders and thighs.

Now she reached the corner and turned briefly to check: the girl outside the pub was gone, the father too; they left empty silhouettes that might be Jamie, might be Will. Grown men, belligerent with loss or shame, shouting at a beloved child. She walked on through lowering light, the same refrain as ever in her head. If her mother hadn't died. If the welfare hadn't taken them. If she'd kept up her visits, not neglected them, left them lonely and vulnerable in that pitiless place. She was no better than all the men in hotel doorways. Indulging their own pain, blind.

July 1965

There was a note on her desk when she arrived: a profile of a visiting English writer. *Born and raised in Sydney*, smiled Judith, *at least until she was nine or ten. Elderly now. But there's a new book coming out, or a reprint or some such, you'll have to check.* She pushed a memo across the desk. *You're interested in these half-forgotten women.*

An accusation, Pearl thought, raising her brows. *What's elderly?* She looked at the note, frowned. *Constance Shaw.*

Never heard of her. Seventy? Judith was looking at the story list, scribbling notes. *A curmudgeon apparently. Contrary. But better than anything else I've got for you here.* She shuffled the other papers on her desk, dismissing her.

Pearl took the memo and stood. *I don't mind contrary,* she said, and went off to check the library for information.

The file on Constance Shaw was thin, most of the clippings old. Short pieces on the novels she'd published in America and England, one in Paris. Well received, mostly. One profile noted her 'short temper' in interviews, her refusal to give straight answers. Shaw was critical of what she called 'the middle ground of England', its irrational fears. In another story a reviewer mentioned socialism in accusatory tones; the word 'cantankerous' was mentioned more than once. Pearl thought she might like her.

She called the number Judith had given her. Was about to give up, and then a voice, low but clear: *Yes?* Within a minute, perhaps, it was arranged. *Come at eleven,* the voice said. *But no photographs, not today.* Pearl rang off and looked at the clock. Ten-fifteen. Jesus. She threw notebook and pencils into her bag and ran for the cab rank.

~

Balmain: Pearl watched through the passenger window as the suburb rolled by. Old, desiccated. It was as if handfuls of Sydney had been seized and scattered here, part handsome, part rotting, flotsam washed up on the shore at the bottom of Darling Street and blown up the hill. Everything and nothing was here, and none of it seemed to match: factories shouldered pubs and houses, lanes pushed up beside terraces and old metal works and down by abandoned shipyards and churches. And through the spires and chimneys and sprays of bougainvillea, past the gables and brick: flashes of blue, slices of harbour. She asked the cab driver to let her off near the shops, so she could walk among the clutter of buildings and noises to the address near Ewenton Street. Years ago, after the move to Manly, she would do this every few months, catch the ferry over, walk up and down. Looking for signs of herself. For a residue of beauty. This was where she'd run as a child.

Did it matter, the absence of beauty? If you grew up in unlovely streets, did you grow unlovely too? There was part of her still that could not answer *no*. A part that knew beauty counted, or at least the form of things. If you were born to the dailiness of the Eiffel Tower, the elegance of its leap, it would surely pierce your dreams, inform your earthly desires. Your ambition. Slipping silently beneath your young skin so you didn't realise, not then, what had made you.

But by the time she was a teenager she knew: a childhood in Balmain meant certain assumptions were made about you. She knew she was appraised by others in a way a North Shore girl was not. As if Balmain was not just where she lived but who she was. As if she'd breathed in squalor, that it leaked out through her pores. For a long time she might have believed it herself, worried that her eyes might filter bleakness, might process it differently to theirs. That she would not know beauty when she saw it. But not any more. Years after her mother's death she saw it for what it was. A kind of social conspiracy. She was relieved; could love it as she always had.

Saw that her preference for odd-shaped houses, for lanes that bent and went nowhere, began here.

It was barely altered. Still down at heel and crumbling. As a child she'd never stopped to appraise the place: it was what it was: her home. All tar and stone and irregularity, the air acrid with tallow and smoke. Now she could see that it was true, there had been no collective urge to beautify, to upkeep. It was rough. The fact wasn't remarkable; no one noticed. Why would they? Everyone lived and worked and went to school within its margins, within its uniform dishevelment.

In her childhood, the whole suburb was at eye level, more or less, except the cranes in the shipyard and the factory chimneys, and even then nothing lined up straight, nothing was plumb. Dog's breakfast, her mother had said, but this was what Pearl loved most, the unpredictability, the sudden dead ends and surprising corners, the wayward streets. And really, so did Amy. *Even the sky is uneven,* she'd say, laughing. And it was true. Its pitch was determined by where you were standing, by what you could smell and hear. Only the harbour was constant. The masts and sails and tugs at the horizon were ever-moving reminders of the sea.

She walked towards Datchett Street. Their own house had been like most others, uneven, squeezed up against another and hemmed by a neighbour's wall. In the scrap of yard her mother grew spinach and carrots. Peas tendrilled on a wire. In spring jasmine splayed and once she'd grown a climbing rose her father named *Pearl*. But its tiny blooms were red, and Pearl was not unhappy when it was dashed to pieces in a storm. She'd wanted creamy white, not red, she'd wanted subtlety and beauty. *Well, I loved them,* her mother said as she gathered the debris that day and one of the twins cried out from a thorn. But Pearl was unmoved.

The little house was different now, partly repaired and extended, its roof replaced. There were roses once more, overblown and languid on a picket fence. Pearl stood on the opposite side of the road and wondered if the new people felt the old beneath their feet, the rough scales of the lives lived here before them. The cries and laughter of children, the plunge and knot of grief. If Suze was right and everyone was linked somehow, the life of every single person drifting through another, then surely these people would feel the rub of her parents' hard days, the relentless grinding hours.

A breeze came up the hill from the water and Pearl adjusted her shoulder bag. Constance Shaw, then.

~

Number 62 was a house of old brick and faded weather-boards. Some kind of vine, its few ragged flowers, crept along the verandah rails, against peeling window frames. But the garden was neat and the bones of the building were good. It held itself well, like a rich dowager refusing the effects of age, or hard times.

Pearl climbed the steps that clung to the side of the house. The woman who answered the door did not look rich or famous. Or act it, at any rate. She didn't wait for Pearl's greeting but turned back into the light-filled flat, shuffling in slippers, a newspaper in her hand. *Not sure about all this,* said Constance Shaw, lowering herself into a cane chair by the window and motioning Pearl towards the other. *But it breaks up the day. What is your name?*

Pearl closed the door and stood for a moment, adjusting her scarf, sweeping the room with a journalist's eye. Thinking: she matches the room, the house. A kind of rough-edged gentility, a studied carelessness: well-cut jacket though the slippers were worn at the heel, sagging cane chairs that looked out over an expensive view. Sidney Nolan hung above a red Laminex table. The carpet worn to nothing beneath it.

Pearl Keogh.

Constance Shaw struck a match to a cigarette held between long fingers. Inhaled in a short breath, leaned back. *Keogh,* she said, exhaling. *Let me guess. Irish Catholic.* She regarded Pearl through smoke as she sat opposite her, retrieving notebook and pencils.

Pearl straightened her skirt. She didn't much like the woman's tone, but looked her in the eye and smiled. *Is it strange to be home?*

Constance looked to the ceiling, where mould bloomed in delicate tracery. *The Catholics run the newspapers here.* She drew once more on the cigarette, blew smoke through an open window sash. *Home. Strange, yes. Discomforting. I find I'm appalled and consoled at the same time.*

The pencil moved noiselessly over Pearl's notebook. She began to prickle with anticipation. Constance was irascible, clever; the usual platitudes had already been forgone. Already they'd run roughshod over the normal rhythm of interviewing: the dissection, the gentle flaying, a subject's skin peeled off so skilfully they didn't see their own fingers at work. Pearl lifted the pencil. *Consoling and discomforting,* she said. *Like your work, perhaps.*

There was a good hour of provocation – *Greene's a misogynist, how could you not see that? You have to get out of*

Sydney, my girl. Give me Brisbane or even Adelaide, Melbourne is so self-conscious. *(Then why are you back?* Pearl ventured. Constance sighed. *At least dignify all this with a decent question, my dear.)* And then Pearl detected a thaw, an adjustment in tone, an occasional flash of humour or warmth. Most surprising, the odd concession to Pearl's own intelligence.

They had been discussing critics, book reviews. Constance waved her hand. *They don't like me here.* Her tone arch, defensive again. *Look, most critics are consumed with envy. Really. It's a coward's game. Why else would you do it? Only if you dearly wanted to write but were too afraid to.*

Pearl let the words hang between them.

Don't you think? Australian newspapers are so … pompous. And male. Full of swagger and certainty. It comes from feeling second grade, I suppose. The suspicion that you're not quite up to it. Constance had been watching the breeze flip leaves and papers along the footpath outside, but now she turned back to Pearl. *I don't know why a girl like you would waste your time with them.*

Pearl thought: 'Affront'. The things women had to do to be published. *Aren't newspapers the same everywhere?* She'd flicked through international editions in the newsroom and already knew they were not. But Constance saw through her. *Rhetorical,* she said, frowning. *Ask me a real question.*

The clock ticked to one-thirty, two. It had taken Pearl that first hour to breach the writer's austerity, to establish a fledgling trust. She knew it was one of her strengths, to set a person at ease. She sought any common ground; it was invariably there, even if it was irrelevant to the interview. In this way she offered up her own vulnerability; they both, interviewer and subject, stepped into the arena together. After nearly a decade in the job, this was the best deal she could offer: to give as much of herself as she asked of the other.

As Constance warmed they spoke about her books, her life in London, the writer in private and in public. About reputation, melancholy, marriage. Love. The possibility of relinquishment.

Of relinquishment. A surprise in the tone Constance had used, making the word sound positive. To Pearl it had always smacked of grief, of loss, of things forgone or given up.

Whatever doesn't work for you, the writer was saying. *Relationships, guilt, shoes that pinch. The past.* She raised her substantial brows. Clicked her fingers. *Get rid of it. Vamoose.*

Pearl watched her pencil press marks onto the page. But saw only the file on the library bench, the stories suggesting Constance had lied about her years in London, about her marriage, about the true subjects of her books. That she invented a history to suit each situation. She'd made no comment on these stories, ever, mounted no defence. (Though later Pearl would ask the literary editor, who remembered a quote in an old interview in *The New York Times*. Quizzed about the allegations, her version of things, Constance had said only: *It is how I see it.*)

Now Pearl glanced up at the woman sitting opposite her, winter sun on skin paled by her years in cold places. Her grey hair was drawn back in a chignon, leaving her face and its lines and shadows exposed. No make up, no artifice; if she was prone to lying it wasn't about her age. And if anyone was exaggerating it was the editor; what exactly was *elderly,* she wondered again. Perhaps it meant something different when applied to a woman, because Constance was, what? Late sixties? No older. It occurred to her then that men like Henry might be confronted by women like Constance. Strong, successful, single, a public figure who called her own tune. Brought to heel by one word – *elderly* – a suitable punishment for breaking the rules. For being the one who got away.

Pearl decided she would not raise the question of lies and inventions now. Partly out of fear, it was true; the woman would eat her alive. But mostly out of respect. Pearl had begun to admire her. She went back to her notebook, thinking: who owns the facts of our lives anyway?

She was weighing the next question, trying to phrase it, when Constance spoke again. *I'm weary,* she said, *and thirsty.* Levering herself up from her chair. A vein in her hand swelled and settled. *Come and have a drink with me.* She shuffled to the kitchen table, pushed off her slippers and pulled on plain street shoes. Moved towards the door. Pearl was sure Constance was more upright than before, propelling herself now with assurance, with determination. She watched her fish in a jar and draw out a wad of notes, which she tucked into a pocket. Smoothed her hair. Desultory. *Come on.* The words spoken over her shoulder. *We'll go to the Royal Oak. You'll need a drink too.*

Pearl rose, suppressed a laugh that bulged in her throat, and followed.

◡

As they reached the street Constance turned into another person. The shuffling gave way to a kind of hurtling walk laced with commentary, on the weather, her brother's children, newspapers. *For pity's sake girl the news pages are as bad as the women's,* she wheezed. The path was uphill, but her pace didn't slow. *At least in women's you can do interviews like this. Something intelligent.* Australian conservatism, American bluster, English naïveté. The compulsion of travel. *Get out of the country.* This as they slid at last into a booth in the ladies' parlour of the hotel. It was almost empty after the lunchtime rush. Constance had ordered gin for them both from the barman before Pearl could speak. *You're a bright girl. Go to London, if you still want newspapers. Or Paris. Can you speak French?*

The drinks arrived in tall glasses, cool to the touch. Pearl winced. So far she hadn't managed a word.

Fleet Street. Constance spoke without looking at her. Chewed ice. *It's a different world. London will — what do they say? — blow your mind.*

Pearl wanted to say: *I can't go to London. Or anywhere. Not now.* But didn't. Moved the conversation back to books, the ban on *Lady Chatterley*, George Johnston's Miles Franklin award.

Constance said: *Should have gone to his wife. Brilliant, but her books are set in Greece. Those columns she writes —* raising her glass to her lips — *she should have got it for those. And for putting up with him.* She lowered her voice. *Let's see if next year's a woman,* she said, as if she was thinking aloud.

They were quiet for a while, drinking, listening to the barman unload beer barrels in the yard. The scrape of wood on concrete, sentences laced with expletives. And above it all, a crow barking.

But the young will triumph. Eventually. Constance had drained her glass. *It's only been days but I can see that, right enough. They'll rise up. Vietnam, Aboriginal people. Women. They won't take it. This young Dane at the Opera House, all the jealous old men. They just wish they'd designed it.*

Pearl thought of Axel, his obsession with the architect, his god-like vision of the man and his cathedral. *Those people,* he'd spat one day, indicating Macquarie Street, *they have no idea. I think they are afraid of Utzon. Of the building. Or ashamed of it. That's how they act.*

Now, above the grunt of men hauling kegs, the sound of singing. Muted, as if someone had opened a car door and left the radio on. The two women leaned in unison towards it. Paul Robeson. 'Joe Hill', the voice thick as molasses, singular. When the song finished Pearl said: *He was here, five years ago, down at the Opera House. He sang to the workers.* The memory of his voice, the men listening. An Italian labourer had said to her, *I will never forget this.* Emotion stark on his wet face. She knew then that Robeson had made a memorial of the building, noun and verb.

He stands for them, Constance said. *And for his people. He's fearless.* She paused. *A shame he loved Stalin.*

Pearl began to ask: *Stalin?* Constance didn't hear. *But he spoke against the fascists in Spain ... You're too young to remember. He said,* 'The artist must take sides'. The words hung between them like a banner.

Then *Yes,* Pearl said, *I know.*

Something like: 'He must choose to fight for freedom or slavery'. Well of course we must, all of us. Constance drained her glass and looked at Pearl levelly. *That, my dear, is why I write. To take a side. If you're looking for something to say about me, say that.*

~

The cab ride back to the office might have taken hours. She sat in the front and urged the car on silently, anxious to be back. Constance had slumped as she left, looked suddenly older, or perhaps it was the gin. *Faith,* she'd said, her smile crooked as Pearl turned to the door. *It's like luck, my girl. You have to make your own. Get lucky and the world will love you.*

Yes, she thought now as the city reared up, shining. Luck. As they'd talked about Robeson, the hero he was, a thunderbolt: the workers. Will and Jamie were workers. And they were their father's sons: they would be in a union. She had no idea why she hadn't thought of it before.

~

In the newsroom she left a note for the industrial roundsman, Peter, and went to the cafeteria for strong coffee. Then sat at her desk. Typed up her notes and began to draft the profile of Constance Shaw. The library file lay beside her notebook, open at the most recent photograph they had:

a grainy portrait, five years old. Pearl consulted it every few minutes, reaching for something that was not in her notes. Something between the imperiousness, the almost regal bearing, and the generosity she allowed as, piece by piece, the carapace was breached. As some original version of Constance was allowed out.

Then Peter was walking towards her through the swarm of typewriters, a piece of folded paper in his hand. *There's the Missos, but start with the Builders and Labourers man*, he said. *Not sure how much he can help, or if he wants to. Stop-work meetings this week*. He proffered the single page, with a single name and a number.

She made the call immediately, her voice contained. The union man, gruff, busy, said he'd see what he could do.

⁓

Axel leaned over the metal casting box. The day before, he and the men had filled the long rectangle with damp sand. This morning the wooden mould, pressed into and against it to create their impression. Now it had been removed; he could see the curves and lines were clean and clear. Sprays of colour, red, the brown of tree bark, flecked the hollows. This was not the most anxious stage of the process but still he felt his breath shorten. As if the weight of air exhaled from a man's chest might affect the texture. Might collapse the shape pressed into the sand, or the idea projected there. The months of thinking and reading this place, of translating vision and emotion, and now this first attempt to turn his thoughts solid. It was a trial only, a scale model – he had still to solve the technical problems of a full-sized piece – but today he would finally move from theory and emotion to the tangible.

Behind him two men moved around the crucible, checking the temperature of the lead crystal glowing crimson within. Twelve hundred degrees centigrade. Axel turned to them; they nodded. He took three small pieces from the shelf beside him, items from his walks and searches, and placed them lightly into the sand. Each movement made with exactitude. When he finished and stood back, one of the men reached into the crucible and filled a ladle with molten glass. The heat was a living thing; sweat pricked their faces, the skin on their arms above the long thick gloves. Their eyes narrowed. But the form was soon full and alight with colour, pulsing with its own life.

It was now a matter of watching, of vigilance.

He left the cast with three of the senior men and walked back to Bennelong Point. The whole day was yellow and blue, Sweden's colours, and the winter air rang. As he walked his lungs opened and he realised that, during the morning, he'd held his breath for long periods as the glass was poured and the pieces settled. Now his body unclenched. A girl smiled as she passed him and he knew he must be smiling too. Must be happy.

He walked through the site, nodding at men who recognised him now. But he was anxious to get to his shed, to the experimental pieces from the small furnace. It was important to test his ideas in this way, trying to feel, between wrist and glass, some expressive potential. The notion of perfection: it was still debated among the glass-makers and also among the students, who had been schooled in its necessity, their work judged against myriad bars, all subjective. Axel grimaced at some of their views and their taste, the hard symmetry that bored him, the cleanliness of it. Some glass artists were happy in that space, but to Axel it felt cold, bloodless. He was trying for something beyond it; for disturbance and emotion, the elusive quality of dreams. Ambiguity. Still, the mastery of skills and techniques was essential: he had to be sure that vision and idea did not collide with the practical matters of the hot shop.

It was most important now. He had been quietly experimenting in the privacy of his small shed with an old-fashioned Swedish method of blasting. Among his tools was a blast-lamp, which used compressed air and sand. First he applied stencils on the parts to remain transparent; the blast-lamp gave a matt finish to the remaining surface of the glass. But it required concentration, and peace.

After two hours of such intensity, he stopped, closed and locked his door, and blinked into sunlight. Turned without thinking towards the lunch shed where Jago and his friends ate their fragrant-smelling food, and the locals pretended theirs was superior. The week before, sitting among the men, Jago had been talking about beaches. Urged him to go to Bondi, the *most beautiful beach in the world.*

White sand, a perfect crescent, he'd said, his hands spread in front of him like a preacher. *The sea cool and clean. And women. Women in bikinis. Boys on surfboards. Everyone happy, playing around like kids.*

Axel had smiled at his enthusiasm. *I like Manly,* he'd shrugged. *The beach is lovely there too, and I can take the ferry.*

But it's famous, my friend!

Coogee. The word rose up, a bit choked, from behind a sandwich. *Got it all, the rocks, the cliffs, the pools. If we're talking beautiful —*

Tania Verstak. Low laughter rolled around the room. Someone said, *I'd like to visit Tania.*

Axel raised his brows, confused, and Jago shook his head. *Beauty queen,* he said. *Miss Australia. Beautiful yes* — his hands made an hourglass in the air — *but really she's Russian.*

Born in China. It was one of the Australians sitting amongst them.

Jago looked at them and grinned. *Then you blokes can't really claim her,* he said.

She's Miss Australia *mate, if you haven't noticed.* The man's friend this time, leaning back with his sandwich, ankles crossed. *We grew her.*

Jago inclined his head to the man, courteous. Let it go.

But today was Saturday; Jago didn't often work the weekend shifts. Remembering the conversation, Axel thought about Bondi. Found he was missing the ocean; more particularly the push and pull of the surf, the build and collapse of waves, their energy as he entered them and the feeling he emerged with. Scrubbed and new. And despite the argument in the lunch shed he'd decided he would not go to Manly after all. It was too much part of his feelings for Pearl, so often like a rough tide that left him winded, beaten.

He looked up the bus timetable and set out with his towel and an orange and a newspaper in a bag. Bondi after all would give him something to write to Per about, to his mother. Everyone wanted to go to Bondi Beach.

When he finally stood on the steps of the pavilion he perused Jago's 'perfect crescent'. There were people on the beach despite the winter cool, but even the crowd could not dilute the deep colours of sand and sky, and in this soft sun the water was storybook blue. He breathed in salt air and stepped off between the beach umbrellas and oiled bodies on towels. As he reached the water he looked out to the horizon. Its endless promise: his father was out there, just beyond it.

⌒

Saturday morning and she'd slept late. Bridget was leaning against the wall near the taxi rank in a pose that said impatient. She twisted her lips and frowned. *You could've rung,* she said. *I left a very cosy bed to get here on time.* She raised her eyebrows.

Lucky you. Pearl tipped her head in the opposite direction and they fell into step together. *Couldn't ring, Bridge.* She told her about the phone tap and Bridget stopped suddenly, forcing two women behind her to stop too. Pearl heard them curse as they manoeuvred around.

But Bridget was motionless, staring at her. *Shit, Pearl. Why didn't you tell me?* She shook her head slowly, then moved forward once more. *Have you been to the cops?*

The cops? The words a harsh cough. Pearl glanced around even as she spoke them, then back at her friend. But Bridget's face was unmoved.

It is the cops! She spoke through pursed lips. *Or ASIO. Same thing. That's what they do, for Christ's sake.* She looked sideways at Bridget. *They tap phones, they follow people, they spy. Never, ever, go to the cops.*

Bridget was quieter now. *My uncle was a sergeant,* she said, *in the country.* Not meeting Pearl's eye. *He was all right.*

They're watching me, Bridge. Listening to everything I say. The words harder than she intended. Pearl watched her friend's eyes dim and her face flush pink beneath freckles. *Just don't trust coppers, okay? Specially uncles.* She reached for her arm, squeezed. *Okay?*

Bridget shrugged, nodded. As they reached Della's street and turned towards the house she said: *Thanks for telling me. No one tells me anything.* Then: *I do the posters and fold leaflets and make lunch. But no one asks what I think.*

They reached the gate of the terrace and its untended front garden. *I hear things though. I'm not stupid. There's something brewing, isn't there?*

There's always something brewing. Pearl pushed the door open. *It's why we're here on Saturday mornings, and not in bed.*

They inched past a bicycle in the hallway and into the empty kitchen.

I don't mean the next demo at Central. Something bigger.

Pearl pulled a typed page from her satchel and filled the jug. She shrugged. *I've been lying a bit low, Bridge. Not in the loop.*

Well, the boys are talking.

They went through the back door to a ramshackle shed. *What are they saying?* Inside they could hear Della at the Roneo machine. Bridget's hand was already on the door knob. She shook her head.

All right, later. But remember, don't call me, not even at work, Pearl said. *Unless I tell you to.*

⌒

Della talked about the new group as they checked the flyers that chugged out of the machine. *All women,* she said, *all middle-aged. Weird, huh?* She held a page up to the light, squinting. *Gary's mother, Tony's.*

Why weird? Pearl stacked flyers in boxes, precise. Patted down edges.

I know it's not a competition, all that. But. Della bit her lip. *Don't want them to mess it up for us, I suppose. Dilute the rhetoric, or something. I mean, they're housewives.* She went back to the flyers. *Anyway. They're calling themselves SOS. Save Our Sons.*

Pearl's hands stilled. She saw rather than heard the words; they hung in the air, waiting to be chosen. Waiting to be plucked down and run with. *Make a great story,* she said. She would get in touch with Tony, speak to his mother. Offer the interview to the news desk. But Della's words were like a string jerking, her heart attached. Her own mother would have leapt into that group.

When Gary told me he was furious, Della said.

What's wrong with it? Pearl pressed the last flyers into the box and pushed it aside. *People might listen to them. They're not listening to us.*

Della shrugged. *He just said, 'Christ, it's embarrassing, your mother trying to save you. We're grown men. We're supposed to be saving them.'*

⌒

Afterwards Pearl walked to the gardens, unwilling to let the day go. Not ready for dark. Lately the nightmares again, brief, chaotic. The images child-shaped, genderless, returning later as she lifted a facecloth or a pen, as if her body had absorbed them, not visitors but part of her. No matter if her eyes were open or closed, or if she raised her voice to them, no matter if her glass was empty or full. They were there.

She climbed a low rise above the water, lay on the grass in fading sun. The sky the colour of pale cornflowers then, though Pearl could think only of eggshells, the blue at the new edges of the Opera House roof. Her father's eyes.

Her brothers. In her dreams, they have no faces. Sometimes eyelashes, curved like a girl's over empty sockets; sometimes the shadow of cheekbone. That is all. No mouths, ever. Twice in her sleep she has chased them, a scream caught in her throat. No sound. Her mouth stretched wide on nothing, and though she is running and they are walking just ahead she cannot reach them. They march on oblivious of her, of the horror hung in the air. When she wakes she is emptied, the panic over. Only the sense of urgency she lives with every day now, and pushes down to a place where it might be useful.

Two birds swept past and dropped into the fig tree below. She sat up to watch them, arm to forehead against the angle of the sun. Another bird, then another, arching their elegant wings in unison as they settled. Pearl laughed out loud. The image in her head sudden, startling: the Danish architect, she thought, watches birds.

~

Birds, plants. Ships. Clouds. Axel wiped his fingers on a handkerchief, leaned back. *He watches everything.* On Pearl's low table scraps of tomato and melted cheese, the remains of the toast they'd made together in her kitchen. He said: *Patterns. The shapes and lines of nature. That's how he works.*

Pearl bit into a cold crust, her own fingers shiny with grease. *I think he's a poser,* she said as she chewed.

I think he is heroic. He lifted his chin. *And really, so do you.*

She grinned, brushed crumbs from her hands. She'd never say it, but she liked this about Axel, this way of speaking. Even when he was wrong. He spoke plainly, firmly, but without challenge or spite. In the mouths of some Australian men, the same words would have been insistent, the glove down. But this way of Axel's forced a civility from her. Or at least, neutralised her anger.

Heroic! she barked. *You've read too many sagas.* This by way of dismissal, but Axel knew. He only smiled and leaned towards her. *You must have been a terrible child,* he said. Something like happiness flashed in her face. In her eyes.

Her eyes: that's where she lived, he thought. Behind them, in their depths. Something fierce there, something fugitive. As if she harboured another version of herself beneath the lids, a Pearl unafraid of love, for a building or a man. A girl who was not bombproof, a girl who might at any moment begin to cry, and not stop.

It had been months, and still no sign of her brothers. This had been their glue: her fear and determination. It underscored each encounter and conversation. She'd found simple comfort in his company, he knew, and distraction. Nothing more. Still, their early lovemaking had been intimate and startling. When he remembered, it was not the pulse and slip of foreplay, the electric charge of their bodies fusing – though that had been deeply satisfying. It was her eyes, open on him, locking them together, sealing them tighter than flesh. Later he would see it was not her vulnerability but his own that startled and held him. The plainness of the offer and of the taking, the intent; it was about something more than pleasure. It was not coy. It was as if in opening her body to him she was sharing more than skin and fluid. It was devastating in its honesty, in its lack of agenda, in what it *wasn't*.

But it didn't happen like that often after the first time, and he began to believe he'd dreamed it. Or imagined it in the stupor of desire. After that she always closed her eyes. It didn't matter. Dream or waking, he knew without question that in the flare of honesty in her eyes, he could see the edge, the cliff, the clear air he fell into. Love. Blind and willing. It gave him enough to withstand this new distance, the brittleness that grew with each dead end, each false lead on her brothers. At some time, he knew, another Pearl would re-emerge, the girl she was before the world intervened. Strong and brave and true. Optimistic. His mother would love that girl.

Tonight there were hints of her. She was softer, and in her movements and her banter he could feel something loosen. She plucked up the oily plates – *Tea?* she asked – and went to the kitchen. While he waited and looked about, noticing. Newspapers and books, and on a small table sheets of drawing paper, pencils, thumbs of charcoal. Some sheets were blank and others filled with the ordinary: a branch of dry twigs, a leaf in close-up, birds. He leaned in, saw the detail of branch and feather, the pencil's minute attentions, and was surprised by tenderness.

You draw.

She came towards him, her fingers looped into the handles of two cups. Sat down and pushed the sketches aside, making a puffing sound, dismissive. She held a cup to her lips with two hands. *Child's play,* she said behind it. *Not like real artists. Not like you.*

Axel shrugged. *But I draw for work,* he said. *It's different.* He leafed through the pencil sketches again. *And I make pictures on the letters I write to my mother. As you say, things a child might draw.*

He raised his own cup, smiling behind it. *But it always starts with a pencil. Like yours.*

They sat quietly. Then Pearl stood and walked to the front windows, drew the blinds. When she turned to him her eyes were steady. She unbuttoned her shirt.

Draw me, she said.

The air turned electric. His stomach unsettled, his hands. But she would not remove her gaze, watching him as she stepped from her skirt. This loosened something in him, and he tipped his head to the side, smiling.

He was unsure what she was asking. It took him a moment. But still he knew it was not Pearl who would be revealed. Nakedness of the body was nothing, he knew that, not compared to the exposure of drawing it. All of his flaws, any residue of fear, any lack: of tenderness or compassion or openness. It would be in the lines he made on the paper she had produced and laid in front of him.

He stared at his hand, gripping the pencil, and at the blankness, the whiteness of the paper. As if he was projecting her outline, as if the shape of her was already there. As if he had already failed her.

She stepped around the room adjusting the lamps and let the last of her clothes slip from her.

~

In the morning he woke early, suddenly sure: he wasn't the only one. He'd felt it in their lovemaking, a subtle distance, and now he remembered how she was around men, how they were around her. It didn't matter. He watched her sleeping, at once afraid and drawn by it, this hard knowledge. A moth to the bright flame of her, not just her body but her confidence, the way she tilted her chin to the world, never hesitating.

Who are you? He waited for her answer. Her voice when it came like a dream sound. Though her eyes were still closed he knew she was awake. A muscle in her neck pulsed, subsided.

Alexander the Great.

Silence.

Plato.

She turned her head. Her face open as a girl's. *I was dreaming about Kennedy. The hole in America.*

He glanced to the long window. Its peeling white edges framed the ocean, bluer than it could be, as close and alive as Pearl. Here in this bed, he thought, it would be possible to be alone without fear, at least without need. The ocean a body breathing beside you, its tempers almost human.

~

On the ferry home he watched the Opera House approach, its shapes looming against the sky. Leaned back against his seat. For months he had done this: absorbed the movement of air and temperature, the drift and call of language. The shape of desire in the city, in the angle of its streets and the eyes of its people. The way its buildings cut into the sky. Stone, he thought, felt odd in this place, where light fell and tumbled like an acrobat, stretched and played in empty spaces. He began to see the city in terms of its light: the way it captured or held it, bounced it back. The way sunlight was swallowed in the throats of the streets, in alleyways, between buildings. The lemony feel of five o'clock, faces coated by dusk. Light was like glass, it changed the way you saw things.

He wondered about the country outside the city. Beyond harbour and headland to the wide stretches of land behind them. Endless acres where cattle ran, and kangaroos. Deserts. A raw, empty centre. He had heard of vast stretches of red sand, and a rock monumental in size, a sacred presence. Was this the equivalent of the temples that erupted from South American jungles? There were Aboriginal people who lived in its shadow, from an ancient culture with story and song and dance at its heart. Then how could this centre be described as empty? He sat upright. And how could anyone represent this place in art without reference to its beginnings?

He drank his coffee at a café near the quay. The liquid was barely drinkable but it was too early for Lorenzo's, and there was little choice. Once more he thought of searching out a coffee pot and bean grinder; Mrs Jarratt might supply hot water from the kitchen at this hour. But he liked to sit near this busy part of the harbour, to feel the morning stutter and start around him, faces untouched by the coming day and still hopeful. The city itself a blank page, uninscribed.

Except that it wasn't. Beneath this layer of living, this past two hundred years, were the traces of that older civilisation, a thick net of pathways and habitation, the tracks of people and animals. Mogens Prip-Buus, Utzon's chief associate and friend, had said that the place was 'storied'. That an entire city had flourished here, different in look and substance — closer to the ground, greener. Look for what isn't there, his mother had always said, for what is missing. Through the layers of concrete and pavement and bitumen of this city, beneath the brick and tile, even the sweep of gardens and lawn, other lives had been lived. He knew little of them. Where were the marks of the old people then? He automatically looked about him, at the quay and its shops and ferries, the city fanning up and out from the harbour's original edge. Where were their traces? He had no idea who to ask.

As he rose to leave his eye caught the open pages of a newspaper on a neighbouring table. He paused, despite himself. There was a short piece about the architect; that was no surprise. He looked more closely: another change in arrangements, and quotes from Minister Hughes. A panel of local architects would be appointed to oversee Utzon's work, and he would not be paid until a task was complete.

He looked around, plucked the paper from the table. Read the story over again as he walked. A straight piece of reporting without any comment from the architect. But surely they would have to get one: this new arrangement meant nothing could be planned now in advance, because each job had to be complete before funds were released. It was staggeringly, outrageously stupid. And so transparent. No architect could work under those conditions.

How could he possibly know how much each individual thing would cost exactly, or how long the building would take? How could anyone even try to put a value on it? There was nothing like it in the world. Any structure that aspired to myth and dream would look broken as it was built; all art was like this. Clearly, they wanted to break Utzon. The truth of this struck Axel like a blow. They wanted to snap his foreign vision and his hold: as if the architect, some kind of magician, had infused Australians with his own way of seeing, revealed their own vaulting potential. Some latent spirit of inquiry and humility and integrity that his opponents found confronting. Politicians especially.

Why should they be afraid of this modern Pied Piper? Or better: why shouldn't they be? Like the old inhabitants of Hamelin, these people had struck a deal, and in their case at least a true bargain. Perhaps their leaders had not anticipated that the people would fall in love with beauty, that they would look into the bright mirror of the Opera House shells and see themselves. This might be dangerous. Who knew what else they might want: kindness, tolerance, more beauty, more.

Of course, they hadn't counted on the power of the piper. The sound of his flute, unworldly, untranslatable. Ethereal. Of course he had to go.

~

The answer from the union man came back the following week. *Surname of Keogh?* The same rough-edged voice, but quieter, business like. *Got a William and a James. Cooma, New South Wales.*

Cooma? Pearl was barely aware she'd spoken.

Shell

Employed by the Snowy Mountains Hydro-electric Authority.

She stared at the desk in front of her. The world shrank to this: the round metal keys of the typewriter, the circled letters, the roller and its paper. The words, paragraphs there suddenly unreadable, insignificant. *They're still current members? At that address?* Her voice a low kind of bark, though she tried for calm. Please, she thought. A prayer to no one but, if needed, to the god of her childhood, of the dour, righteous Protestantism of her mother. *Good things come,* she heard her say. She closed her eyes.

A brief pause down the line. The sound of pages turning. *Yep. Paid up, both of them.*

Pearl blinked at the walls around her, the ceiling above. Everything changed and nothing did. The world turned benign, ordinary, and her body released its hold, the defensive certainty of bad news. She breathed.

The man's voice again. *All I can tell you mate. More than I should. Good luck eh?*

And he was gone.

She sat for a moment and let the information settle. Looked at the scatter of paper and notebooks in front of her, all suddenly edged in light. In her head, alps, snow, bright rivers and men, heroic, forging new shapes in the landscape, holding back the force of water with their bare hands. Jamie and Will, with the faces of children.

Finally she stood, walked again into the library, found the right phone book, asked for the files on the Snowy scheme. Scurried with them back to her desk, a witch with her hoard, with the makings of a spell to find them, to bind them. There were people to tell, but she wanted to sit with this feeling, let it settle in her, the joy and relief of it – and the trepidation.

She thumbed through the files. The folders were thick with stories and speeches, sentences and sentiments that puffed up on the page like blancmange. The fervour, the righteous clamour that accompanied such projects, the building of a nation. Images of mountains tunnelled by men, moles working in deep dark earth, slinking from their holes at shift's end with exhausted smiles. The camera recorded it all. Men with faces marked by exile and immigration, the surprise of comradeship with old enemies and a decent wage.

Newcomers and locals, stunned by cold, threw arms around each other's shoulders for the camera, stepping into symbolism. They looked too tired to be cynical, too grateful. Too needy. Thumbing through endless clippings, this is what she realised: for the migrant men, war weary, whatever happened to their hands here, to the soles of their feet, their backs, these things didn't matter. This was work for pay and for good. The war was in the distant past. In this place they were all one nationality.

But then the regular reports of accidents in tunnels and on roads. Just two years earlier, three men in a tunnel had been caught in an avalanche of liquid concrete, were pinned by it as it set in the bottom of a shaft. There were rock falls, mistimed detonations. She turned from the clippings of accident reports with their images of ambulance bearers and faces frozen in shock. Could not meet their eyes. The thick skin she had grown as a reporter allowed her this, at least.

Until suddenly, it didn't. She wanted to weep: the lives of working men and women. The duty and acceptance. All over the world, men went down dark mines, laboured with picks and shovels, in tunnels and sewers and abattoirs and in unforgiving fields. Women in the stink of factories and laundries, the relentless fist of the machine. Skivvying in the kitchens of the rich. Her own mother at the steam press and the cannery; she could not bear the smell of asparagus for the rest of her life. All without choice and little reward.

Among them, her brothers. Were they grateful too for these jobs, this forging of an icon, for this fellowship of damaged men? Like those from the shredded countries of

Europe, were they grateful, were they happy? Up there in the Snowy – even as labourers, or digging the earth, hewing rock – they would have a new identity, recast as builders of the new Australia. As useful. As brave. But still at the mercy of a pitiless landscape, a pitiless machine.

⁓

There was the urge to borrow a car, find a map, drive south. But alongside it, needles of terror. She had wanted to protect them from the bludgeoning hand of government and war. But were they safer where they were, tucked away in snowbound villages, than they would be in Sydney? They might be. And their jobs might be exempt from the ballot. Even if they weren't, it might be easier to avoid the draft up there, where news was harder to get and the thicket of nationalities might disguise you. There was the irony of big cities: everyone was connected in some way, and eyes were everywhere. She'd found that out those months ago as she marched in the first protest; the middle of the mob and still she was caught, seen by a random camera that turned the moment into an image.

And then there was the fear: she may not know these brothers any more. Their moods and ideas, their personalities, how the grief of their childhood played out in them now. How they expressed anger, or worry, or love. How the hard scrabble toward manhood had marked them. Part of her was afraid she wouldn't like them; they wouldn't like her. That they would not want to be found.

Depends who you're doing all this for, said Suze that night, playing with the ends of a buttery plait that snaked down from her shoulder and across her breast. She examined the spikes of hair for splits, then dropped it. *For them or for you.*

She had no answer. But the next day she called Jeanne, said she could stop searching. Asked if she could borrow the car Jeanne used to drive around the parish.

~

Out on the site the night shift was not yet in full swing. Axel surveyed the forest of concrete and steel, the giant cranes in their crucifix shape, the erection arches along the soaring lines of the roof shells. The shells themselves like cupped hands, open and poised for prayer. Everything was cross-hatched, an artist's impression. But now the moon, rising, turned the apex of the shells luminous, silvering the wide-hipped ribs. He followed their line upwards and there – like a show-reel, like a magician's trick – the stars of the Southern Cross. Above the crane, unmistakable even to a man who had grown up beneath the northern sky: two pointers and a crucifix. What did it signify to these people?

He didn't know. The shape of it, hung there like a symbol, like a promise.

Now he wandered slowly through the darkness towards the concourse, readying himself for the blaze of industrial light, the blunt power of it, indiscriminately flooding the yards and corners, the shells and the main auditorium, the concrete and metal. A brutal sun in this forest of steel. In a real forest on the other side of the world, Utzon had walked and walked, around the lakes, through trees in thick drifts of leaves. Every day before he moved to Australia, he took his architects into this forest and out onto the frozen lake to sketch their ideas on ice.

Axel had walked these paths too, but alone, and much later. Looking for signs and messages, clues to the architect's mind, or his dreams. He had heard a story about Utzon's children, how they had run at full pelt through this forest one afternoon to meet their father off the train, their bodies flickering through trees, their chests heaving, each dying to be the one who told him: he had won the competition, his design for the Opera House. Their own father. The best in the world.

This was the man he wanted to find. The architect, the father. At first it felt like a waste of time; he couldn't feel the man there or, when he did, it was just his shadow. But now, walking this dreamscape of steel and concrete and unworldly shapes, he could imagine himself back to Hellebæk, to the shores and the forests, walking beside Utzon, speaking of poetry and the sacred, clouds and canopies, the recurrent shapes of nature at the service of the artist. Here, beneath the darkened concourse, the evidence of this conversation was all about him.

It was cold now; he pressed his hands beneath his pullover, looked out beyond the empty yard with its crouching shapes, unknowable in moonlight. Muted sounds from the handful of night workers reached him, and it felt very agreeable to be here, alone, surveying the richness of the scene. He leaned back in the quiet. Then he saw him: a mere shadow but tall, unmistakable, moving slowly against the fence, hands dug into the pockets of his overcoat. A noble silhouette. Axel was up before he realised, took several steps and stopped. Would he seem like a lunatic, approaching the man in the dark? He glanced down at his clothes: respectable, ordinary. Stepped out again. But in those seconds of hesitation the figure had gone. He hurried then, searching each section, and finally asked the guard if Mr Utzon had dropped by. He shook his head, no, went back to his paper. But Axel knew what he had seen.

When he reached the far end of the quay on his way

home, he turned. From a distance and in a shimmer of night light, the sails themselves might be new celestial forms, a new constellation or galaxy in the southern sky. Might do the same work as the Southern Cross, he thought, guiding people home.

~

Saturday morning dawned cool and clear. She caught the bus to St Joseph's, watching old women in cardigans and scarves subside in their seats, their faces unreadable. Outside, the winter paradox of Sydney: a cold wind snatching leaves from trees, overcoats held tight to waists, and the sun striking gold angles through lanes and windows, mocking. The city, grey, gaunt, was sliced with light.

At St Joseph's Jeanne met her in the car park, clutching keys and a road map for the Alps. They embraced, Jeanne's arms hard around her. It brought back the maddening tears she'd been crying since Thursday, some bottomless well of new emotion. When they pulled away from each other Pearl turned quickly to go. But as she drove through the gate she could see the nun in her rear-view mirror, standing straight and still. She was there, hands in pockets, watching, when Pearl turned the car south. The early breeze picked up her hair, briefly curtained her face. Pearl blinked, pursed her lips, but the image hung before her as she drove.

⌒

Cooma was hard and grubby with snow. Pearl was self-conscious, a pale figure in a pale landscape, pushing into the wind. Despite jumpers and coat, her bones were cold. The air particled with pieces of things, torn leaves, bus tickets, a scrap of fabric that might be a hat band, and the wind itself projectile, stinging her eyes. She wiped at them savagely as she walked.

At the office of the Hydro-electric Authority, the unabashed gazes of men. The day manager did not remember her call. Apparently. He rifled through lists.

Keogh, eh? You're a relative?

She regarded his bent head, Brylcreemed, and ignored the question. Dandruff littered his shoulders, the dark wool. *James,* she said evenly, *and William.*

The stub of his finger pressed and sought. And then stopped.

Here we are. Hut 27, Island Bend. He looked up at her with a loose smile. *Your brothers, you say?*

She moved her head infinitesimally.

Well then, if you go and talk to Wendy over there – he nodded towards a blonde beehive across the corridor – *she'll fill you in*. He swivelled to look at the clock above his desk. *The next transport up there leaves in fifteen. You'll want to leave your car here, unless you've got chains.*

Later, standing outside the office beneath the threat of a new snowfall, she thought: Island Bend. So they're tunnellers? Human machines clawing rock and mud. Though in her head they were animal, boring into darkness, inching towards the sun. Their muscles fired and brutish, their eyes forgetting light. When she climbed into the jeep she looked quickly around, checking faces and bodies for signs. Of what? She wasn't sure. Hair and feathers, something scaly or raw? But they were just tired-looking men, two wives carrying shopping. When she told the driver who she was, he said, *Keogh lads? Done for the day. They'll be up at the ski jump with the others.* And before she could reply: *I'll drop you up there.*

⌒

From a distance, the ski jump itself was not intimidating. An oversized ladle, a scoop of snow and wood. The men on the jump were not men but figures in a child's wind-up toy, sliding, leaping, landing one after the other. Their timing and movements uniform and almost mechanical, the push, the lean, the flight. From a few hundred yards away she could hear the occasional whoop carried through the clear, still air.

Pearl stood for a long time and watched, imagining this one Jamie, that one Will. Identifying profile and body shape, the angle of a crouch. Absorbing the irony: these boys, born to Sydney sun and summer heat, who had, she assumed, spent years in the parched landscapes of the bush: now trusting the angle and weight of their bodies to this air, this frozen ground. One after the other: the crouch, knees bent, chin up; poles firm for the push, the acceleration, the world rushing up. Then the leap, feet together, bodies merging with skis, they became boys with feet of wood, thinking through their soles and the palms of their hands, their knees, because these are what will save them, re-attach them to earth. Without skulls and bones smashing as their balance fails and the world spins and splinters.

She moved off towards the jump. Up closer of course it was bigger, more fearful to the eye. Its curve like the outstretched paw of a monstrous bear. Now she could see there were others like her, standing still to watch, trying to interpret the language of this. This flight. This bodily tunnelling through air.

⁓

She waited among the small group of spectators until the jumpers began to thin, until her brothers were two among the last four or five unbuckling their skis, pulling boots from packs. She could hear their voices now, the deep, easy voices of men. But unmistakably theirs; she knew them in a second. The cadences of their speech, the way Will's sentences tipped up at the end. Still she waited behind several others, fiddling with the strap of her bag, attempting invisibility. She thought this was for them, not to embarrass or startle them. Her belly roiled with anxiety, a girl on a blind date.

Then they were shouldering their skis and packs and the other men speared off, and she was standing in their path. Their eyes not quite registering. It was Will who broke first. *Pearlie?* He stopped, they both did. Staring. There were three feet and six years between them. Then Jamie tipped his head to the side, a smile twitching at the corner of his mouth.

She was struck dumb, looking. They were taller. Their faces sharpened by manhood and perhaps by life. Weathered, she'd think later, though in that moment she saw only eyes and skin alive with risk, with the force of the elements they'd been daring. They were grown up, relaxed, limbs loose. With five o'clock shadows. She wanted to rub her hands over their chins, kiss their rough cheeks, say, *You need a shave.*

But of course, didn't. Her chest heaved, she swallowed tears that might change things. There was so much she didn't know. But then their faces were against hers, she felt their arms about her, their voices. *Is it you?* one said. *It is you.* And the other: *Pearlie.* Which was which? It didn't matter. They patted her cheeks, smudged with their own tears, wiped their eyes. Then pulled back. Laughed. *How the hell?* Jamie was holding her hand, shaking his head. *How – ?*

Nothing came. The words in her were gone. She stood mute, not trusting herself. Then Jamie stopped suddenly, the smile contracting, closing him up. He looked into her eyes. *What's wrong? Is it – ?*

She stood squarely, eyeing them both. *No. Nothing.* She shook her head. *Your Da's okay. Not up to leaping off a ski jump, but he's all right.*

She saw his chest expand with a breath finally taken. His lips part as he blew it out.

Then, in the silence, Will's slow grin. *Did you see us up there?* Tipping his head to the jump. *Were you watching?* As if it wasn't real unless she saw it. He was the boy in the tree once more, about to leap from a high branch, or from the woodshed roof, needing her as witness. As admirer.

She nodded. *Yes of course I was watching.* Her body returning to itself, to what she always had been: their sister. She beamed. *Bloody terrifying.* She looked from one to the other as both faces flushed with happiness. They were delighted and gratified by her fear for them. As they always had been.

—

Back in the village, she walked between them towards their quarters in the single men's huts. The sun faded to apricot, the cold like a fist tightening. The next shift began at ten; they'd change and take her to eat at a café in Cooma, their favourite, Jamie said.

She glanced at her watch; five hours together, five hours to win them back.

She sat in the mess to wait. A wooden shed, flimsy as cardboard, marginally warmer inside than out. At the end of a long table she watched men, dirt-smeared, fill their plates from tureens at the far side. They slid along the benches and immediately dipped their faces to their food. Occasional conversation sputtered into the air, low grunts of laughter against a background of cutlery scraping, plates and glasses banged down, the soft crack of bones as limbs were stretched. Pearl had learned the best approach in such places, where she was outnumbered by men by a hundred to one, was to assume a proprietorial air. She tilted her chin up to the space above the table, where industrial lights hung low above the rows of bent heads. But she stole glances at the faces and profiles: the olive-skinned, the swarthy, the bearded; bodies of every shape.

She recognised Axel's way of speaking, or something like it, in the mix of languages that flowed like a braided river across the room, voices rising and falling and drifting into quiet. Beginning again. She tried to pick up the sentences of the Scandinavians, but they were lost in the robust cadences of the locals and the Italians. She watched them speaking and eating and drawing pictures in the air. Even dirt-streaked they were glossy, these Mediterranean men. Their skin shone. The pale-haired northerners looked washed out in comparison.

The men drifted in and out. Through the staccato of conversation she heard her own internal voice, her fretting questions. How to say what she'd come to say? She'd rehearsed lines in the car as she drove, plain-spoken sentences firmly put. *There's a war on and you need to come home. Will, especially. I'll get you jobs, good ones.* Or: what? As the miles had fallen away so had her confidence. She was, she realised, far more nervous about talking to her brothers than she'd ever been with politicians. It wasn't just the matters of conscription, of war; it was the matter of love. Love and negligence, love and judgment.

Now, at the end of this long table of men, she saw she'd expected to find them still boys. Even at 19 and 20. But their hardscrabble years alone had grown them up; it was in their demeanour, their acceptance of hard things. Their refusal of pity. They were men now, working men, who wore the mantle of hard labour as their father had. She recognised his approach, his attitude: they were workers and proud of it. Hard labour was their fate and their strength. But they were not subservient. She could see it in the way they held themselves, the way they spoke. They were not slaves. They were good at what they did, and they were paid for it. They had found dignity in it, in this bargain. That is what would save them. They would work, they would work hard. But they would not be trodden into the ground.

And they would ski! A reminder that their bodies were not merely forms to be bent to the company line, but free, strong. And in the miraculous air of the mountains, in the recklessness of the jump, completely their own.

So how to speak of government and policy and war in this place? Here in this mess hut – perhaps over the whole immense project – politics had been abandoned. Exactly twenty years before, these men were dropping bombs on each other's countries, aiming rifles at each other, manufacturing hate. Now, many of them were refugees, without homes or countries except here, in this company of outsiders.

Others had left families in shattered cities to seek work to feed them. Somehow they managed to sit at this table and eat together, to work the long night shifts side by side.

And then there was this: how to say *come with me, you're in danger,* when they worked in the face of danger every day? And in company with these men. Who had seen the very notion of it redrawn in the last war, and the notion of belief, of allegiance. She felt the chill wind of her own naïveté, her own failure to think things through.

⌒

She looked up to see them striding into the hut, self-conscious in their clean clothes, their hair slicked down and combed. Some of the men wolf-whistled and one called out: *Eh Jamie hot date huh? You like older woman?* Pearl could see the colour rise furiously in their faces. Jamie grimaced. And Will, over his shoulder and stern: *Shut up you idiot. She's our* sister. But they enjoyed it, she could tell, it was in the looseness of their bodies as they approached her, their mocking smiles.

She stood and inhaled the soapy smell of them. Then turned and linked her arms in theirs. She said: *Take me to the swankiest place in town.*

You're in it, said Will, deadpan. And steered her through the door and out into the mugging cold.

The landscape was muffled, hard to read. Night had absorbed forms and shapes, but the snow, Pearl thought, was lit from within, as if some great fire burned beneath it. The sky was a million points of light. They walked down a path towards another jeep. *But you're in luck,* Jamie said, squeezing her hand, *it's lamb roast night at the Cooma sports club.*

~

She sat opposite them at a vinyl-topped table. Everything was lighter here: the décor and faces, the sounds. Plain white walls with posters and photographs, conversations and laughter. There was a party air. Family groups, couples, faces open and flushed pink. The sounds of a jukebox in a distant corner. No one wore work clothes or dour expressions; like her brothers, the men had shed roughened skins and reverted to ordinariness. There was once more the choir song of languages.

Lamb and vegetables and gravy. *On us,* Will said lightly. *Shandy?* He tilted his head towards her, hesitant, uncertain of the proprieties. *Or – sherry?* She bit her lip in a pretence of choosing. *I'll have a beer,* she said, *whatever you have, Will,* and watched him lope away. Jamie pulled out a stackable steel chair and Pearl realised it was for her. She slid onto the cold seat, let Jamie manoeuvre it towards the table. He sat across from her and beamed. Will returned with a jug and three glasses and sat down beside her. *Watch this, sis,* he grinned, pouring beer. *The head on a beer should never be more than an inch.*

It wasn't. *I'm impressed,* she said, and drained half the glass in one go. *That's good,* she said. They exchanged swift glances, and grinned.

When their meals came she watched them eat, as she had the men in the mess. Their energetic jaws, scrubbed faces. They ate quickly, speaking as they chewed, pausing only to shake more salt over the meat or to nod at someone they knew. They talked about the township, the weather, and began to ask questions they didn't know they had. Pearl's work. Their father. The twins and their children. Jane. Pearl chewed thick slices of overcooked lamb, cold beneath the warm gravy, and felt the conversation as the same texture. They were muffled, all of them. Everything unspoken. They exchanged surface pleasantries, like people on a bus. No one mentioned the real thing. All the missing years.

But of course, their disappearance, her own, was like a net thrown over them, Pearl thought; they could wriggle around beneath it, but it caught and trapped them, confined them to a particular space, a particular way of being with each other. She pushed soggy roast pumpkin around her plate. In the oily residue she could see it: there was only one way she could say what she had come to say.

She struggled with the last piece of meat and finally pushed the plate away. Picked up her beer. *There's something I need to talk to you about,* she said, both hands around the glass. Her brothers flicked a look at each other. *Knew it,* the look said. Then their eyes settled on her.

You ran away. Didn't know where you were. Took some finding.

Their eyes blank, shifting.

It's all right, she said, trying to hold them. *It was my fault. I ran away first.*

She checked them for any sign they might bolt now. But they sat with their hands in their laps, docile as infants at story time. She breathed in, out. *So. Let's see. I think I got the job on the Tele a couple of years before you left. Can't remember exactly.*

In the pause Jamie lifted his head. His doe eyes. He said: *Something like that. You cut out your first stories and brought them to show us.*

Will said: *Yeah, we'd sit around and look at them and think, geez, Pearlie's hit the big time.*

She smiled at him. *Yeah. I thought I was big time. Ordinary old Pearlie. This big important job at the newspaper. People wanted to talk to me, read my stories.*

In their faces she could see the patience they'd had as children. Waiting for her to come and play with them, or get them out of the bath. Dress them. Their eyes lifting to her from the tub or from their beds. *I loved looking after you two when you were little,* she said. Though she hadn't expected to. *As if you were mine. You were, in a way.* She didn't wait for a response. *But that job. It switched something on in me. Something that had gone off.*

You were good at it. Will's voice encouraging. *And the money. That was good too.*

The words fell into the empty space above the plates, the smears of gravy and fat. She looked at them, their faces open, unbetrayed. Then why did she feel she was in a witness stand? Will shrugged. Two seconds, three. *It's okay,* he said. *We knew you were busy at work, Pearlie.*

And then after a while we — Pearl watched Jamie's Adam's apple rise and fall in his throat. *We had to get out of there.* He was a teenager again, lifting his shoulders in answer to a question.

We hated it, Pearlie. Will's voice matter-of-fact, as it always was.

She could barely look at them. But did. *I know. And I'm sorry. I'm sorry I didn't come.*

They looked back at her. Not angry. But there was an equation on the table: the extent of their suffering, she saw, had to match the heft of her actions, her reasons. It was clear she was still in debt.

I lived a pretty wild life for a while there. She leaned back, preparing. *Worked hard, played hard. Being the child I didn't get to be.* She shrugged. *Stupid.*

Perhaps it was her surroundings, these icy fields of labour, hard labour, or just her brothers, finally. Because it was suddenly plain to her: the impetuous leaps she'd taken, the self-gratification. She thought, there was something in me, and still is, that allowed me to do all that; the risks, the forgetting. She had put herself first. Occasionally, she could still feel it: a pure selfishness kicked in, a blindness to others. It drove her then; she went after what she wanted. And usually, she got it.

Her fingers on a white paper napkin now; she rubbed it over an imaginary spill. *And. I got pregnant. To a married man.* The gaps between words meant to ease them, but still she shocked even herself. Again, it was more than she'd expected to say.

In their faces, the fight for words, or equanimity. Selfish, she thought, I've said too much. A cheap shot to clear the debt; to make the debt *theirs.* It wasn't fair, the equation was wrong. *But that's nothing to do with you.* The distress in their eyes. *Nothing at all. And anyway, it's all in the past,* she said.

Trying to absolve them of the need to respond. *A long time ago.* A thin smile. *I've grown up now.*

Out of the long silence: *Bloody 'ell.* It was Will. His lips moved to speak again but nothing came.

You're ok then? Jamie's head was down; he looked up through dark eyelashes.

I'm fine.

The baby?

Lost it, she lied. Though it wasn't a lie, not really.

Then Will's fist against the table. *Jesus, Pearlie.*

They finished the jug of beer. Will fetched tea. Pearl watched them stir sugar into their cups and turned the talk to them. Their lives since she'd seen them. Fruit-picking, labouring. Then the miracle of the Snowy. It didn't take long to realise how their experiences and their workmates had changed them. The Labor Party was full of communists; Menzies has saved them, the whole bloody country. Students and protesters were louts. *They should get a job,* said Will. *See what real work feels like.* He rubbed his shoulders as he spoke. *What do they know? Sitting on their arses all day. Do they even know what they're talking about?*

Pearl's lips pressed together. Keeping her feelings behind them. *So you get the news up here, people talk about it?* she said. *Politics, protests.*

The wireless. Jamie nodded. *And the papers get shared around.*

All ripped and greasy by the time we get 'em, Will said.

Jamie lowered his glass, thoughtful. *I do like a fresh paper.*
He looked to Pearl, suddenly shy. *You know, with a cuppa and a
smoke. Like Da.*

They grinned at each other. But her pleasure was
smothered by the way they spoke, their odd opinions. Her
brothers had turned into Tories.

But if they read the papers they'd have to know about the
war. About Vietnam. Still she struggled with a way to speak.
A way to put things. Will got up to get trifle and when he
returned she blurted: *So you've read about Vietnam? This war?
Menzies is sending our men now, conscripts too.*

Jamie poured more tea.

Pearl said: *Twenty-year-olds.* Accepted the full cup he slid
to her. *Like you.* The tea burned in her throat. She pulled her
coat tighter.

They exchanged a glance. *Yeah, we know Pearlie.* Will
lowered his spoon, licked crumbs from his lips.

Later, she'd see that was the moment when knowledge
struck. When they spoke again she already knew the words.
How they would sound. A cold stone sinking in her belly.
The room collapsed in to their small table, the three of them,
their hands.

Jamie examined his palms. *We're going too, Pearlie,* he said, then dared to look at her. *We've enlisted. Just waiting to be called.*

Yep! A grin cracked across Will's face. *Reckon Da would be proud.*

She was aware of her mouth opening and shutting. No sound. It was like a dream that was hard to wake from, one without voices. She was frozen, mute, powerless against them. For several seconds she understood this as the truth.

Then Will spoke again. *What do you reckon? A couple of tours of Vietnam and then they'll train us in a trade. Metalwork maybe.* The smile hadn't left him. But it wasn't the Will of a moment ago, who could still smile like a child. Suddenly in front of her he was a man. With a future. And a mission: to save the country. Himself. Her.

It's the commos, sis. They're like insects up there, hordes of 'em, taking over the world —

For Christ's sake. She was barely aware of speaking. Her head moving slowly, side to side. She opened her mouth, unsure if she could trust her voice. *You've signed up?* She tried for calm. *Both of you?* And looked at Jamie.

Didn't get drafted, he shrugged. *Had to volunteer.*

She turned to Will. *Couldn't let him go alone.* Grinning. Happy.

Her voice when it came was a muted cry. *You're too young, Will. They won't take you.* Then to Jamie: *And you don't have to go.*

I'm in Pearlie. At that moment a man appeared at their table, confusing her. She didn't know who had spoken, Jamie or Will.

Evening, he said. *Who's this?* She looked up into leery eyes and immediately looked away. The boys must have warned him off; when she looked up again he was gone.

Why? she said, the word shocked out of her into unsteady air. *It's not even our war, we don't belong there.* She looked from one to the other. *You don't belong there. And* – her trump card – *you're wrong about your Da. He'd be appalled. Shocked. And your mother* – But it was too hard to continue. She squeezed her lips together. Looked away.

They seemed devoid of a response to this. *None of them have been our wars, Pearlie.* It was Jamie, rubbing his thighs as he leaned forward at the table. *We're lucky, living here. We haven't had a war. But we could, all that stuff happening up there. In Asia.*

She frowned at him.

All this shit, Korea, Indonesia. That bloody mob in China, it's them. They'll work their way down.

What did he mean by this? What did he know of Asia, of Europe, he hadn't even finished school. She wanted to shake him. Instead she dropped her hands to her lap, and her voice took on a kind of pleading. *But Vietnam.* She looked from one to the other. *It's like eating your own. Those boys in the north, they're just like you.*

Still don't want 'em here, said Will.

What do you mean?

Jamie's right, they're on the march, Pearlie. All that empty country up there, Cape York, the Territory. We've been in those places, they're as empty as the sea. We wouldn't even know they were here 'til they were. He shrugged. *Gotta be stopped. See?*

~

They stepped outside, their bodies changed by the conversation, their limbs stiffer, hands at a loss. So they were surprised by cold, by shapes made precise, unarguable. The hard beauty of frost, and silence.

The night sky wheeled above them. Jagged stars, light colliding. Pearl looked away from it, nauseous. Found, once more, that she could not speak. Not struck dumb so much as quieted by her own reluctance to say hard things. And by what she had seen as she sat there with them: that her absence had removed her right to admonish, even to advise. She had relinquished it when she left them to find their own way.

War's a disgusting thing, she said finally. *It's not cowboys and Indians, Will. It's not toy guns and nice uniforms and girls.*

We know.

Even if they don't kill you. It's your mate dying horribly in the dirt next to you. It's mothers and children blown up by bombs and mines.

Silence.

Bloke got killed on the job up here not that long ago. Buried alive. Jamie pushed the top of his boot against dirt. *Had a wife and kid. We knew 'em.* He stopped, looked at her. *That was a horrible way to die, Pearlie.*

She suddenly saw where he was taking this. Dying in Vietnam would be better. Braver. She wanted to say: this *is* brave, what you do here. You've been brave all your lives. But couldn't. Could not humiliate them, diminish their fledgling sense of worth. *You want to defend the country, is that it? Protect us.*

They both looked at her blankly. Then Will shrugged. *Dunno, Pearlie,* he said. *It's just the right thing to do.*

⌒

They stood together at the door of her motel room. Hands pressed into pockets. Pearl felt numb, her body deadened, her heart scooped out of her chest. They stood in the kind of silence that precedes a parting. Jamie turned then, peered up at the cold sky. Flung out an arm to take in the mountains, iced with snow and luminous in the dark, the dark shape of their world.

Camped out for nights, looking up at that sky.

Three heads tilted to the stars. In the silence Pearl fancied she could hear them, the stars, the sky, the bare rasp of ice beneath water, or snow forming as it falls.

Will said: *Had to find the Cross. Every night, before we went to sleep, like it was a lucky charm or something.* He wrapped his arms around himself. *And if we woke up and couldn't sleep, it was still there, low and kind of –* he looked at the ground.

What?

Kind of, reassuring. Reliable. You know?

Pearl stole a glance at his face. He was blushing. *Just there,* he said, *night after night.*

⁓

The new day dawned crystalline. Pearl stood at the window and could see only a cruel beauty. The blue and white clarity of it mocked her; she would have preferred a grey rain, a mournful air. When the boys came to her after their shift, their faces emptied by the night's labour and bodies sagging towards sleep, she tried, as she knew she had to, one last time. In the mess hall she said: *You don't have to do this.*

I've got a friend at the Opera House, there'd be jobs there, good ones.
She was aware of the pleading in her voice. Tried to smile.
Brave jobs. You'd be serving your country too, working on that.

They grimaced over weak tea. Jamie said: *Serving the country here, Pearlie.*

Finally she had to concede.

They wandered towards the car, each step slow, tentative.
You sure you gotta go now, today? Will pouted, his face returned to the eight-year-old.

Pearl kicked a front tyre. *I have to get this back to Jeanne.*
Matter-of-fact now, already girding herself, and she lowered her head, realising. She softened. *And you two have to sleep.*

They dug their hands in their pockets. Will grimaced.
S'pose.

As she threw her few things in through the back door:
So when is all this nonsense happening, then? And turned to smile at them, her arms open.

But when she slid into the car her whole body turned to lead.
She twisted the key in the ignition, pushed the gear stick into first and moved off while her volition lasted. Raised her hand in farewell, and drove. Still, the crying took her by surprise. It convulsed her chest and throat, unstoppable, releasing waves

that blurred her vision, weakened her limbs. But she drove. Needing to. Realised too late that she'd taken a wrong turn — she was heading south-east, towards the coast. She slowed, wiped a sleeve across her face, got her bearings. To hell with it. She would just drive. Take the coast road. Longer, but no matter. So long as she was back by the morning.

She was careful in Jeanne's wheezing motor, pulling up when she thought of it to check its water and tyres. Bega, Narooma. At Nowra she stopped to eat an early dinner at a Greek café, chops and egg and lemony potatoes. Strong Greek coffee. Scraped the plate with bread and butter and realised she hadn't eaten all day. Then drove to a beach to walk it off in the just-dark.

The strip of sand was empty apart from the distant figures of a man and a dog. Too far up the beach to know if they were moving towards her or away, but the memory came unbidden of the conversation about Wanda Beach those weeks before. She dismissed it, walked deliberately as a man would. Deliberate as Della's new boyfriend, pushing himself into her when she confessed she'd taken the new contraceptive pill. As if that was consent. But up ahead the figures were shrinking into distance and the night. Pearl slowed her pace, felt her muscles loosen. Looked up to the mess of stars, until all she could see was the Cross. Then turned back to the car.

All the way to Sydney she could see only the shapes of two boys in swags, a dying fire, and the million-acre sky careering above them. Their eyes hunting the Cross, elusive as a dream. Until they saw the pointers, undeniable, flashing like a sign, and recognised the womanly shape, the head and feet and hips. A reliable mother, above them every night, reassuring, protective. A shuffle to east or west, up or down but the same Cross in any case, her meanings alive and bigger than she was. No wonder the boys sought her, Pearl thought, and no wonder that every Australian government, of every stripe, had kept her on the flag. The flag that flew them to governance, to servitude, to war. That validated everything.

Night was evaporating when she pulled into the convent. She sat in the car and watched darkness leach from the horizon, her eyes gritty with the drive and the aftermath of crying. Sadness fought off anger and then swung back, until she could no longer read her own emotions, no longer knew what she felt. There was only an endless emptiness, a desolation, and the certainty of her own culpability. She pushed back the seat and closed her eyes.

And woke to brightness, to the sound of a thousand car engines speeding people to town, to jobs. The stars had retreated, the sky already milky with winter sun. She felt bruised, her bones chilled. But as her eyes and ears adjusted, another sound, soft but insistent through the closed car windows. The bells were ringing.

Pearl walked towards the path Jeanne would take to chapel. She was numb, hollowed out, but the bells pulled her like ropes thrown to the drowning, the sound coiling softly around her. She was once more the child craving touch, a consoling hand on her head or her arm. A voice that spoke forgiveness. Absolution. The path skirted the ancient graveyard and its bent, tired trees. Pearl moved slowly, her head down. The bells sharpened in the cold air, a chisel striking granite, and when she raised her eyes there was Jeanne stepping quickly between gravestones. Pearl stopped still on the path. As Jeanne neared her she lifted her hands to cover her face. What Jeanne would see there.

August 1965

He walked in new light towards the harbour, grey now like a whale's back, quiet. Too early for breakfast at Noah's, though Mrs Jarratt, *call me Olive*, was up and making tea. Here love, she'd said, pushing a thick white cup towards him. He'd thanked her and stirred in sugar to make it drinkable – she seemed not to have heard of coffee – as he stood in the dim dining room with its square tables and sideboards, the stacked saucers and plates. Then he drained the cup, nodded, handed it back. Turned to the door. *Good luck with it*, she said to his back, *Don't let 'em give you any crap*. The waking street, the damp footpath gave no clues to what she meant.

From Bennelong Point he turned and looked towards the city. His back to the harbour. His eyes grazed colour and contour: the sweep of green that was the gardens, stands of sandstone and concrete and rock. And the bridge. He could never stand on the point without feeling its pull, the audacity of its leap across water. *The emotion of it. As if it spans time,* he'd said to Pearl one day. *And feeling, as well as space. You might be a*

different person at each end of it. Don't you think? In just a glance.
She'd only smiled at him in her maddening way, crossed her
arms. But Axel knew the bridge across the harbour informed
his work each day, the great bowl of water at his elbow, the
miracle of steel and light in his eyes.

The feeling dissipated later in the shed at Woolloomooloo. As he arrived the craftsmen were in conversation
about Davis Hughes and his new arrangements with Utzon,
whether the latest controversy would mean they themselves
would not get paid. *You could starve,* one said over his shoulder
as he passed a drawing to Axel. Axel frowned and held his
eye. As he turned away the man said, *Ah just some bloody spat.
Cheque book control or something.*

Axel called to Barry. *What is a 'spat', what does it mean?
Exactly what is this cheque book thing?* His tongue made *cheque*
into *sheque.*

Barry grimaced and sighed. *It means the government is taking
control of Mr Utzon's pay, instead of the Opera House committee.
Means they can withhold payments whenever they feel like it.* He
pulled on his gloves and walked towards the kiln. Over his
shoulder he said: *No idea why they think he'll take that lying down.*

The men gathered near the smaller prototypes they'd
produced over the past month. There were still problems with

proportion, with the contrast of textures, the transparent and the coarse. And ahead of them the technical challenges of producing the full-sized piece, the length and tapering, the capture – the encapsulation of – light. Usually, Axel loved this part of the process. Loved the paradox, the uncertainty created by transparency, the illusions inherent in the glass, and its opposite effect, the rough, sandy surfaces. The contrast, the ambiguity, of two opposing states held within the one idea. Two ways of seeing reality, the deep truths within each.

⁓

But now there were days when the glass was all he could manage. Was all that could save him. The darkness arrived without notice; today it was a bleak wash over his vision, across the very surface of his eyes. It coated everything, turned the world to a negative, black and white. The face of the architect came and went inside it. At these times he would work for hours without respite, his thoughts as viscous as new glass. There was the furnace and the fire. There was the inchoate and his hands, shaping. His arms, the cords of tendon, the muscle and blood. The bright bone of intention. He concentrated hard: this was the only way he could dilute the terror. The fear that lived in the bleak depths of the water and even the streets, the menace of their shadows and their variousness.

If he could capture it like a sea monster. If he could contain it.

For hours at a time, the rawness. He was turned inside out. Emotions not so much on his sleeve but stretched like a thin skin over bones, ghostly, permeable. Organs beating pink and grey beneath this transparent sheath. Like the jellyfish he'd seen washed up after storms: they pulsed in the wash of waves, a mere blueness, beating. As if that's all they were, these gelatine hearts. As if that's all he was.

At night, in his bed at the Mercantile, he dreamed of watery worlds and amphibious creatures, people at home in sea or lake or land. Of long ships, bark canoes, vessels that encapsulated life and death and the journey between them. Vessels of rescue and escape. That, upturned on a beach, could provide shelter from a storm. From the dark recesses of water, its subterfuge and strength, its promises. He would wake in terror of the shifting light of the harbour, its beguiling surface.

He fought these feelings in himself. It was not, he knew, the way Utzon saw it. To him the clean light, the water, were creatures with benign intentions. So Axel worked on, ashamed, as if this feeling might be visible. Hid himself from view, so no one should know this about him. This duplicity, this darkness. His feelings betrayed all that Utzon himself felt and saw and said.

These feelings rushed in with every new crisis around the Opera House. It was the plywood for the ceilings now, the contract and its price. The government wanted tenders, the job offered to the cheapest bidder. To Axel, this was confounding. At home the best craftsmen would be consulted first, the cost negotiated as the process proceeded. Anyone could produce the cheapest price. But only one or two could produce the highest standards, the result of a lifetime of experience, of integrity. You always went to those who knew best.

So many here did not see what Axel saw, or pretended they didn't. The Opera House was their second miracle; he was not sure they deserved it. The new government behaved as if the building was a millstone rather than a monument. A shining symbol of what might be. For months they'd pursued the architect on every point, from his pricing to his planning, humiliated him publicly and privately. Rejected his drawn plans for his own house in Sydney. Utzon's own family house. The man had emigrated, brought his wife and children here; had designed a house for them to live in. To put down roots. This man who was leading them out of cultural darkness, who had been chosen for that reason.

But in this country, he saw, it was a kind of sport to belittle those with vision, to treat art with disdain. He wasn't sure what benefit it brought, but it was something to do with this flattening out, this shuffle towards sameness, to a life lived on the surface, without any depth. Was that why people clung so hard to the edges of the country, their backs to its beating red heart? Were they afraid to look in, to hear the old stories, to see what was inscribed on their own hearts and land?

One day, Axel knew, he must see Utzon and tell him: the critics were blind. That the locals had no myths and therefore could not understand him or his building. Some time in the future, they might. When they needed a symbol, a narrative that explained them, that stood for them, they would look to the Opera House and see themselves. When he saw Utzon he would tell him: you cannot give up.

⌣

Don't take this on, Pearl. It isn't yours. Suze leaned back on the bench and stretched her bare legs, her arms. The park was awash in late winter sun, the air clear and still; Suze had rolled up her loose pants and tilted her face skywards.

Pearl was bound up in scarf and coat, and still her jeans felt too thin, as if all her skin was exposed, goose-fleshed. She crossed her arms, tucked her hands beneath them. *Of course it's mine,* she said. She looked steadily at the bare branches of a peppermint tree.

Christ's sake. The faint thread of impatience in Suze's voice. *You didn't see them much for a few years. You think that changed everything, the whole course of their lives? Their personalities?*

Of course it did. It damaged them, turned them hard.

They grew up. That's all. Happens to us all, in case you hadn't noticed.

Suze. Pearl swivelled her body towards her friend. Fought for composure. Still her voice cracked open, her lips contorted to contain it. *I was as good as their mother. The closest thing they had. So they lost her a second time.* She looked away, fighting hard. Her body an edifice that might crumble at any time. Then Suze's warm hand was on her neck, and even this was too much, too kind. Her heart contracted, a fist in her chest.

I fucking abandoned them Suze, and they knew it. And they were kids. How do they deal with that? They turn themselves into different people, that's how. Who can't be hurt any more. Her voice broke on the words and she stopped. Pulled at threads on the old scarf. Tears that might be anger or might be grief pricked at her eyes. She sniffed.

Suze produced a handkerchief. *Ironed it myself,* she said.

Pearl held it to her face, but couldn't feign a smile.

I suppose you blame your mother for everything that happened to you. Suze pulled her knees up, wrapped her arms around them.

Pearl frowned. *She died, Suze. She didn't do it deliberately.*

No, she didn't. But you. You hurt the boys deliberately. Sat down and worked it all out, the best way to cause them pain.

Pearl pursed her lips.

You gave up school for them, gave up your chances, your youth. Then you got a job you loved. Or weren't you supposed to feel any joy? Suze stopped, looked at her sharply. *Because your mother didn't get to? Is that it?*

Don't psychoanalyse me Suze.

For God's sake. She dropped her arm around Pearl's shoulders. *You deserved a life. No one can predict how things will turn out. How people will think or react. Not even you.*

They sat in silence then as a light breeze picked up and sparrows picked at the ground around them. Occasional sounds drifted to them from King Street, a bike revving, a shout, the low bass of traffic. Pearl watched the birds and thought of her father, the magpies he fed in the early morning garden of her childhood, breadcrumbs scattered as he left for work. In his old man's chair near the door now, the birds watched him, as if they knew. The word *fidelity* crept towards her with the sparrows.

You know darling — Suze lifted her arm and tipped her face to the sun once more, her voice slow, as if she was half asleep — *it can be a bit self-indulgent, this self blame. As if you're the centre of the world, all powerful, inflicting or withholding blows. Fixing stuff.*

Pearl had no reply. She stuck her hands in her jeans pockets, crossed her ankles. A sparrow had crept close to her boots and now startled away.

But you're not, and you can't. Suze spoke to the sky. *You're just a feeble bloody human like the rest of us. You can't cause calamities unless you try really hard, and you can't fix 'em.*

You saying I'm on some sort of power trip? And enjoying it?

I'm saying it's strangely satisfying, putting yourself at the centre of things. Seeing yourself as the cause of everything, bad or good. It's playing God. And that's the thing — if you've signed up for the wrongs, you also have to concede the rights. If you made them suffer you must also have made them happy. Sorry, but it's true.

Pearl swung around to look Suze in the eye. But Suze was ready. *So pull yourself out of your hole.*

Those boys, Pearl said slowly, *were born good. I was there, I saw it.*

They were born imperfect, as we all are.

But Pearl was seeing their toddler bodies bent to the spinach leaves in the garden, Will's palm turned up to show his brother the ladybird teetering there, his eyes shining. And later Jamie with his baby sister, crying when she did, and his plump hand on his mother's, stroking. *And it's still there,* she said. *It's obvious.*

Well. I rest my case. Suze lowered her feet, pulled herself upright. She was smiling. An odd, incalculable smile.

Pearl was still, conceding nothing. Then she turned, lifted her arms, breathing in the herby smell of Suze's hair, her skin. When she was away from her paints, Suze always smelled as if she'd grown from a patch of thyme and sage. Pearl leaned in, pressed her nose to Suze's neck, and felt calmer somehow, earthed. *If I had to pick you out of a lineup and I was blindfolded,* she said, pulling away, *I'd still know you in an instant.*

They stood and stretched. Suze said, *I'd be the one lecturing you.* She tucked her arm through Pearl's, and they walked off across the grass.

When they reached Enmore Road Pearl stopped. *You know what they said? Will and Jamie. They said it was the right thing to do. Signing up. Like cleaning their teeth at night or standing up for an old woman on the tram.* A car cruised past, its driver's elbow protruding, his eyes moving from the road to Suze and then to her. He raised his brows, puckered his lips into a silent whistle. *How do you go from that to killing the commos?*

Suze shrugged. *They're probably polite in bed too.* She smiled and raised her hand and walked off towards home.

⁓

She caught a bus to Blue Skies straight from work the next day. Visiting wasn't encouraged at that hour, when evening meals were almost finished and medications were administered. The staff favoured late mornings, or mid-afternoons. They made it sound as if any appearance outside routine times might turn her father, or any one of them, into a crazed monster. Or worse, that he would be unsettled at bed time. But Pearl knew the opposite was more likely. If she simply sat with him for half an hour, spoke about this and that, read aloud to him, he would be happy. The orderly would get him into bed. But she would smooth his sheets and blankets as he had once smoothed hers, stroke his forehead, sing softly as he had once done. *Black Velvet Band.* Then he'd sleep like a baby until morning.

Shell

Several nurses eyed her as she came through the door. But they were too busy to remonstrate; one was urging an ancient man in a wheelchair to open his mouth, the others rattling medication trays. The odour of boiled cabbage hung in the room. Pearl went to the dining table where her father sat staring at his near-empty plate. Leaned over his shoulder, kissed his cheek. *Hello Da.* She waited, her face against his, until she felt him relax. Then tilted her head around to meet his eyes. *Got time for a brew?* Odd how the rhythm of her speech tilted to Irish when she was with him. She was a ventriloquist, speaking for him, keeping his voice alive.

Before she moved him she went to the nearest nurse. *If he's had his pills,* she said, *I'll get him some Milo. Settle him into bed.*

Sometimes they would grizzle at her for interrupting routine, but they rarely objected. Pearl looked at her watch; they were running late, medications were usually done by now. The nurse, young, tired, looked from her list towards Patrick. She didn't smile. *Yep, all right,* she said. *But not too hot. And get a bib.*

Pearl translated this as *Thank God yes you do it but don't get me into trouble.* She mixed the warm drink in the kitchen and returned to Patrick without the bib. She pushed his chair to the window. Pressed his hand around the mug, then hers on top, and raised it to his lips. He blinked slowly with the pleasure of it.

She watched his face and knew she couldn't speak the words she had come with. And neither could she lie outright. She spooned the milky granules into her father's mouth and said she was sure she'd soon have news of Jamie and Will. *Got a lead on them, at last.* But Patrick's eyes were blank. Only his mouth moved as he ground and sucked the bits of chocolate. *Scallywags. Why are boys so bad at letters? Eh?* Did he understand what she was saying? Had he even heard her? For one elongated moment she felt he hadn't, that the numbness had widened between visits, gouging more of the Patrick-ness from him. *Dadda?* Louder, though she hadn't meant to be. *Reckon you might see your boys soon.* A hand on his cheek.

He swallowed. Then his eyelids fluttered; perhaps he understood.

~

Tell me about your father.

It was the end of a warm day, but a breeze had come in from the sea and he'd walked with his face raised to it, and to the paling sky. Some evenings were like this: the vague threat of emptiness. It was easy here to feel without a compass, that there might be a hidden edge you could walk over, blind, and disappear. Now his eyes sought something to fix on. He did not immediately answer her question.

Below the cliff path the ocean was a giant's chest, bronchial, heaving itself over rock. They'd climbed up from Coogee in the strengthening wind, both quiet. Her hair whipped at her neck, at her face; he wanted to scrape it back, hold it, hold her. But she walked steadily forward, unaware.

He blinked into uncertain air. So much he didn't know. Could not remember. *I was only a child,* he said.

There were flashes of memory, snapshots smeared with colour, with sound. Walks in the woods, his father naming trees. Crouching to the petals of early spring, or fluted ice on a stream's edge, the music of water melting. These were not images he could easily call up. Rather they would come to him unbidden, unlooked for, and often unwanted. They made him uneasy. He would try then to summon others, earlier or from certain times, and these weren't memories so much as points of colour, or pleats in the air. Some were insistent: his tenth birthday. His father's face grave, his unknowable eyes. Just that, his face. And a child's intuition of change.

He liked to walk, he said. *He started taking me out with him when I was just four or five. He wasn't a man who spoke much, and*

I was a quiet child. But I loved those walks. He slowed his pace to mine and we went along together for miles like that. His words spoken in the same rhythm as his feet, moving him forwards and backwards in time, his thoughts shuffling between the boy and his adult self.

Every now and then he would say, how are the legs? Or point out a rabbit or a deer. He'd know when I was tired, so I never had to complain. He must have felt it in my movements or my breathing. But he wouldn't say. He'd just find a tree for sitting under, or a good outlook, and say it was time for a pipe.

He was aware of Pearl keeping step with him, her deep concentration. There was only the sound of the sea, its regular breathing, and birds. Gulls. And crows, black as night, that swept into trees, settled. He dug his hands into his pockets, shrugged.

Lately I've wondered if he might have preferred a different kind of son. Perhaps a boy who liked ice hockey, or was clever with algebra, or played practical jokes. Like Per. He was always in trouble for something, climbing the chimney at the cement factory, throwing rotten eggs at the women as they came to work. But I wasn't that sort of child.

Pearl had been quiet, listening, but now she said: *He didn't disappear because you were the wrong boy, Axel.*

They had begun the descent to the tiny arc of Gordon's Bay, where wooden boats rested on shingle. The water gentler here, shushing like a mother with a crying child. His legs moved him past it as if they were not his own.

Axel? You don't really think you made him disappear?

His own breathing crashed in his chest. Her hand on him now, shoulder, arm, and it pulled him back to the past. His father's absences, the sour air in the house when he returned, brittle. His mother was different then, preoccupied, no longer his own, soothing the air around her husband. Axel would be sent to his grandmother.

Into the curve of Clovelly then, across a platform of rock, and once more the reassuring crack of waves, like the clatter of dropped porcelain.

Sometimes I wished him away, you see. Wished he hadn't come home. We were happy without him, my mother and me.

The words fell into different air; they had come up to the cemetery, a sea of old stones and grass waving between them. He turned to face the ocean, the sightlines of the dead. This surely would console you as you buried your beloved: their infinite view across moving water, its maternal harmonies, and at night the chatter of stars. Pearl stood beside him, squinting through blades of sunlight to the uncertain horizon.

Once, he'd watched as his father moved heavily through the room wearing the backpack he used for their walks. His boy's heart leapt. He was half out of his reading chair before he realised: his father was going out alone. He paused only to take down his coat from the rack; the door sighed and clicked shut. Axel's book slipped from his hand. He stared at the back of the door, as if it wasn't quite solid, as if his father might materialise through wood and steel and retrace his steps back through the house, laughing at his own magic. Saying: *The snow's stopped, get your boots!* But the door was just the door, and the ordinary air fell back into the room.

He needs the quiet, Axel, he needs the whiteness. His mother's voice from the dinner table, where she sat mending his father's shirt. He turned to her, bent to the task. *And the trees.* Her needle pierced cloth, came up, went in again. She made a knot in the dark cotton, sliced it with scissors. *He has been far away. And seen hard things.* She looked at him across the room. *I think,* she said, *he's trying to save us from that. From what he can't forget.*

Now Pearl took his hand and they turned away, up the rise. As they trod the haphazard tracks she stooped to pull frail flowers hidden among long grass. Then she walked ahead and bent to a grave on the landward side of the rise. Tore at errant weeds and grasses there, tossing them to the side, and pressed her palms to flatten the ground. Scattered the confetti of petals.

Amy Erin Keogh. Beloved wife and mother. Left us 18-7-1947, aged 36. Forever missed.

She stood and backed away then, paused for a moment. Turned to walk through the field of old gravestones arranged on the slope like rows of rotting teeth. He followed at a distance, letting her be. Finally they reached the cliff path and a projectile wind; it pushed the ocean towards them, caught hair, salt, leaves. But still he heard it, something whispered like a secret, or perhaps it was the wind, dissolving words: *My brothers have joined the army.* He turned his head, as if they'd flown past him. Expecting the dead to wail.

Later, as they lay on their backs in the flat, hands held, he waited. But she would say no more about it.

⁓

In the morning rain coated the window, blurring the world. Moisture gathered at its edges, swelling into thin streams that turned the glass delicate, ornate.

Pearl said: *How often did your father go away?*

He took so long to answer that she assumed he hadn't heard. She turned her face to him.

He spoke then as if he was not fully awake, though they had been lying together silently for long minutes: *I don't know. Often, I suppose. I learned not to notice. I was content at home with my mother.* When she pressed him his face became clouded. His voice barely sounding in the room.

Did your mother search for him? Did anyone?

I suppose so.

Axel?

The room listened. Finally: *I don't remember. I was only ten.*

~

Axel stared through the misted window, where the world moved in smudged outline and nothing was absolute. And relaxed, breathed. He might have said more then, might have slid beneath her question and spoken of earlier years, different years that, like the world beyond the window, were incidental, arbitrary. *What I do remember* – he might say – *what I remember meticulously, is the year before my father disappeared. The year of my tenth birthday. It was my lucky number, ten. The day I was born: November ten. Our house: 210 Assarsgatan. It became my measure of things, more than, less than.*

Later, of course, it would intensify: distances, volumes, heights and depths. Multiples of ten, divisions. A way to contain the world. But before that birthday the number was merely one of the clues he assembled for reassurance, part of the pattern he was making himself from. He was, that year, beginning to see that self in the world. Tentatively, but as a definite shape that moved through the landscape, visible and solid. He had begun to sense the power of his own volition.

Beside him, Pearl closed her eyes, opened them, closed them again. The rain was a weight now against the window, pressing in. It might be safe to speak, to try out words in certain sequences, careful, testing the air between them: his early days in the glass shed, the intimation that it would be his life, would save him. How he hadn't known the work of it then, the making of a watery reality, a solidity, fluid made hard so it could be held in the hand. The power of it, the consolation. He knew only the feeling of transformation, a kind of magic, worked by his own hand. It was the elementary, the ordinary, the danger, the heat, not just on his skin but within him. When he first broke a piece, shattering a perfect globe, he gathered up the glass and kept a shard of it in his pocket, carried it with him for years.

His mother had been surprised by his devotion to the glass world, his uncles too, the old glassmakers who had understood, even when he was a child, that Axel's life would be one of the mind. That he would not be encouraged to join them. Lars had found it difficult to accept. *He's the only one,* he'd said to his sister when her attitude became clear. *Then get married,* she'd said evenly. *Have your own son.*

But Axel had chosen for them. And later, Lars would smile and say, *See? It was in him. He chose it. I knew he would.* Axel, listening, watched his mother shake her head. *How much free choice is there when something is all around you?* she asked her brother. *When it seeps beneath your skin and enters your heart in stealth? He didn't choose, Lars. It was there, waiting, too obvious.*

Lars had shoved his hands in his pockets, rocked back on his heels. *Then the glass chose him,* he said.

So in the years that followed, Axel kept on at school but spent every holiday with his uncles, and many weekends. He never spoke to them of his father. That might disturb the thin membrane they survived beneath, all of them. This caul of safety and silence they had made or submitted to, who would know? When he was in the shed he thought of nothing but the glass. He entered not just the room but the feeling of it. The qualities comforted him, this hard, hard thing that could be strong enough to contain heat and wind, that could reflect or change light – it *eats* light, his teacher would later tell him – but at the same time was so fine it could be shattered by a voice. By shock waves travelling a kilometre through the air, more.

For Axel the glass itself was a place to enter, an atmosphere. A kind of membrane too, a thin protective shell. An insect casing, the hull of a bark boat. A shelter where no one could get you.

Spring 1965

And he says, 'What's wrong with you? You young blokes are all the same. Good jobs, good pay. Live in the best country in the bloody world.' And he sticks his finger in my chest — John jabbed a forefinger towards Ray — *and he says, 'You oughta be proud to be called up, defend your country. You oughta grow up.'*

The party was a celebration: Bridget's boyfriend had been thrown out of home. News travelled fast; people stood shoulder to shoulder, music twisting through the maze of rooms that was Della's flat in a crumbling house in Potts Point. In the lounge John laughed as he told them, the fights, his father's fury. Bridget leaned away from the shouts of encouragement and said to Pearl: *He cried that night. His father called him a coward.*

Pearl reached down to a side table and filled her glass from someone's flagon. *Let me guess. He's a veteran.*

Bridget nodded. Though the party was just a couple of hours old, she looked weary. *It won't change John, he won't register.* They leaned against the wall and drank. *My father's the same,* Bridget said. *It's like being young is some kind of crime.*

All the young men in the room. Clean-shaven, most of them, hair cropped and boyish. Pearl looked away towards the back door. Was that part of the unease about Utzon, one of his crimes? That he was young, especially compared to those lined up against him. And good looking. It was hard to avoid the face of the architect; it smiled or grimaced from the pages of her own newspaper several times a week. The face of a young interloper, brilliant, handsome. *The country's run by stupid old men,* she sighed. *Ugly, too.* She looked at Bridget. They burst into loud, choking laughter, wine spilling from their mouths and hands. As they subsided Pearl wiped her sleeve across her mouth, looked out to the warm dark. Wondered if Axel would come.

She found Ray filling a tumbler from an unlabelled bottle on the kitchen bench. Held out her glass. They sat on the back steps, arms on knees, drinking, quiet. Then in the sobering spring air Pearl said: *My brothers have signed up.* Surprising herself. From behind them came slices of some facile political discussion – *and I said you're fucking joking. Holt's a fucking idiot* – and the odd bark of disagreement.

Didn't know you had any. Ray's voice uninflected by anger or surprise or booze. He was always like this, come hell or high water. It made her aware of the volatility around her and her own disordered thoughts.

Two. She pulled out her pouch. *Didn't even wait for the call. Just joined.*

That's shit, man.

She pinched out tobacco, fastidious. Tongue steady along the edge of the paper.

And nothin' from your man?

She shook her head. The question seemed out of sequence, or time. She flicked him a look, but he was staring out to the night sky, smoking a tailor-made as if it was his last.

There had been one telephone message, somewhere near the end of winter. *The six-thirty bus has been cancelled.* She'd been hoping the call would contain information about training and departures, and had composed an oblique question, ready. There was a finality in his voice, and more, something that brooked no reply. It took a moment to understand: they were on to him, or were about to be.

Fuck it. Ray's head rocked forward with the force of the words.

Pearl spread the fingers of her free hand in the air as if she was letting something go. Shrugged.

There was a hand on each of their shoulders, sudden. *Then we need someone else.* Della squatted behind them, leaned in. The sweet and sour smell of rum. From this position neither Pearl nor Ray could twist around; they glanced at each other, the same question in their eyes. *We need dates,* Della said. *Or they'll humiliate us, like last time.* She used their shoulders as levers and stood.

The sentence sat amongst them, pulsing like a live thing. Della moved off, back through the kitchen and its charged air, voices loud with insurrection and dull with cheap wine.

Busted. Ray stood. *First rule of secrets: never talk with your back to a room.* As he turned to go he said, *You coming to the big march next month?*

She leaned her arms on her knees and lowered her head. *You know I can't,* she said.

~

Axel stepped through the door into unsettled candlelight and a roar of noise. Felt momentarily unbalanced, the room pitching like a ferry on waves of sound. He stood still to orient himself; fought an impulse to flee. The room dipped and shifted, the faces unfamiliar and distorted by smoke and shadow. Beyond them a doorway and a lozenge of pale light. He'd drunk whisky for courage before he left home, but now he clutched beer bottles to his chest and stepped across the carpet, trying for confidence.

Hey, man. The words at his ear soft despite the thump of noise in the room. He turned to a half-familiar face, a grimacing smile in the gloom.

Ray, the man said, without taking his hands from his pockets. An Australian habit, but still Axel's own hand levered up instinctively, and then dropped.

Met you at Pearl's.

Ah. He remembered. A cool afternoon and the surprise of her, sitting with a man under a tree in the yard. Sunlight fell through the branches. Axel had stopped in the driveway, but she'd caught his eye and smiled.

Neither had moved as he approached. Pearl introduced them across the peeling cast iron table, cigarettes and ashtray, a biro. Then and later she gave no explanation. *A friend.* Just that. Ray had left minutes later, and Axel lowered himself onto the edge of the fraying wicker chair. He wanted badly to ask, but of course did not. Pearl leaned back, closed her eyes. Stretched her bare legs in mottled shade.

Axel lit a cigarette, tried not to look at her. Cast his eye instead to the back of the flats, anonymous wood and brick. He had never been in the yard, was surprised by space, this big spreading tree. An incinerator and a pile of grass clippings, a rotary line like every other yard he'd seen here, a rough garden bed edged by concrete. He leaned forward, rested his forearms on his knees, cigarette between thumb and forefinger. Overblown roses tangled with long grass. Profligate Sydney.

It might have been minutes. So when her voice came: *Axel?* he turned slowly to her and it might have been his mother's voice, his mother's arm raised languidly, the fine wrist. Her eyes opened onto his. *Let's go upstairs.*

Now he regarded the man beside him and wondered. Had he been waiting for the same invitation? Surely, he thought, he wasn't her type. He watched Ray wander away towards the kitchen. Stood still to locate himself in the myriad conversations, the battery of words, all mixed with music from another room. He saw a space beside a long window and took refuge there, leaning against the sill. Drank a glass of beer, fast. And thought, if I had been born to this language, would it have sounded so comical? His breath a grey circle on the glass.

He had seen Pearl only from a distance. Or rather, heard her. Strained to pick out phrases, a sentence, but instead her words at the graveyard came to him, sharp and sudden:

My brothers have joined the army. He hadn't pursued it, conceding to her own questions that day. Stupid, stupid. No doubt she was talking about it now, with these people who seemed so different to him, careless, confident. He poured a second drink and was halfway through it when another man swerved towards him out of the haze. Axel was unsettled by whisky and beer, stronger than he was used to, but even so he could tell this man was completely, utterly drunk. His eyes. Like raisins in dough, his mother would say, but oily somehow, damp. He clutched a drink in one hand, the fingers of the other crooked in his belt. Were they? Hard to tell behind the swell of his belly. A word accompanied him as he approached, one Pearl had used the day before: belligerent.

Pearl's mate. An accusation. He tipped back his glass. *Swiss, eh? Or Siberian. Don't suppose it matters.*

Axel weighed the words. They were deliberate. At that moment the alcohol sharpened his view; he knew precisely what the man intended. So he merely looked at him, inclined his head. A smile began and ended.

Or did she say Danish? They're in vogue now. He coughed out a laugh. *But maybe not for long.*

The man hadn't introduced himself. *I'm not sure what you mean,* Axel said.

Your countryman isn't he? The great architect. He was trying to look Axel in the eye. Failing. *On the nose now.* He swayed, turned to the window, gestured with his glass. Beer tipped, slopped onto the floor. *All that fucking money, and my kids jammed thirty-odd to a classroom. Bloody queues at the hospital –* he stopped, lowered his glass. *I've never even heard a bloody opera.*

Axel fought for civility. *I don't think the architect jammed up the classroom.* His mouth refusing the *j*.

But there was Ray suddenly beside him again, so that Axel wondered if he'd been there all the time. *You right, Brian?* His hand on the other man's shoulder.

Brian's head flopped forward. *Talking a bit of politics to Switzerland here.*

Sweden. Ray looked to Axel. *You're talking to Sweden.*

Brian's face jerked on his neck. *That's it. Glass man.* Then his eyes narrowed. *Well you're clever, Sweden, you know what you're doing. No wars for you eh.* His voice like gravel now, the words deformed. He raised his beer to Axel. *Here's to you.* He tipped the drink towards his mouth, lowered it. *Back in a minute,* he said, pulling away from Ray's hand.

Axel saw his chance to leave. But Ray was talking, his voice steady. *Yeah, here's to you. Here's to not takin' a side. Bein' neutral. Or is it neutered?* Whatever he'd imbibed earlier had left him, his face clear now, his tone even. He raised his glass, drank, pressed his lips together.

Axel wasn't sure if he was expected to answer. He put down the glass he'd been holding for an hour and made ready to go. But Ray was still talking.

You make glass.

Again, his voice impossibly even. Though Axel was tired, dulled by whisky, he could hear the false note. He tilted his head again, questioning.

Glass is kind of neutral too, Ray said. *Don't you think?* He glanced to the window, a bland rectangle. *It's kind of. Nothing.*

The insult was subtle, allowing several possibilities. But there, in the man's eyes, there was only one. So when Axel spoke his own voice matched Ray's. Bland, ingratiating. *No, not at all,* he said. *In fact, the opposite. It's one of the solidest things I know.*

Nah. His mouth a gentle grimace. But he kept eye contact. *It's the absence of something. Like silence.*

But Axel knew something about silence. About new snow, and ice that held the memory of sound. *Silence isn't absence,* he said, taking a step away. *Not a lack, not something missing.* The words, and his memory, making him brave. As he moved off he looked back and smiled. There was a mild pity in it. For the man, his double-talk. *You think the whole of Sweden was a vacuum?*

Ray allowed one beat, one second to pass, so Axel's words reverberated softly between them. Then: *I'm saying it was mute,* he said.

~

By the time he reached the door a familiar chill had entered his chest, his bones. He felt it as colour, white and ice green. Hard. Then he felt her hand on his shoulder. *Mr Jansson.* And turned to her wine-washed eyes. Her voice through an odd smile: *Leaving?* He could not detect an invitation to stay.

His own voice was steel. His body stiff. He did not move though she was very close to him; her hair smelled of smoke and something else. Acrid, like stale aftershave. *You people,* he said. And stopped, foiled by language. *All this talk of war, the Americans, what they do. But you are all thieves.* The words calm, a quiet detonation. *You stole a country too. You are all ...* He pressed his lips together, searching without result.

He turned then, dug his hands in his pockets, stepped into the night. As he reached the gate he heard her. *Hypocrites,* she said. The gate squealed as he closed it behind him. *Yes,* he wanted to say. *You annihilated a culture. You let it happen.* But he knew he'd be speaking into thin air.

~

Pearl woke to glass splintering. Was it? Her body was curled into an *S* on an armchair; her right foot was numb. The party was over and the lights dimmed, but there was a hum of voices from the kitchen, plates being stacked. Bottles dropped carelessly in a bin. She slipped her shoes off and rubbed the tingling foot, checked for handbag and scarf. Stepped like a thief to the front door and slipped out.

Her stomach flipped around. In her mouth an acrid taste, sour lemon or worse. She raised her arm as a cab rounded the corner, and as the door opened she remembered the kiss. What he'd said: *Got a car outside. We could park somewhere.* John, putridly drunk. He kissed her and she'd let him, and then told him to go home. *I am home,* he'd laughed, and went to find Bridget out the back.

She managed the ride to Manly without asking the driver to stop. Then vomited helplessly against the back fence of the flats, clutching brick. Groaned as her stomach emptied and blades of memory pierced her head: the anger, the regret. One drink for the losses, ten more for the sacrifice. Hadn't she loved that newspaper, given it everything she had? The boys. Her politics. There'd been no fair exchange. She was imprisoned in the women's section, the boys were lost, and she couldn't march or stand publicly with her comrades.

Couldn't speak. She finally stood upright and wiped her mouth. Axel's words throbbed in her head. She had been made mute.

—

The forecourt was chaotic with steel and machinery and pieces of a building slowly finding its shape. Axel crouched in the shade and watched. Every day now he walked from Woolloomooloo to Bennelong Point to do this, to watch and listen, and the scale and intricacy of the work made his breathing change. Every movement and shape, snatched phrases, the rhythm of a man's hands as he tightened bolts or reached for the load on a crane. Axel took up a different position each time, near the water, under the concourse, in the casting yard. Sometimes in the same general area he'd been the week before, to see if the perspective had changed. Every week, it had. That was the only thing about the place that was predictable.

A team of men had just guided a rib section into place. He'd watched as they each attended to their own tasks, the concentration in their hands. The building, he thought, was an accumulation of thousands of such movements, thousands of such tasks; pieces of energy and unspoken prayers expressed through the hands of workers. Imaginations and dreams, loves and hates, energy and boredom, eyes open and half shut. So many different perspectives and notions. The whole was like a song, a story, nothing without all these parts.

The men had made the building their own now. They climbed and clambered over it, hung from steel bars, balanced in flimsy shoes to adjust formwork. Now and again he would see a man with his hard hat tipped back, his legs apart, staring up to where the erection arch clung like a praying mantis over the highest shell. Was he staking a claim to the glory of it, the confounding beauty of it? It was the work of one and of ten thousand.

Sometimes, he could see, the work was crushing in its repetitiveness. The sun streaming onto backs bent to the same nailing or smoothing or planing or glueing. At these times he could feel a numbness in the air, a kind of stasis. He felt glad for his own work, which had its own heat but was at least out of the sun. But other times the days passed in a stream of languid energy, effortless, and he saw that the men went home with as much energy as they'd come with. Their work made them feel fully alive.

Previous jobs, Armand had once told him, had made him feel less than he was. It was the same, he knew, for the others. The tunnels were the worst. *Mud and dark,* he said.

And cold. But the sameness, he shook his head. *All day every day, just digging.* The seconds ticked. *But you know the worst of it, Axel? No colour. It made me realise. Night is full of colour, in comparison.*

Axel understood immediately. He had thought candle-light a colour when he was a small child, when darkness lived with them for months, even inside.

He leaned back now so that only the points of the biggest shell were visible over the mayhem, bringing thumb and forefinger of both hands together in a rectangle before his eyes, a camera frame. Each time he moved, this way or that, the shells changed, now soaring now crouching, their interiors eerily hollow like empty hoods. Or pearl shells. Or waves.

Suddenly, Jago's clean-shaven face in his frame. Smiling like a fool. He folded his long limbs onto the ground beside Axel, arms around his knees. *You can stop doing that now.* He cocked his head in the direction of Axel's gaze. *They have a computer for such calculations.*

Axel sat upright and grinned. *Not like these,* he said. And tapped a forefinger to his head. *These are my own.* It was only Jago's humour, he knew that, but he felt caught out somehow, exposed. *My own kind of algebra. A way to look at this thing.*

But Jago was gazing up to where the curves of the building met like hands in contemplation. *My brother-in-law,* he said. *The electrician. He's seen this computer.* He laid his own hand on Axel's arm for emphasis. *Up there in York Street. These men, engineers, programmers. They know calculation.* He swung around to look Axel in the eye. *They feed bits of paper into the machine at night and in the morning it tells them things. As if it's human. Like it's, you know, alive.*

Axel listened and tried to follow. He'd heard of this computer, as big as a room, a whole team of people to tend to it. Its calculations for the positions of the concrete ribs within the shell structure of the roof. Surveyors would take readings at the end of each day, from four different places around the site, and these would be fed to the magic machine in the city. The next day there would be a thousand minuscule actions and adjustments, according to what the computer said. How it spoke.

It's all steel and points of light, Jago said. *Nothing like a fusebox. Or any ordinary engine. It is truly a living thing.* His face alive. *It's intelligent. It has a language, you know, like mine, and yours.* He smiled. *My brother-in-law is an ordinary man in every way, but he loves these things. The idea of them, that they do the work of men, their brains. He said to me, 'It's beautiful, Jago.' He said, 'I wanted to put my ear to it, hear its heart.'*

Axel had little knowledge of electronics or how the machine worked, but he understood what he was hearing. He felt the same listening to Jago and the other Yugoslavs. He loved the rhythms of their speech, the inflections, the energy, he loved their faces as they spoke, alive like the machine Jago spoke of. They brought the same qualities to their work with concrete and steel, a kind of reverence for detail, for perfection. He loved their fidelity to the task, their attention to it. He would not have been surprised to see them lay their hands on a finished beam, or a curved concrete rib, to feel a heart beating beneath its perfect surface.

He felt safe with these men. They spoke about the heart of a job as easily as they talked about the weather. Their mothers, their fathers. Everything was expressed with their bodies. He'd watched one of the men produce a letter from his family in Split, and read part of it aloud as tears coursed down his cheeks. Later Axel heard the same man singing in his language as he brushed plywood with fibreglass. Each stroke precise, assured, coaxed by the steady notes, the control of pitch and breath.

⌒

But something in Jago's face, in his words about the computer and his brother-in-law, pushed an acute loneliness through him.

Later, on his way home, he stopped at a phone box, fumbled in his pocket for coins. Hesitated with his fingers poised. He had been determined to leave Pearl alone – with her friends and probably her lovers – but there was an ache in him for touch, for closeness. He wanted to be near her. Even if their connection with each other was a fiction, something he had concocted in his head. Was it? He didn't care. He dropped coins into the slot and spun the dial. There was no answer on her work number so he left a message: *Mr Jansson called.*

⌒

That night she opened her door and smiled as if she'd expected him, took the bottle of whisky from his hands. Fetched glasses from the kitchen and stood in front of him as she poured, her eyes on the liquid. *You haven't finished my drawing,* she said.

She went to a low table and pulled the rectangle of cream paper with its half-made shapes from beneath a weight of books. Dimmed the lamp, watched him over the top of her glass.

He held her gaze. The obliqueness, the refusal of what might be expected, of predictability. As she unzipped her skirt he swallowed whisky and reached for the cup of pencils: *And you haven't told me about your brothers,* he said.

⌒

She sat sideways on an armchair as she had the time before, her body draped and sinuous as soft fabric, one arm over the chair back and her head resting on it. Later Axel would wonder if posture, a particular arrangement of limb and muscle, could influence mood, or attitude, because her words were soft, unexpected. He listened as the pencil touched line and shape, picking up where he'd left off, leaned in to the shadow below her neck, her breast. Feeling his own rhythm change, the cadence of his hands. The pencil light between his fingers, its weight on the paper.

She was using words like *sorrow, fairness, atone.* She said: *I want to be angry with them. But find I can't.* Calm, no emotion, or none he could detect. *Because they're not pretending, you see. They believe it, all the rhetoric. They believe they're doing something good.* She was staring at the wall in front of her, nothing moving but her lips. *But it's all politics, this war. There's no moral imperative.*

He didn't raise his head. *Every war is political,* he said.

She hesitated. *Yes,* she said. *But the Holocaust was a moral imperative.*

He ignored her last sentence. *What does it mean, to atone?* His eyes flickered between Pearl and the pencil. Her body was cupped in the chair so that each line and curve was accentuated. He closed his eyes briefly, wanting to arrange his own body beneath her, to cup her with his own flesh, to abandon the picture and hold the curve of hip and shoulder in his palm, unmistakably female.

To make amends, she said. *To make up for something, an error or a wrong.*

Then what are you atoning for?

A flicker of hesitation. *My own failures, I suppose. For everything that brought them to this point, all the decisions that meant they had no choice, not really. No free will.*

But they did have a choice, didn't they? It wasn't the ballot, they weren't forced to join.

That's too easy. What is free will, Axel? That's what I'd like to know. Who can say? We bring our whole histories to every decision we make. Don't you think?

He left the line of buttock and leg, deepened the muscle's shadow on a calf, the rim of belly. *I suppose so.* He tried to concentrate on seeing, tried to forget himself. But 'atonement': the word lodged in him like a thorn, irritating. And the idea that a person's actions, even their thoughts, were not completely their own. He kept moving the pencil, deepening the give in her arms and neck, the generosity in her open palms. After a struggle with her wrists, at once strong and fine, he stopped.

Laid down his pencil. Poured more whisky, took a glass and sat on the floor in front of her, his back to the chair. Her hand on his shoulder then, a subtle weight. That's what she had meant: your whole history was a subtle weight on you, or in you. He knew then what the drawing was missing.

They were both quiet. Axel looked up. From here on the floor he could see the true dimensions of the flat and what was in it. High walls and ceilings, so it felt bigger than it was, airy, but still clamorous with things, rugs on the floor, a table, a bowl with apples. A sofa with cushions and strewn newspapers, its fabric unravelling. Her mother's cups and plates, blue and white. These struck him, the first time. The blue and white plates at home, commonplace, beautiful.

Tonight, the smell of salt and old paper. And something else, sweet and savoury and foreign. *Lemon gum,* she'd told him weeks before, tipping her head to the backyard. *And someone at the incinerator.* He'd looked to the window, doubtful. He was still getting used to the outside snaking in here, or gusting in through windows open to breezes and other voices and smells.

But the newspapers: not just on the sofa but on the bed and on the floors, on tables and surfaces. The chaos of the world and all its events, there in the paper she helped write every day. They were important to many people, he could see that, but they had stopped making sense of the world. They confused him, the daily insistence on information too much for him. So he looked only at pieces of them. One page, one story. It was easy to be overwhelmed.

Had she been following his gaze? *You should read the papers, Axel,* she said now, her mouth close to his ear. Then he felt her lean back. *They are at least a partial record. And it's good for your English.*

He hesitated, searching for a way. He didn't want to sound evasive. How to tell her the very dailiness of it destroyed something in him? Diminished the small animal of his art in him, which was, finally, about questions, about trying to make sense. In this he was like a child encircling the shattered pieces of a puzzle with his arms and pulling them towards him. Seeing what might be possible there, meaning, order. The present, the future.

I think, he said carefully, *that I use art to work things out. And this* — he used the glass in his hand to indicate a folded newspaper — *is a kind of camouflage. It's not real. Surely people don't think it's real. Don't think it's their life.*

It is their life. An undertow of impatience in her voice. *And it is real.* She threw her arm out. *Here, all around us. Sometimes it can't wait for art.*

But Axel heard the defence in her voice, saw it in her eyes. It wasn't him she was trying to convince.

⌒

In the morning he stood at the window with his back to her, stretching his arms above his head. She watched him dress. As he pulled on his trousers, the familiar blue of airmail paper in his back pocket. When he turned she nodded towards it: *A letter from your mother,* she said.

Surprising him: he avoided her eye. She frowned. *What does she write?*

It's just the usual letter. Like the others.

In English?

He buttoned his flies, concentrating. Pursing his lips as he always did. She smiled behind her hand.

Swedish. Then: *It's a little sad. I won't read it now.*

She spoke softly, as if she was talking to a child. *Axel? Read me some, just a sentence or two.* She watched him but didn't shift from the pillow.

He lowered himself onto the bed, his back bent. Something had altered in him during the night. As if he had been in pain in his dreams, or as if the pencil had drawn something from him, brought it to the surface. He said, *It's only the weather, and* – not looking at her.

That will do. The weather.

He sighed, hesitated. Then began, faltering immediately. '*The year — the year turns, Axel. The early snow*' — he frowned, self-conscious. *Fizzes?* — '*and dies in a rain shower, withdrawing. The autumn sun will take the rest.*' He looked up to the ceiling. *It's not precise, I'm sorry.*

It doesn't matter.

'*There it is, shy*' — *I think she means the sun* — '*glancing through trees. It will show itself soon enough in spring, and we will be flooded by light, nowhere to hide. When I think of coming to see you, this is what stops me. The —* ' He hesitated once more, lips pursed. '*Exposure.*' *For some words there is nothing exact in English.* He was still addressing the wall, the page. *And it does matter, Pearl.*

She was thinking of the last words he'd read; meaning hovered above her, not settling.

But I might as well finish it. '*I am used to this aloneness now, this ache. You know how it is. There is a part of me that welcomes it; the ache becomes its own company. In truth I think I would miss it. This is who I am now, this person, here in my house, cooking, reading, talking to Aldous. Only outside, wandering about in the woods, do I lose that sense. As if I leave my conscious mind and enter another. As if I am just another tree. I think you understand this Axel. It is only lately that I see how like me you are.*'

He lowered the pages and sat staring at his hands, shoulders slumped, his body conceding. Pearl reached for her tin of rolled cigarettes, extracted one. Struck a match and leaned towards him, offering it. Then lit another. A thin trail of smoke from her fingers. The calibration of time.

Finally she said: *It's like a conversation. As if she's here in the room, speaking to you.*

Axel shrugged, smoked the cigarette, spoke without turning. *She just writes as she thinks,* he said. *Sometimes she thinks too much.*

But what Pearl had heard was Axel's own assessment of himself. Not in his own words but his mother's. There it was on the page, a pencil sketch of a body growing around a wound. Its movements protective, the pain like an infant who must be placated. Kept safe. What had Suze said about pain? That it was like a child who just wants to be understood.

Axel said: *She — how do you say it — lives inside herself.*

Pearl pulled the last from her cigarette. Blew smoke. *It's understandable,* she said. Inched forward across the bed to look at him. His face was blank.

Yes, he said finally. *It is.*

⁓

In the office that day, after she had filed two stories, she went into the library. Browsed the day's *Herald* at the bench and waited for a lull. *You right, Pearl?* asked Wanda, the head librarian, who'd been at the paper even longer than Pearl had. She barely lifted her eyes from the newspapers she was clipping. *Raoul Wallenberg,* Pearl said. *Swedish resistance in the war. Do we have anything on that? Or the White Bus movement?* And as Wanda consulted the card file: *and the Jørn Utzon photo file, if it isn't out.*

Back at her desk she turned first to the slim packet marked 'Sweden, World War II'. A Red Cross booklet, some clippings about the country's trade in iron ore since the turn of the century, stories about the disappearance of the emissary, Raoul Wallenberg, and Swedish merchant shipping in the Baltic Sea. She opened the Red Cross booklet. There, on the first page, a black and white photograph of a line of buses with the Red Cross insignia, and an essay about the Swede Folke Bernadotte. Secret negotiations with Heinrich Himmler and the rescue of prisoners from German concentration camps near the end of the war. She skimmed it front to back, and found herself staring down at a picture of Bernadotte as he was in 1944. The Scandinavian cheekbones, the clear eyes.

Shell

There was a fat file of photographs of Jørn Utzon. On the Opera House site, in his home village, Hellebæk, a speck on a map between lake and sea. With premiers and politicians, with Arup, the engineer. He was a good-looking man, in a hard hat or a suit. Genial, at ease in any company, the workers, the Queen, Patrick White. She wondered what his wife was like, his children, if they were as impossibly sunny as he was. Did they also look so … what? So not Australian. As she thought this, Utzon's face on the page slowly became Axel's, which morphed into Bernadotte's. The smile that hinted at patience, intelligence, an even disposition. Or perhaps it was just the Nordic bones, she thought, closing the folder.

Because Axel had a different look, and it occurred to her suddenly that it was slightly furtive. The look of someone who was ashamed. But didn't know. She knew that look. He would glance down, or away, at certain points in a conversation, shove his hands in his pockets, look at the sky or the road behind or bite his lip and stare at a nearby street sign or flower.

She tidied the clippings and photos. As she shuffled and checked, her eye fell on a timeline of Bernadotte's life. The last line: *Assassinated in Jerusalem in 1948.*

The phone rang and she answered it in her newsroom manner, holding the receiver with her chin as she read.

Pearl here. Careless, peremptory. So her heart banged when she heard a boy's voice: *Pearlie?* He sounded ten years younger than he was.

Jamie! She slammed shut the file on Swedish resistance and pushed it to the side.

You said to call.

Well you took long enough.

Ah y'know. Not good at phones.

No. How's your brother?

A jostling noise and then Will: *I'm good Pearlie. Never better. We're finishing up here this week.* Static as the phone changed hands again.

Thought we'd better let you know. Jamie calm, adult, though there was something behind his voice, some caution. He let a moment tick by. She imagined him taking a breath, then diving: *We're going into camp.* She felt the words coming before he said them but still, the shock of it. She wasn't prepared, despite the weeks since she'd seen them. Wasn't ready.

Really? What about medicals and things?

Yeah, but we'll be right.

More silence. Then: *Will?*

What?

Come on.

Can't say too much sis, so don't ask.

I'm asking, dammit. Then she lowered her voice and hissed: *You're too young.*

What does it matter Pearlie? I'm in. Don't do this.

Your mother —

Or that.

Fuck. On a breath to stop herself crying, or crying out.

We're coming through Sydney.

Where? Where's your training?

Pookie something?

Kapooka.

That's it.

They were coming to Sydney. *You'll want to see your Da,* she said. Felt a hesitation over the line. *It's all right,* she said. *We won't tell him.* She couldn't bear to think of her father's face if he knew. Despite his ravaged mind he would understand immediately, and it would break his heart. That they had *chosen* it. Her own heart had not yet recovered.

$\sim$

Still, when they walked off the platform at Central Station she felt an old happiness wash through her, something comforting and true. The years collapsed inwards. For a while they beamed at each other. They might never have been apart.

They found a locker for their bags and went to find a beer. Their faces flushed with pleasure and, she understood, an anxiety they were trying to hide. *It's some city,* smiled Jamie as they settled in a bar near the station. And it was true: Sydney had turned itself on for them. Spring had finally arrived in full colour. Each day a movie played out, a spectacle for the eye: trees greening, and lawns, the sun bright but benign on harbour and sandstone and faces turned up to its warmth. Even here on these rough streets, it played on walls and bitumen and people's faces, lifting them. On late afternoons like these, everything glowed with it, this soft light that transformed the winter-dull city into a place of optimism and energy.

Jamie looked around and said: *It really feels solid, or something. Serious. Different to other places.*

Pearl looked at him closely. He might have been talking about himself. This new, adult version. His face: more grown up, though it had been a matter of weeks. *Solid, serious.* She frowned: *How?*

Well, Melbourne is so kind of —

Cold, Will said.

Heavy. Jamie turned his glass in his hands. *And Brisbane's the opposite, like those towns out west, only bigger. Wooden houses on sticks, big verandahs. Feel like they might blow away in the next storm.* He sat back with his beer. Smiling, Pearl thought, like a man.

Will said: *Brisbane's hot, I love that. It doesn't even feel like a city. It's a lazy kind of town.*

So Sydney's like a real city? She was grinning at this side of her brothers she hadn't seen.

Yeah. Will tilted his head, thinking. *But the harbour makes it different. Makes it a bit mysterious. I used to think there was something under there, like that Atlantis place.* He blushed. Picked up his beer. She'd never heard him say so much in one breath.

⁓

They walked to the bus stop. There were so many things to say, and she wanted to say some of them before they saw Patrick. As they blinked into lowering light she spoke in a rush: *Before we go, I want to say I'm sorry. That you were lonely, that you had to run away. I should have been there more.*

Two pairs of eyes on her. Not angry, not forgiving. Finally: *We weren't running away from you, Pearlie.* Will's face broke open; he looked from her to his brother and back.

No, said Jamie. And frowned. *We were running away from them. St Joseph's.* He breathed in, audibly. *It was horrible. More than horrible. And besides, we wanted our own life.*

Nothin' to do with you, Pearlie. Will put an arm around her shoulders and squeezed, an old uncle who has told a lame joke. *Thought we'd do a summer out bush and come back. All cashed up, you know. But then there was another job and another —*

A girl here and there. Jamie smiled, at last. *But I'm sorry you worried. I'm sorry about Da.*

We wanted to make good, Pearlie, Will said then. *You know, get rich, buy a cattle station or something. To make him proud, yeah?* He shrugged again, a new habit. *You too.*

She looked from one to the other. *Christ,* she said.

⌒

They got off the bus outside the nursing home. The boys stood, hands in pockets, regarding the dull brick, ramps, the scuffed grass. Already Jamie was struggling, Pearl could see; he looked away up the street, averting his eyes. Getting his emotions under control. Will looked straight ahead at the entry, blinking. *Let's go,* she said.

It was visiting time, busy, and Pearl was glad of it. The presence of other families, the general hubbub of tea trolleys and children and conversation: an absorbent backdrop for everything they were feeling. She led them through the corridors, watched their mounting unease at the uniformity of it, the drabness, the smell. The utter lack of cheer. Their father in its hold.

The week before, she'd come by to prepare him. Knelt in front of him and tried to hold his eyes with hers. *The boys are coming, Da,* she said evenly, trying for calm. *Jamie and Will.* She waited a moment. *Next week.*

She watched his face for signs. At first he was blank, returning her gaze, registering nothing. But she'd learned something from the accumulated hours with him here: patience. It could take minutes for understanding or recognition to dawn. She shifted her weight from one knee to the other, waited again. Then: *Your sons, Da.*

There was barely a twitch from him. Then without warning, tears. No sound. Only a glassiness, his eyes full and then overflowing. The tears ran down his cheeks, across his lips. She stood and took his handkerchief from his pocket, dabbed at the creased cheeks. Kissed his forehead.

Next Wednesday. Knowing it meant nothing, the days or the weeks, the months. They were a series of punctuation marks, that was all, sleep, eat, watch the birds, sleep. *Ok? I'll tell them to get out your best shirt.*

She'd told the night sister. *The blue checks. His sons are coming.*

Now they reached the common room and halted in the doorway. Scanning among the patients and staff and families for his face, his chair. And then Will was walking away towards a corner, slowly, as if he was pulled by a string. Pearl and Jamie stood for several seconds, watching. Will's shoulders collapsed forward a little as he moved closer to his father's chair. As if he was making himself smaller, more boy than man. Pearl took Jamie's hand. They followed.

She watched her father's face. Said a prayer to no one in particular: please see him. Please recognise him. She saw Patrick lift his head as the figure approached. As Will dropped to his knees, his hands on his father's face. *Hello Da,* they heard, and then Jamie was there, his arms around him. Patrick's head on his shoulder. Pearl watched a sob shudder through him, silent. He closed his eyes.

The staff had placed extra chairs around, pulled a table over for tea. Patrick was indeed wearing his best checked shirt and trousers. He was shaved and combed. This in itself nearly undid her. She let the boys settle themselves and went to fetch cups, glad of a distraction. Some of the aides had paused to watch the scene in the corner unfold; they smiled as she approached, and she thanked them for what they'd done. In the kitchen a nurse passed her a plate of fruitcake. *He likes that,* she said.

When she returned the boys had worked out what to do, how it was. What their father could hear and take in, what he could understand. What he couldn't. So they spoke to him as if they were down at the Federal, spinning yarns. No matter that he could not reply; they spoke into the space, imagined what he might say, replied to questions he could never ask. They sat and told their father their lives since they'd seen him; stories of the great Snowy, of wild bulls and horses, of drought and flood and fire, of the men and women who had come their way. There was Will learning to ride and tame a brumby, there was Jamie cooking for the shearers. *That would surprise you, Da,* he smiled as he told him. *It surprised me.*

He can do a mutton stew and a roast, Will said, *a pudding. Scones.* He poked Pearl in the ribs. *Better scones than you did.*

I never did, she said.

I know, he said.

And all the while Patrick Keogh sat, tea going cold in his hands. Occasionally one of the boys would lean over and ask him: *How's that then?* Help lift the cup to his lips. Or cut a square of cake and put it in his good right hand. Then continue on with whatever they were saying, making nothing of it. Making nothing of their father's muteness, his thin wrists, the heartbreak of it. He was their old Da. They spoke to him of the past rather than the present, not out of avoidance, or what was left unsaid, but because the past was where their father lived.

⁓

The boys grew quieter as the afternoon closed in. The tea things were cleared away and most of the visitors gone. The nurses had been patient but now they looked at Pearl and motioned towards the big clock. Again it was Will who moved first. He bent to Patrick. *We have to go now, Da.* Speaking to Patrick's eyes. He put his hand on his father's shoulder. *We'll be back. We'll be here to see you.*

But Patrick was worn out. His head drooped. As Will stood he might have nodded, Pearl wasn't sure. But when Jamie put his arms about him, Patrick raised his own right hand to hover over his son's back. Somewhere in the depths of his unknowing, Pearl thought, he felt it, this intimation of farewell.

We'll see you soon. Jamie half choking on the words, withdrawing quickly, walking away. Then turning, unashamed of his tears. *I love you Da.* Then Will. They walked from the room, heads down, wiping their faces, as unlike soldiers as you could get, Pearl thought. She kissed her father and moved to join them, looked back from the door. Patrick had turned his face to the window, where the sun was setting, where his beloved birds were scissoring home through the sky, home to their nests and their broods.

～

In her flat they ate cheese on toast and refused the offer of her bed, opting for the lounge room floor. *It's what we're used to,* Jamie laughed, patting it. *Only this is too soft.*

We'll sleep like stones, Will said.

And when she woke in the dark night and walked out, she saw it was true, they were peaceful as babies. Their men's features subsided and gentle, returned to those of boys. Their bodies soft and vulnerable. It was this she couldn't bear, not their laughter or their openness, but their goodness. She went back to her bed, pulled the spare pillow close, lay staring at the window, her own eyes staring back. There were no stars, she could not consult Acrux. She was alone with it, her own face, fearful but open, so she let the thought come. Is goodness, she asked silently, retrievable? Not theirs but her own. Because of course they'd run away from her. From the empty space where she should have been.

Instead, she'd been with Henry.

～

The affair had begun while he was still a senior reporter. She knew he was married; but in the environment of the newsroom it mattered less than it should. It was, they felt, an affair of the heart. But they both knew the score. Hearts or no, it was what it was: illicit, secret, charged. He would not leave his wife. When he became chief of staff it only served to heighten the risk and the obsession; time was more scarce, but they shared the intricate and unnatural world of the newspaper and for both of them, no one else would do.

Of course, word got about. Telephonists and secretaries narrowed their eyes when she passed. But when a new female cadet did the same, turned away from her in groups, refused to address her directly, she felt burned, chastened, diminished. Even then she felt more hurt at the censure of women. If a man found out it didn't surprise her when he looked at her a certain way, and though she felt cheapened by it, she didn't feel ashamed. The women's looks burned shame into her. But none of it was enough to make her stop.

They're jealous, Henry would joke as they lay together in cheap hotel rooms at lunchtime, or an hour at night after the edition went to print or the occasional late afternoon.

But Pearl knew it was something much deeper. Part of it was cynicism: the assumption it was sex for advancement.

When in fact the reverse was true: Henry bypassed her for jobs that should have been hers, just to be sure. But there was something else she couldn't quite locate. Some unspoken rule had been broken, one the women themselves had concocted. It came, Pearl thought, from their own deep-seated frustration at the world. That much was obvious, their anger at men and their own inferior place. Regardless of it all, she despised them.

How dare they. She sat on the edge of the bed, its hollowing mattress, and lit another cigarette. Exhaled extravagantly. The slats of the Venetian striated the night, the sky smeared behind dirty glass. *Fucking little North Shore saints.*

Minutes earlier she had knelt over Henry as he quietly came onto the handkerchief he always kept at the ready. He'd groaned, laughed, said *Jesus.* Now he was silent, propped on a pillow, the handkerchief still spread on the rise of his stomach.

So righteous and chaste. Pearl handed him the cigarette. *They're probably home tatting, embroidering doilies for their glory boxes.*

Henry blew smoke towards the ceiling. *It's because you're good at the job. One of the best reporters we've had.* His eyes on the smoke that didn't quite dissipate, but hung in the air like a question. *And lovely. They wouldn't care if you were ugly.*

Pearl turned to him, frowning. *No,* she said. *It's something more. I mean, do they look at you as if you're the devil when you walk into the room? It's something about me as, what?* She stared at the pattern on the quilt, swirling vines of cabbage rose or some such. *As a sexual being. It's okay for you to be sexual, to like sex, even to sleep with the staff. Because you're a man.*

And because I'm the boss.

She thought about this. *Only partly that.* Took the cigarette back, examined it, looking for some kind of reason or explanation. Then put it to her lips. *I give up.*

She stubbed it in the ashtray on the bedside table, dropped the damp handkerchief beside it. Then laid her head on his chest, closed her eyes for the brief moments before he would rise, wash semen from his belly, re-button his shirt and his suit. Becoming once more the responsible chief of staff, going home to his sleeping wife after another big day of news.

But weeks after this conversation, they'd slipped up. There was no time for the handkerchief. Or they didn't allow it. Later, that was what Pearl told herself: it was an act of love and passion, they were helpless before it, overcome. How else to relieve the nagging fear, or the suspicion that Henry had been wilfully careless and she had not stopped him? Had not wanted to dilute his pleasure, risk his *dis*pleasure, by making him stop and withdraw. Still, even in the moment, and those that followed, they knew what they had done. Every second that ticked by was laced with it. They'd been stupid.

When the pregnancy was confirmed she held the news close, walking with it, sleeping with it for days until she told him. And when she did, in a crooked side street in Woolloo-mooloo where he'd parked his car, there was no surprise or horror in his eyes. Only a fleeting sorrow, or so she thought. A look you might adopt for any bad news. *What can I do?* he said, and she heard the tone of inevitability in his voice, realised he was speaking as if it was already decided. That there was only one thing to be done.

He was right, of course. Then why did she hate him in those minutes? She sat next to him and felt her body fill with a revulsion and an anger that surprised her. She wanted to strike him, spit at him. So this is what you are, she wanted to say. Just a pillar of male flesh, impotent in all ways but one. What do you mean, *What can I do?* You can climb inside my skin and feel it from here, feel the life there and know you have to discard it. Wilfully, violently, excise it. A part of you. A finger of flesh that already had a brain, eye sockets, a heart. That was imprinted with Henry's or her own likeness, in flesh or temperament. To say nothing of her own flesh, the webbing between the two. The terrible procedure itself.

Nothing. When the words emerged they themselves were lifeless, grey. *Just sign off on my sick leave next week. Tell people I've got the flu.*

When she walked away, hands in her jeans pockets, shoulders set, she was calm. An odd relief washed through her: that was that then. It was over. Done.

Suze knew a woman in Newtown. Pearl didn't ask how. Or if she trusted her. They walked together through the grubby back streets on a cold winter morning, quiet, both women eyeing their feet as they carried them forward, each step heavy with dread. But Pearl had decided days before: she'd be composed, businesslike. It was a task to be done and got through. A lesson. She would never be so stupid again. As she walked beside Suze she was aware that part of her had flown to the roofs of the buildings they passed, and was watching her bodily self with interest. Noting detail and feeling – she, the woman in the green woollen coat, walked a dank street. Imagining a scene: an anonymous room, a smell of disinfectant. Where another woman, aproned, faceless, cleaved flesh. Her gimlet eye.

But as they reached the back gate of the terrace house – no more rough or ramshackle than its neighbours, perhaps less so – she froze. *Women die of this,* she said stonily, her hand on the sharp end of a paling. She didn't look at Suze. *Tell me, what is it that kills them?*

Haemorrhage. Beside her Suze was still. She spoke plainly. *Septicaemia.*

My mother died of septicaemia.

I know.

Pearl shivered in the long green coat. Her top lip beaded with sweat. It wasn't her mother's death that consumed her but her life, her choices. Pearl was alive because of them. She knew then she would take one self, her bodily self, into the house, into the room, and subject it to whatever was coming. But another would emerge. Her better self, her surviving self, to be rejoined as soon as the other had finished its business inside. She raised her chin, opened the gate. In this way she knew she would survive.

⌒

Later, as she lay bleeding in bed, she clutched a hot water bottle to her belly and tried to imagine the ache and pull and slice as just period pain, no worse. But she wept with the humiliation and the relief and the grief of it, glad her mother was not alive to know. Amy Keogh would not have been harsh, would not have judged or blamed. She would have been startled, as Pearl was, and horrified, knowing that what had been prised from her daughter's body was more than a lump of blood and sinew. It was part of the girl who had waited at the gate, the one who sang to her brothers at bed time. The smart, optimistic one, who nevertheless believed in souls. It was that girl, as well as her body, who would not be the same again.

In those first two weeks she barely left the flat. Lay like an obedient patient in her bed, trying to hear the sea. The elongated *shhhhh,* a mother soothing her child. The loudest sound a baby heard in the womb, someone had told her, was the whoosh of its mother's blood. Had her scrap of a foetus, fingerless, blind, heard the regret, the treachery in her own blood? She read and slept, watched rain sluice down the bedroom window.

One early morning a weak sun, sickly yellow, spilled into the room, and she pushed herself up and through the back door. Her bare feet pressed into wet leaf mulch beneath the trees in the yard, a rich compost of decay and renewal. The earth shed its skin, she thought, and ate itself. In the thin air each step released the thick, organic odour. She stopped, breathed, recognising it: the smell of her own body as it discharged its pathetic cargo. Every day for two weeks, as part of her lived and part of her died. But she would not cry.

As her body mended she looked around the flat and was filled with a revulsion for the dusty, the grubby, for the worn and moth-eaten. Filled buckets with hot water, scrubbed walls and floors and pushed a cloth into cobwebbed corners. Wiped and polished windows. Stood on stools to sweep ceilings. Pulled lost and forgotten things from the darkened recesses of cupboards and appraised them: cracked cups, ugly vases, a too-small cardigan, broken-heeled shoes. A pile for the bin and one for St Vincent's. Dragged rugs into the sun. Remembering her mother's methods, she scrubbed soap into them on the ground, then hung them on the hoist and hosed them hard, watching with physical pleasure as dirty water streamed away into rivulets among the blades of grass.

Once she would have listened to the wireless as she worked, her ear primed for news bulletins. But found she had no appetite for the world. Instead she played records, Ray Charles, Peggy Lee, turning up the volume so their voices filled her head and infused the air. At night Suze would come and they would lie in her bed and talk, switching to Louis Armstrong or Paul Robeson, the depth of bass and compassion soothing her to sleep. Once, Suze had found an older Robeson in the stack, one of Patrick's. She lowered the needle and climbed back in beside her. 'Sometimes I Feel

Like a Motherless Child'. Pearl had turned and curled into Suze like a baby and, winded by its beauty and grief, she cried.

In the morning she caught the ferry to the city with her brothers for the troop transport to Kapooka. Their faces to the wind and the brine, sun in their eyes. Pearl said: *You bloody well better call me*. And tried to smile. *Or* – she stopped, grimacing over the impossibility of the moment, the day. Of their faces, here now and then gone. The irony: when they disappeared this time, she might prefer not to know where they were.

~

In the glass shed light played over the casting frame like a bow over an instrument. A violin, a cello. Points of light, delicate, struck the surface of the glass, picking out strands of deeper colour, the miniature shapes and figures within. Axel remembered what his teacher had said: glass swallows light. Eats it. Then redirects it, diffuses it, throughout the vessel. Bertil Vallien, not much older than Axel was, but already a master. An intellectual and a craftsman, a man who thought his way in. Axel had tried to emulate him in his approach to material, to experimentation, the preponderance of narrative and myth.

Now he sat back with coffee and wondered again what Vallien would think of his work. The master had been on his shoulder the entire time, that was undeniable. *When you're at your best,* he had said once, *you are just the instrument of your thoughts and courage and all you've seen, all you've refused. Then what you create is better than you are.* As the light thinned and the shed fell into shadow, he felt suddenly unsure. Felt he was not even close to it: a piece of work that was better than he was, better than the sum of him, of all his efforts. The sense of doubt dragged at him, but he was no stranger to it. He thrust his legs out and reminded himself: this fear was part of the process, and useful. But at this moment he could not let it win.

The evening wore on and he kept working. Time passed in scraping, polishing, fixing, and then experimenting with the arrangement of the various items to be encased in the glass. Here or there, this angle or that. He placed and replaced, moved an inch and took it back. Occasional sounds echoed from the empty heights of the shed, the rows of louvre windows below the roof. As he worked he thought of his mother, of the emptiness around her, the snow that disguised and revealed in turn. The sounds it obliterated, those it sharpened: voices, singing, weeping. He saw her moving around the house, in the kitchen, at the window, curled up before the fire with her books. On a good day stepping into her skis, pushing off towards the village or out across the field path to visit her own mother or Tove, friend of her childhood, who grew flax and potatoes near Orrefors and – thrillingly for young Axel – always kept a whole pig salting in a bathtub in her cellar. Tove, his mother said, liked to do things the old way.

It was Tove who made the celebratory *spettkåka* for his tenth birthday. She spun rings of potato flour batter around a conical mould and baked them, then wreathed the tower in sugary frosting. Every birthday with a zero an important marker now; when he was twenty, his father had said, there would be akvavit for toasting. Axel had cut the top layer of cake and watched his father, how he fought for composure; his smile evaporated with the coffee and singing and he trembled when his wife touched his arm. But on this day her smile was only for Axel. He chewed the sweet dough and wondered when his father would go away again, back to his work.

The *spettkåka* lasted for months. His mother separated the layers and stored them in tins. They ate it with coffee, or at midday when, finally, his father went away. But it wasn't long before they forgot it, and when it was clear his father wasn't returning his mother had other things on her mind. The cake was left to grow hard and rock-like, and when Axel happened upon it a year or more later, it had shrunk into itself like an exhibit in a museum, a dead thing you might find in the snow, preserved by cold.

~

They met at Lorenzo's to plan the big march and protest for October. Pearl sat with Bridget and Therese towards the back of the room, visualising: the knock-off crowds in Martin Place, tired public servants trying to ignore anything that might impede their flight. The air fidgety, unsettled. What she'd give to be there, amongst it. Bridget looked at her and lowered her glass. *You're quiet,* she said. *Uncharacteristically.* Pearl blinked into the gloom. There was a misery that washed between grief and guilt. A catalytic sorrow she recognised, as old as her mother's grave, and still as dangerous. It arrived as anger, and she took it as an ally. She looked into Bridget's face and might have said anything, as long as it dislodged the pain. Stopped herself.

Just visualising the march. Pissed off I can't be in it.

She glanced towards Ray. Despite the energetic conversation and laughter around them he'd been silent too, and though that wasn't unusual – he rarely made a lot of noise – tonight he seemed distracted, detached. He stood apart most of the time, she noticed, blowing smoke towards the ceiling, staring at his shoes. *And tired,* she added. *Sorry.* She stood. Gathered bag and coat and drained her glass. *Need some sleep.* She looped around to walk past Ray, touched his shoulder, indicated the door. He turned and fell into step beside her without query.

He said nothing as she led him up George Street and turned left at Argyle, climbing up past battered terraces and boarded shopfronts. Up through The Rocks, through its air of general disorder, its dishevelled streets. At the top of the rise Pearl stopped, looked out to the harbour and the ferries, lit by the light of early evening. Across Sydney Cove to the bizarre silhouette that might be a bombed cathedral rather than an opera house. In her mind the uncertainty around the building, its ambiguous place in the city's imagination, had attached itself to Axel, his own mysteries and ambiguities. His way of being in the world.

They walked on. Ray finished one cigarette and lit another. The others saw him as taciturn, she knew, but really it was only a refusal to be provoked. Instead this quiet, itself a prod for others to speak, to argue. He made room for that, she thought, for their intelligence. Only occasionally led an argument, or a call for aggressive action. A rare trait among men. So she was surprised when, as they sat on the grass on Observatory Hill, looking over the city and the harbour, he said: *What would it actually take, do you reckon, to stop a troop ship?*

In the distance a ferry slid away from the quay, its lights festive against the deepening navy blue of harbour, of sky. The idea sounded new in Ray's mouth, though Della had been talking about it for months. *Depends what you mean by stop.* She wrapped her arms around her knees, the evening breeze sparking her skin. *Prevent, postpone, or just play havoc.*

His fingers picked at blades of grass. *All the above,* he said.

She turned to look at him. His implacable face. *Is this Della? What's she up to?*

Dunno. He leaned back on his elbows. *But she's talking to people.*

You mean Brian.

They both fell silent as the dark came down around them. The suddenness of stars. Then Pearl said: *Block it with sailboats. Chain ourselves to the wharf.* Her voice low in the cool, still air.

They sat with the words between them until, by some tacit agreement, they stood and began the walk back down. *Yeah.* Ray's face was turned to the bridge, the stream of car lights. *But is it enough? Some biffo with the coppers and a few arrests.*

Pearl followed his gaze. The bridge leapt miraculous from one side of the harbour to the other. He was right. There was no risk in passive protest; and usually no result, except the scorn of the establishment. *Disable its engines,* she said evenly. *Disable the wharf.* Her own words surprising her. They hung in the air between them, solid as chain link; Pearl could feel them in her chest, her forearms, her wrists.

But Ray said nothing. He was quiet until they reached George Street, where he paused, his shoulders turned towards the ferry terminal. Tourists and commuters streamed around them. *Keep an eye on Della eh?* he said, and disappeared into the crowd.

～

Axel was meant to go to Pearl's. There was a drawing to finish, but first he needed air, to walk with the harbour at his elbow. He locked the shed and set off around the wharf. His memories of Tove and her *spettkåka*, her old ways, stayed in his head, mingling with all the day's uncertainties, all its fears. His feet pressed into the earth marked by old ways too, the old people of this place.

He could not un-know what he had learned over the past months and finally understood. The intrinsic importance of legacy. Personal, cultural. The passage of time, of life, from one realm to another, the traces left for others. The thought made him more anxious, unsettled: how to take the work to this stage, how to contain and represent these thoughts in glass? He turned and hurried back to the shed.

The work in front of him was clearly deficient, mute. He looked at its fine lines, its suggestion of newness, of potential. Saw that it could not speak for him. Nausea growled in his belly. He went back to the lunchroom then, picked up the fallen sketches and laid them flat on the table. Stared at them. His glasses slipped on his nose and he pushed them up with a forefinger. He felt he was only just learning to see.

Later, in the low light of Pearl's sitting room, he put his first drawing aside.

It's as if I did this with my eyes closed, he said. And began again.

⌒

Axel woke before Pearl from a sleep so deep that he felt inhabited rather than rested, as if the heavy body of an animal had entered his own, stretched its limbs inside his, weighing him down. It took some time before he could escape it, move his legs and arms freely, to convince himself his body was his own. But he could not escape his head. Inside, the blackness: the animal now a fat grinning infant with triumphant eyes. I'm here, the eyes said, marble smooth, terrible.

He glanced down as Pearl stirred and reached for him. Her face as fresh as a child's, washed with sleep. Her hand on his chest now, her eyes closed, so that his nipples contracted and he almost lost his nerve. She was not, he saw, properly awake; soon her arm slipped and she turned in her sleep, her spine curved against him, her feet on his calves. (She could sleep like a child too; deep, long, undisturbed by noise.) He waited until her breathing was steady again, moved his legs infinitesimally. Then eased his body away and off the bed.

On the ferry his stomach flipped like a sick fish as it had in the shed the day before; he grasped the rear rail and kept his eyes to the horizon. He knew it was plain terror: he felt dislocated, truly without location, unable to direct himself forward or back. Where to go, how to get there. He longed for the boat to reach the quay but as it approached he felt no better. His whole world fluid, he could not find any holds.

The quay was all moving faces, oceans with eyes. He turned towards home, his body alien, his head bizarre. His thoughts urgent: he wanted tea. Tea! This made him smile. Mrs Jarratt's tea. But it was true, he was certain, that the murky brew would help to dilute this feeling, steady his stomach. And plain biscuits to dip into it, the tasteless arrowroot biscuits perhaps, or those coated in sugar that always reminded him of *spettkåka*. He wondered again about its fate. The tin itself had frozen in place and time along with speech and memory after that birthday. His mother's terrible blankness, and then this own, descending like night, like winter; it could not be negotiated or moved. He'd been sent to his grandmother's, though he preferred the glass shed, even then. He wondered if anyone ever opened that biscuit tin, or if it too disappeared, with the coiled dough and syrupy icing he could never contemplate again, ever.

George Street: he raised his eyes for the first time, and for the first time looked around him. Information slowly pierced his brain. A bus heaved past, then another. They were full. And there were people on the street, walking with purpose, their faces earnest. He stopped in mid-stride. So it was a work day. A woman bumped his side, others looked at him askance as he stood on the footpath, pedestrians streaming around him.

He barely noticed. He made himself think, counting back through the week.

Thursday. It was Thursday. The realisation like a shot of pure adrenalin. He spun around, cut back through the oncoming crowd, turning his shoulder to them, their fierce faces. He didn't care. Today he had a meeting with Utzon's senior man, Prip-Buus. And Utzon himself would be at Bennelong Point, as he was every Thursday. He walked quickly, threading, darting, breaking into a run as he made the quay. The nausea evaporated, his head cleared. The grinning infant quieted. He rushed down Macquarie Street towards the giant nautilus of the Opera House. That was it! As if the architect had once held a shell to his ear, and heard as well as seen his design. The image reassured him, made him certain: Utzon would listen. Axel would speak and Utzon would listen, Prip-Buus would make sure of it. He would finally understand.

~

Axel's buoyant feeling intensified as he approached the security gate. He looked around and up; his heart swelled with immensity. He himself felt immense. Other buildings that soared skywards towered *over* people, he thought, shrank them. The Opera House would expand them. Allow them to open out, rather than close down. It was the idea of the building as much as the physical thing; though its manifestation was beautiful and confronting, it was the scope of Utzon's thinking that held him now, the breadth and generosity of the man's imagination.

Still, there was the old trepidation. How to approach such a man. Why Utzon would bother to listen.

He walked, slump-shouldered, across the forecourt. This country! Though it was only spring the sun warmed every surface, struck bright on steel and concrete, heated a man's skin. Already there were some stripped to shorts and boots and hard hats; without shirts they might be overgrown boys at play, climbing roofs and ladders, larking about with machines. This made him smile once more. These men would not baulk before the architect; would speak to him in their own way, man to man. This, he supposed, was where their odd culture of mateship might be redeemed: Utzon as just another *bloke,* like them. And like them he needed help now and then, a word in his ear.

The heaviness slipped from him. He stopped in a pool of sunlight and closed his eyes. Here he could feel the cauldron of energy held within the shells; it shimmered around the roof like some electric field, connecting every single worker, he knew that now. It entered each man and his language, the language he spoke and the language of his hands as he worked. The building's energy infused each inflection of voice or wrist, every heft of hammer or wrench. It was in each of the thousand different chores they performed each day, gladly, resentfully, whatever its nature or theirs. Whatever their level of skill. Every minuscule movement, step, every task performed, made up this bowl of energy, this pool of intent from which they all drew. From which Axel drew too.

This, he realised as the insect whine of machines met the crash of hammer on steel and men's voices rose and fell, was what happened in the glass shed once a piece had evolved, advanced. This collective intent, and its potential to buoy and push each individual, so that what emerged was more than the sum of its parts. At the beginning of a project, working alone, he had to dip into this pool in a different way. He'd never thought about it before. But as he opened his eyes again to vastness, he felt himself inside the swarm of labour, inside simultaneous movements both brute and minuscule, all part of the one. Alone, he had to make himself multiple, Axel saw this now. Each individual movement had to represent the many, and what emerged under his hand had to speak for the many, ask all their unvoiced questions.

He looked about at the men working in pairs and groups, or alone on the cranes, and it was plain: this was why they needed Utzon so much. Why it was imperative he stayed. The architect understood the tension between the individual and the collective, where they came together and where they were separate. How this all worked for every person, and for tribes, for countries. There was so much misunderstanding of this, so much fear. But in the right hands – generous, far-sighted, humane – the one could speak for the many, could open the way, enabling the many to speak for themselves.

It was exactly where this short-sighted, naïve, cynical government had gone wrong. They could not see past the one. They did not understand the Opera House but at the same time understood it completely. What it meant, the seat of its true power. He shivered, exhilarated by certainty. This is what they knew, the critics, the cynics, the politicians: that left alone, the building might make them mute. It spoke to and of the people in a way they could not. Of course they were afraid; they were fearful that the Opera House itself was a bloodless coup. Might overturn them, might stand in their place.

〜

Pearl woke to the sound of her door closing. Just a faint *click* but since the phone tap her ears were tuned to subtlety, to noises not meant to be heard. He'd left, then. The bed bereft of his weight and his breathing, but alive with all that its emptiness meant. Might mean. She lay and listened to the ocean, its sounds more knowable than he was. She'd gone to sleep sure of his body next to hers, that in the morning he would reach for her: hips, breasts, face, his hands like a blind man's, intent, seeking. She loved this slow foraging, almost unconscious, almost innocent, like children playing in blindfolds. But at the same time carnal, interrogating; as it progressed they were less and less restrained, pushing unspoken limits, rampant.

And afterwards, completely exposed, stripped of every layer of artifice, of pretence. Their bodies used up, shrivelled, but flesh shining with effort, grand, banal: a hand an ordinary thing, despite the pleasure it could arouse, mouth and lips merely organs for speaking. Their bodies emptied out.

But today he had left without touching her. Without speaking. She turned onto her side and watched daylight drench the air, her skin stinging in the unfamiliar and solitary sheets. She thought: so much is unspoken. What did she know of him, really? A scattering of things. None of them telling or easily pinned down. His work for Jørn Utzon was secret; this above all might reveal him, but he would not breach secrecy to say. There was his mother, her letters. His missing father.

Around the subject of his family he was diffident, and when she asked his eyes grew masked, opaque. A Scandinavian despondence, perhaps. She did not push him for answers.

The thought pushed an image into her head: the face of Folke Bernadotte in the news clipping, as Aryan as Utzon, as Axel, the clarity of eye and the universal fairness, the tolerant mouth, the ironic smile which did not completely disguise the steel in them. Only the set of cheekbone and chin hinted at it, some rigidity, unyielding; they would not say, or give, or do what they didn't want to. All these added up to a particular sensibility, but she wondered if she'd been drawn to Axel because of the things he wasn't, rather than those he was.

Mainly: that he wasn't Australian. Didn't feel compelled to prove himself, to other men or to women; didn't regard women as secondary, accessories to the main game. He showed no propensity to violence or to swagger after more than two schnapps; did not shrink from beauty. Did not shrink from the female in himself, the female in general. Did not regard himself as superior; was in fact the opposite of that. How did a man grow to be like this? One who made meaning with his hands, who shaped the world and his place in it with such delicate art. Was it his mother?

Pearl's mind looped back over scenes, images of him, looking for clues. She sat upright. The suddenness of connection: Bernadotte. Killed in 1947 or 1948, she couldn't remember which, after numerous missions to Germany near the end of the war. Surely just a coincidence of dates, of events. Still, the room shrank around her, the walls drew in; there was only the sheet rucked on her thighs, her hands in fists beside her. She stared down at them, the new strangeness of ridged knuckles, of wrists. Then flew into the bathroom to shower; the next ferry would get her to work an hour early.

He unlocked the door to the site shed. At this hour sun streamed in to warm the concrete floors and air chilled by the absence of bodies and activity. He needed to consult the site maps and timetables for an indication of where the architect might be, where his attention might be focused. But the pages were interleaved with old sketches for the pieces the young glassmakers had been assigned. He'd fought hard for their involvement; it was their building, after all. And now they had all produced new sketches and preliminary work that was informed, at last, by their own narratives, by the building and Utzon's example.

He sat at his table and felt a vast tiredness engulf him. His head too heavy for his neck. He tried to continue, stared hard at the timetables, then reared back blinking as the pages swam and multiplied before his eyes. Just two seconds but he'd been gone in sleep. Someone was pounding on the door.

It opened before he could reach it and James, a junior architect in Utzon's team, almost fell over the threshold. He'd clearly been running. Seconds ticked as Axel observed him: young, short of stature, fresh-faced; a boy at the end of a long chain of command. Despite his own irritation and disappointment, Axel could not be rude. He raised his brows. Pressed his lips into a half-smile.

Mr Lindquist, James said, clutching his hard hat and catching his breath. His eyes caught momentarily by something to his right. Axel followed his gaze to the pinboard, enormous now, and the hundreds of news clippings and press photos, each one pinned so that, in this lightest breeze from the door, the entire wall appeared to lift and undulate. Then James' head snapped back around to Axel, and he blinked as if he'd just woken, as if he hadn't just seen what he had seen.

Axel regarded the young man. He wore a long-sleeved white shirt and a tie, the field uniform of the professional team, and he was nervous: in the pause his hand went to his throat, to the knot in his tie, its neat shape a reassurance. He swallowed. *Mr Utzon is unavailable today. As I think you know*, he said. *And I regret that Mr Prip-Buus is, ah* ... He looked up, searched the ceiling. *Rather occupied. He sends his apologies*. He moved his hard hat in a circle with his fingertips.

Axel bent his head. He was beyond resentment now. The boy in front of him, agitated, embarrassed, was just the messenger from people with more problems than he had. Still, he wanted to extract reasons, information, he wanted something as recompense for his botched morning. He wanted an indication he was a vital and valued cog in this creaky wheel.

I'm sure, he said carefully, *that Mr Prip-Buus would not have ignored a meeting with me. Unless, of course, something important had intervened*. He let two, three seconds go by. *I am aware, James, that there are some tensions in the air.*

The two men stood and looked at each other. Then James turned his eyes to the window. Avoiding the bizarre wall of newsprint. *I'm afraid*, he said, *that we have a crisis on our hands*. He turned back. *A real and significant crisis, if I may say so.*

⌒

As James left – *fled*, more like it – Axel consulted his watch. It was nearly midday. Despite the heaviness in his limbs he felt a new sense of urgency: half the day was gone. And with it, another chance to intervene, to help Utzon. James had as good as said it – every move by the government had been designed to get rid of the architect. They'd starved him of funds, appointed overseers to scrutinise him, and now the engineers had bypassed him with a report on the plywood ceilings. It was another betrayal in a long line of them.

He washed his face in the basin, plucked a hard hat from the hook near the door and hurried outside. His direction arbitrary. But he would find him; he would search all day. Near the pedestal of a side shell arch he recognised one of the engineers. Who? Another white shirt and a tie loosened against the sun. Jenkins, Lewis, Zunz? He looked more closely. Glasses. Lewis then. Perhaps. Others milled around him, some in shirts, some in singlets; they followed the line of his arm as he indicated a point along the curve of the shell.

Mr Lewis.

Michael Lewis twisted his torso to Axel. His arm still hung in the air; he frowned.

Axel Lindquist. Still the man frowned. *Glassmaker. We've met before, I think.*

The engineer faced him then. He offered a half-smile. *Yes.* A moment. *How can I help?*

Axel squared his shoulders. *I've been trying to locate Mr Utzon. Is he on site today?* His belly a tossing sea.

But Lewis was already turning away. Was it relief Axel saw on his face? *No. He left an hour ago, Mr Lindquist.* He was about to resume his conversation with the others, but glanced again at Axel and said lightly: *Any problems?* And over his shoulder to the men: *Everyone else has got one.*

~

The face again. She placed the photograph of Bernadotte on the broad library bench to view it in isolation. Her awareness of his death made the picture opaque, layered with unreachable meaning. But today it was likenesses she was after, the set of cheekbones and mouth, the depths of his eyes. She plucked a magnifying glass from the bench. Moved the lens in increments from hairline to brow to the bridge of nose and ledge of cheekbone. The half dozen photographs played tricks on her eye: she kept seeing Jørn Utzon in Bernadotte's face. The architect and the count shared neither nationality nor blood; the lens merely magnified her suspicions, she knew, her own desire for a neat answer. She lowered the glass, shuffled the photographs: Bernadotte in military attire, his funeral, and one of his wife, Estelle, and their sons. Axel, of course, was not one of them.

She went back to the clippings file for the White Buses and paged through it. The few stories varied in their tone and content: the enterprise had been either heroic, saving twenty thousand lives, or Sweden's attempt to save face: too little, too late. There was no mention of anyone called Lindquist. She read fast, skimming details, forgetting the clock, until a voice startled her back to the present. *You hiding in here?* Henry was by her side, smiling thinly. He looked over to the librarian, asked for the Opera House file – *Just this year's,* he said, *not the whole wheelbarrow.* Then he turned again to Pearl. *Hughes looks hellbent on getting rid of Utzon. Not even bothering to pretend. Refusing to pay him.* He shook his head. *Big story.*

As the librarian handed him a bundle of files he peered over at Pearl's. *Spring fashion shows?* And saw the clipping in her hand. 'Himmler and the Swedish royal.' His eyes turned serious. He cocked his head, frowned.

Just trying to track someone down. Pearl kept her voice light, closed the file, signed it out.

Henry was leafing through the top folder in his own pile. *Did Constance tell you about her husband?* He glanced up at her. *He was involved in all that.*

Pearl tried for calm, for unsurprised. She had no idea what he was getting at.

But he was distracted now, and began to walk away. He said over his shoulder: *The White Buses, that's right. Is it an anniversary or something?* Then he was gone; he did not see her face lose its colour, her look sharpen. Constance. Back at her desk she scrabbled around for the writer's number and immediately dialled it.

—

Later that afternoon Axel stepped off a bus at Palm Beach. The sun's heat had dissipated, but beneath his bare feet he could feel warmth stored in the pale sand. He rolled up his trousers and walked close to the shoreline, though the sea hurled itself towards him, each wave explosive, detonated by wind. There was no room in his head for anything but this, the need to keep his body moving forward, against the wall of sound. To find a path, any path, from the beach to Pittwater. *Up across the top of the hill and down*, the bus driver had said, to where old boatsheds were scattered like birds on the water's edge. *Mate, it's a bit of a trek. Could have dropped you there on the way in.*

Axel had frowned, confused. But nothing should delay him now. It was imperative he find the architect, speak to him, ascertain his level of awareness. Had Utzon felt the strength of the animosity against him, the depth of the misunderstandings? Even the engineers spoke scurrilously about him. Did he know? He may not have heard the word on the street, or read the newspapers. The objectionable newspapers. He had to be warned.

The wind whipped up dry sand and the air turned sharp, needling his eyes. He had to walk with his face averted. So he was startled when the lighthouse reared up within minutes, or so it seemed. He knew he had walked too far. He turned, looked at his watch, stared back towards the bus stop and the small beach kiosk, veiled now by porous curtains of sandy air. Anxiety knotted his stomach. It had to be today. Each morning and afternoon brought the danger closer, made it darker. Out past the waves, clouds threw black pools of shadow on the ocean. They were omens, he knew that; why did no one else? He stared as they grew and spread across the heaving surface. Then looked back to the line of trees on the hill, pleaded for some guidance, some clue to the right way.

But the sun was already faded, watery, an ineffective guide. He shuffled towards the low dunes, sank to his knees in the sand. He could not lose Utzon now! Tears burned beneath his eyelids, and he swiped at them savagely, hating himself. There was no room for self-pity. All his energies must be in service of this task now, in circumventing the forces gathered against the architect. It was they who must go, not Utzon. He breathed deeply, drawing on all his strength and the certainty that Utzon could be saved. He had to think carefully. Be strategic.

He rolled onto his stomach and looked through dune grasses towards the other end of the beach. As Utzon had done, trying to see. He'd directed the architects in his team to lie or crouch behind sand dunes, and see the scene partial. Fractional. Its place and shape in the whole. It left room for imagination, to show pieces rather than entirety. And allowed perspective, angles of sight: the way light and shadow played against the fabric of sky, of salt-strafed air, the effect of looking through lines of foreground. The way meaning bulged from shapes so familiar to the eye that they were unseen, disregarded.

~

She caught the ferry this time. The city muted, benign in its spring dusk, but there was an oiliness to the harbour, as if some ugliness had been secreted below. She shivered and pulled her coat close, lifted her eyes from the water to the bridge. Remembered the first time she'd walked across with Axel, his face grave and words stumbling in his attempt to describe wonder. *It leaps across the water,* he said, slowing as they reached the northern end. He turned to look back, and then forward again. *But also time. You could be one person at that end, and another at this.* His eyes shone with emotion. *Don't you think?*

Now the ferry passed beneath the arches made carnival with lights, and she thought she finally understood. Here is a threshold; she had known it as a child. The realisation like a balloon inflating inside her as she looked up at the dark expanse. The fretwork of brute steel and bolts thick as a man's thigh, all somehow bent to elegance, to grace. She knew absolutely that the person she was before the ferry slipped beneath it, becoming part of its shadow, absorbed in its shape, would be different to the one who rode the ferry home. The woman who walked off the boat in Manly would be someone else.

She had, she saw, been waiting for this person, and the knowledge that transformed her, for a long time.

⁓

Axel stood on warm sand, squinted towards the horizon, watched the tide withdraw. He thought: what the land knows. Knowledge of this place had entered his head incrementally, as water pushed over sand. Whatever had happened here had entered the soil: blood, water, bones — all beneath his feet. Every intention, won or lost. Just as it was at home. He shivered, watching children play in the shallows. Realising that these people had grown from the very dirt they were born to. As he had. Swallowed the air and the water and the minerals in the earth. These people had absorbed sea water and the drift of desert at their backs. Felt the weight of it on their shoulders. The weight of history, of all they had come to and all they had inflicted on this place. Perhaps, he thought suddenly, that weight stopped them welcoming others here. They themselves had been the newcomers once; at a cellular level, they knew what they were capable of.

But no. They were blinded by sun; it meant they didn't have to look. Where Axel came from, you had to look hard. Work for your visions, your insights. Set free in the immense southern ocean, this country sprawled like a sunbather. Without borders, it imagined its enemies, was free to create them. Looked only at themselves rather than over their shoulders. Found it too easy to be right.

It came to him then, suddenly. That he had approached this place like a child looking for a gift hidden in a wide field. There was something it held for him, something lay waiting, the answer to a question, the exact shape of absence. Had he arrived here expecting to become whole, to grow the missing limb? To feel something numb reawaken to feeling? As if this place might give something back, and he could return home complete. But that meant learning a new language that was not a spoken one, rather one that explained where he was, what he saw and heard and felt.

He turned once more to the sea. Pulled off his shirt.

~

Constance opened the door with a perfunctory hello and turned back into the flat, as she had the first time. Once again the plain house dress, loose and belted at the waist, the slippers, but her hair elegant, swept up in a neat French roll. Pearl followed her into the room, noticing all this but mostly the hunch in her shoulders, the slight curve in her back. Tonight, Constance looked old.

The White Buses eh? Wasting no time on preliminaries. *Haven't heard the phrase for years. Years.* She slumped onto a chair at the small kitchen table, leaned back. Elbow bent, cigarette between her fingers, so that smoke tendrilled in a strand of hair around her ear. *What do you want to know?* She picked up her drink. Indicated the chair opposite, the whisky bottle on the table and the empty glass next to it. *Ice in the fridge.*

Pearl poured a finger and held up the glass. *Everything,* she said. *Whatever you know. Your health.* She tipped it back and let the liquid warm her chest. *It's just a personal interest. I'm trying to track someone down.* Her words a momentary, ghostly echo of finding her brothers' tracks. Too late.

Constance drew on her cigarette, swallowed the last of her whisky, pushed the empty glass towards Pearl. *Well, my dear. It's a long time ago. And I was only on the periphery of it all.* She tapped her cigarette on the edge of a glass ashtray. *But my husband was a Swede. High up in the Red Cross. He felt a responsibility.* She watched smoke rise and dissipate against the high ceiling. *He was a fastidious man. Had a conscience.*

Pearl sat with this last sentence, letting 'fastidious' find its place. *How did he feel,* she said carefully, *about Sweden staying out of the war?*

Divided. Sawn in two. She waited a beat. *Those countries are so close together, you don't realise it here. Sweden, Norway, Denmark. They were all neutral at the outbreak of war, it was their policy. But it was obvious that Denmark and Norway would fall.* Constance glanced towards her. *Only Sweden was left. Doing a mad soft-shoe shuffle to stay out. To keep both sides happy.* She let out a breath. *I suppose that's what neutrality is.*

Neutrality is not taking a side. Pearl's voice calm, clear.

Constance looked suddenly sober. *It's staying out of conflict,* she said, the words edged with iron. *It grows out of pacifism. A dislike of war.* She looked at Pearl with a steady eye. *A bit like your own distaste for sending Australians to Vietnam.*

Forcing them to go to Vietnam, she said. *Or encouraging them.*
She bit her lip. *But there was an ethical dilemma in Europe, wasn't
there, Constance? A whole race of people was being exterminated.
How do you remain impartial to that?*

You are very naïve, my girl, but I'll tell you. You don't.

Remain impartial?

*Of course you don't. Do you think they were monsters? Without
morals or virtue? Of course they took a side.*

Pearl was silent.

Besides, Constance continued, *there were many Swedish Jews,
or Jewish Swedes, I don't know, but many of them were caught up in
this too.*

Which brings us back to the White Buses. Pearl's voice quieter
now. *Some say* —

*And how would these 'some' know? It's all politics and expedience,
my dear Pearl* — *Australia didn't go into the last war to save the Jews,
it went in to save itself. It followed Britain in as they're following
America in now. There's no difference.*

An uneasy silence hung over the table. Then Constance
went on, as if she had rehearsed: *At any rate in 1944 and '45
the Swedes were the right people at the right time. The Allies were
getting the upper hand, the Germans could see it. They were going
to blow up the concentration camps, kill everyone.* She took a

deep breath. *My husband was involved in the plan to get people out. It involved talks with Himmler, so who else could do it? Only a nation that was neutral.*

Pearl lifted her empty glass. Put it down. *I'm sorry, Constance, but you might say they had to do it.* Pearl looked the older woman in the eye. *Who else had trade contacts with the Germans?*

For God's sake. Are we going over that old ground? It's all there in the records. If people want to read it. Constance waved her hand as if she was conjuring the facts. The proof. *Look. My husband knew Bernadotte. It was all down to him really.* She looked once more towards the ceiling. *He did most of the negotiating with Himmler for the release of prisoners, for their transport on the buses.* She turned her own glass around and around on the table. *Back and forward to Germany, talking to that pig. He was fearless.*

Talking to Himmler? Names like that, spoken aloud, still carried a chill. Pearl felt it in the hairs on her arms, on her scalp.

Yes. Himmler could see how things were. He tried to ingratiate himself with the Allies. Constance was lost for long seconds, staring into thin air. *But the secrecy was like a deadlock, the logistics, the strategy. There had to be absolute silence in the press, a complete blackout. Any publicity and Hitler would be apoplectic. The whole game would be up.*

Constance looked across at Pearl, perhaps for the first time. *And you know, no one broke it. The silence. Every newspaper and radio station stood firm.* She pursed her lips. *I admired them for that; all those lives were saved.* She shrugged. *But call a spade a spade. At the time the press was almost an organ of government. In Sweden I mean, as well as elsewhere. They could be shut down for publishing anything anti-German. Anything. It was shameful.* Her cigarette had burned down to nothing. She stared down at it as she spoke. *I said to my husband, they should be ashamed.*

Pearl had smelled the alcohol around her as she'd come in the door, but now she saw Constance had been drinking solidly for a while. She was just this side of drunk, trying to keep her eyes focused, her words crisp. Not quite succeeding. *I mean it's easy enough in retrospect,* she said now. *At the time it was terrifying. Bloody terrifying. But had to be done.* She glanced up. *Know what I'm saying?*

The conversation had taken the edge off her imperiousness, gave her something else — not quite softness, but a fine vein of nostalgia, perhaps. Pearl softened in return. *Hitler,* she said. *Here he was just a word, rather than a man. A fearful idea.*

He was mad, demonic. Every one of those missions was mined with danger, one slip and boom! They could all be lost.

They sat and drank. Occasionally the yellow beam of headlights flashed on the window and across the wall like a message. Constance drew a new cigarette from the pack, tapped it on the table. Lit up. After minutes of silence, she spoke. *But you know.* She picked up her drink. Gazed through the thick glass as if it might talk. *For the drivers and volunteers, the most frightening thing, I think, wasn't the Führer at all. It was the faces.* She turned the glass in her hand. *When they got to the camps. The faces, the emaciated bodies, the empty eyes. It was like they were collecting ghosts. That's what the drivers said. They got them onto the buses and it was as if they were alive but not alive. They'd shrivelled away, they were husks.*

Pearl let the words sit like stones between them.

And then there were the bodies, the bones. The children.

⌐

His first wave found him too early and unprepared, harder than he recalled, more solid. He picked himself up, pushed hair from his eyes. Now his body remembered: watch the wave, watch it build. Wait for the peak. At the last moment: dive. Under and up. Under and up. Each wave different, with a subtly different mood. Each one a live thing, with its own beat and rhythm. Each one a challenge: dive and surface, concede and resist, breathe, fight. The sea itself irresistible, capricious.

This, he thought, was what he loved most: that in the sea's urgent attempt to pitch its energies against his, there was give as well as take. His mother believed that nature had a conscience, that this was implicit. It had a will, almost human. Axel did not agree. Nature was ruthless, insatiable, blind. But there were times when he could feel something else in its moods. Not human, not anthropomorphic, but driven by its own forces, accumulated over millennia. Not a will, but a memory. An unfailing memory.

He staggered from the water, his arms clasped across his chest, holding himself. When his feet met soft sand he turned. From here the current was invisible, the strong fingers of tide and channel; it was benign, a blue pool rimmed by the horizon, pulling, pushing, giving, taking. He watched waves build by increments, gathering themselves. The ocean before him, he thought, was an equation, a fair one. It might take his body and pummel it and might suck out its life; but eventually it would return that body, rolling him clean, white, salt-encrusted, back to the waiting shore.

Finally: *Were you involved with the buses? I mean the operation itself.* Pearl needed to keep Constance talking now, before the rest of her words slid away.

Oh God no, not really. Peripheral, as I said. She squinted at Pearl through smoke from the last long pull and exhalation from her cigarette. *Accommodation, food, things like that. Liaison with the Swedish Red Cross. I had some language then.* She barked a laugh. Raised her glass again. *Now I'm flat out saying akvavit. Skål!*

Did you ever hear of a man called Anders Lindquist?

In the resistance?

I think so. Maybe the White Buses, not sure. He and his wife lived in southern Sweden. He did missions to Europe, perhaps to the camps.

Constance tipped her head back, closed her eyes. Pearl looked at the ropy neck, the incongruous string of amethysts and opals. Seeing the elegant younger woman now, lending her fierce brain to the movement, her eye on its narrative shape, its possibilities.

Lindquist rings a bell. There was a definite lisp, if not a slur, in the words now. *But it's a common name, Lindquist.* She bent her head, perhaps a whole minute went by; she might have been thinking and she might have been sleeping.

No matter, Constance. Pearl was quiet. *It was a long shot. So many people and so long ago.*

Wait, wait. Her head tipped up again. Constance placed both hands, palm down, on the table, leaned forward. *Southern Sweden, you said? Not Malmö but further up.*

Near some of the glass —

Yes, yes. She pursed her lips, admonishing herself. *Anders Lindquist. He and his wife helped with the Danish Jews, put people up. But he also drove with the White Buses. I remember now.* She leaned back, frowned. *They volunteered, all of them.*

Pearl held her breath.

The things they saw. Christ.

What happened to Anders Lindquist?

Constance paused, her eyes on Pearl. *Killed himself after the war.*

The air unstable now, the room an island at tide's turn, a storm wind rising, unreadable. Pearl looked hard at Constance to make sure she herself wasn't dreaming, that Constance was indeed speaking. Looked down at her own glass: just one measure. Not enough. And now more words, reaching her across the expanse of Laminex, an ocean of space. Constance said: *A few of them did. Good people, lost. Survived the war but not the peace.*

Pearl heard her own voice, thin, and questions for their own sake. *Are you sure, Constance? Are you certain of the name? Anders Lindquist? Could there be others with that name?*

Others with that name, sure, but not with that history. Not that I recall. And you said he came from up country, near the glass villages. What do they call it. She bowed her head. Pearl wondered if she would raise it again or give in to sleep. But it came rearing up. *Småland! That's it. Glass. All through the place. And water, everywhere.*

Right. A hesitation. *You're sure?*

Sure as I can be at my advanced age. She laughed suddenly, stopped. *Yes. He drowned himself. In a lake, I think.* Constance paused, following the vein of memory. *I have an image of myself, hearing that news. I don't know where, just my husband, speaking into a telephone, repeating the words he was hearing as if they weren't true. But I was hearing with a writer's ears. You know. I could only think about the connection, of course. Drowning. A return to the beginning, to water.*

Pearl pushed back her chair. Images filled her own head now, too many. *I have to go, Constance,* she said, and stood. *Thank you.*

Constance eyed her. *Stay for another. Look like you need it.*

But Pearl was moving around the table. Picking up her things.

So that's who you're trying to track down? Constance picked up the bottle. *You're a bit late my dear.* That laugh again. She frowned. Then: *Sorry. A few drinks. You didn't know he'd died?*

No. Though I should have guessed.

And may I ask —

A friend. Thinking on her feet. *His father had known the man. Lost track of him after the war.* She wanted to leave now, quickly. *You look tired, Constance. I'll leave you in peace. But thank you, I'm grateful.*

Constance stood, planted her feet to stay upright. *Was in the Swedish papers, as I recall. People knew of his work by then.* She grimaced as she moved away towards the bathroom. *Though probably not here. Eh?* She turned and raised her eyebrows, then her hand. *Good night.* And shuffled away into dimness.

⌣

He sat on a dune in dry clothes and watched the day fade. Then rose and brushed the sand from his trousers, his shirt, and set off with his back to the lighthouse, his shoelaces looped on his hand. On the gravel path to the village people were walking their dogs. A man and a woman smiled as he approached, their poodle pausing to sniff his bare feet. Once more he noticed how pale they were, the veins quite blue. Remembered what he'd said to Pearl: *They're like fish!* He was suddenly and stupidly happy. Bent to the dog, smiled up at its owners, asked about the path over the hill.

They indicated a road, perhaps twenty metres away. *Up there,* said the woman, waving a bangled arm and shuffling as the dog pulled at its leash. *At the top follow it around to the right, then up the hill to the left. You'll see the road down, there's only one.* She smiled and let the dog lead her away.

Fifteen minutes later he stood on high ground, looking across at calm water. Laughing to himself. Because in the end that's what it had taken. Fifteen minutes to find what he'd already spent weeks searching for. In dying light, across rooftops and through trees, the outlines of small structures at the water's edge. Just three or four, each indistinguishable from the others, and unlit, so that though he stared, willing one and then another to reveal itself as special – surely it would glow or announce itself to him in some way – they all looked the same.

He ran down the path, his feet scrambling to keep up with the speed and forward pitch of his body, to the road that curved steeply to still water. At the bottom he slowed, stopped. His hands hanging at his sides. Fear pricked his skin. He watched water lap at the legs of the boathouses and knew he had to decide. What? Before he could name it he pushed his legs into motion, strode to the first door, made a fist and knocked.

Nothing.

The second, more loudly, but even as his knuckles struck wood, he knew. The water beyond it was drained of light, its secrets dispersed. Too late: no one was here.

He turned away. Disappointment sat heavy in his limbs. Embarrassment too: he should have looked at his watch. He retraced his steps, began the slow climb, shadows creasing the ground beneath his feet. Still. He knew now where the architect was, and though his own mission was urgent it could wait another day. Besides, there was the consolation that, as the place was so well disguised, hidden in plain view, no one else would find Utzon here either.

At the top he stopped to catch his breath, looked beyond the boathouses as the expanse of water and the small islands, the treed shores, were slowly absorbed by dark. There, on a surface that might be glass, or ice, a sail. White, and it cupped the last breeze and filled, full as the Opera House sails, the hull shining beneath it. In the unearthly seconds between day and night it was utterly alone, ghosting among the elements, wind and air, water and sky. The silhouette of a man at its helm.

The world softened a little, the compulsion and dis-appointment. There was the suddenness of night, of cold icing his skin, a tenderness in the soles of his feet from the rough ground he had walked. And a scouring hunger. He turned towards the beach, one last glance back to where Pittwater had all but dissolved to silver. The boat was gone and the thin moon was a false smile as he found his way back to the main street. Stopped to re-lace his shoes, straightened his clothes, looked for a hotel. He had high hopes of whisky.

~

There was nothing in the newspaper's library about young Swedish glassmakers. Pearl looked under every likely heading: 'Lindquist, Swedish glass, glassmaking – general'. Finally she picked up the phone and dialled the switchboard. *I need an international number,* she said. *Please.* Then waited until after her shift finished, until the work day in Sweden had begun. A telephonist at Konstfack in Stockholm picked up on the first ring.

The man in the glass and ceramics department spoke in halting English. *Axel Lindquist, yes.* He paused. But any infor-mation about him would be in Swedish, he said. A pause on the line. *At the moment he is in Sydney, I think? You can speak to the man himself.*

She tried to explain the notion of background, of reading about a subject before an interview. The man listened. *One moment.* Pearl could hear a flurry of Swedish in two voices. She bit her lip. Watched the clock tick another expensive minute away; she'd have to answer to Judith. Then some static, as he took his hand from the mouthpiece and raised the receiver to his ear. *We have two booklets from exhibitions in the United States and in Denmark,* he said. *Both in English. If you have a facsimile machine I will send you the relevant pages.*

⌒

It was her first inkling of the kind of art he made. His position in the glass world, the things that were said.

Copenhagen, September 1959: Lindquist is one of the most interesting glass craftsmen to come out of Sweden and most probably the best of his generation. His work is visionary, refractory; he works with light to recompose dream and waking. In these pieces — goblets and vases with swirling figures, some winged, insect-like — he embraces myth and the subconscious. But Lindquist's work is never literal.

Another, in a catalogue from an exhibition in New York, was exactly two years old.

Kristina Olsson

*Axel Lindquist: Here glass and glasswork can be seen as illusory,
a metaphor for life or death, the passage between them. Light
is enclosed and redistributed in these pieces that range from
the sculptural – a head emerging from a block of glass, its face
aged by sandblasting, to the voluptuous vases and arks. All in
some way suggest fathomless depths, the lure of vast waters,
rescue or retrieval. They are curious, alive, deeply ambiguous.*

*But it is the spheres, spinning like planets, deeply creased
with negative imprints and shapes – endings, extinction – that
edge Lindquist towards something more disturbing, something
that hints at nihilism. We want disturbance in glass art; we
want work that turns our heads. But these are increasingly
personal. The pieces are radiant, sea-blue to umber to the
colour of dug earth, and devoid of whimsy or pretence. But
loaded, like a Viking burial ship, with dark symbol. As if each
piece has a soul. Or a map of the underworld.*

Pearl lowered the sheets and looked to the ceiling,
trying to see Axel in the words, the bodily reality rather
than the ethereal presence he emerged as in the catalogue.
As he sometimes seemed to her. At first she had thought
the gentleness, his quiet, was merely his nature, or perhaps
an aspect of his nationality, his upbringing in the isolation

of rural Scandinavia. Now his demeanour, and the implications of the paragraph from New York, suggested something else. *Unearthly*.

She went back to the clipping from Copenhagen, to the third page. The image was not distinct; she leaned in to make out its lines, to read any feeling that might rise from the paper. A reflection, a confirmation of the comments in the New York catalogue. The disturbance, the nihilism, the soul. But the facsimile was not clear enough; the lines between Stockholm and Sydney themselves were too disturbed.

Later that day, she picked up the midday edition to read the political roundup. Most of it familiar: the predictions that Menzies would resign, Askin's troubles, the growing nervousness over decimal currency, whether five cents really would be as much as sixpence. Amongst it, the regular scorecard on the Opera House. For once she read it carefully. Unaware the relationship between Utzon and Hughes had deteriorated so sharply. The government's divide and rule approach had worked: the engineers had taken their latest report on the interior ceilings directly to Hughes, bypassing Utzon altogether. Even she could see the betrayal.

And Axel, she thought suddenly. She hoped he hadn't read it. Axel would feel it like a wound.

⁓

The rough, intimate space of the shed on Bennelong Point: this was where it all felt right, where his skin pricked and flushed with thoughts, with notions of the work, of above and below, of open and closed, the weight of water and glass. In the soaring spaces of the big warehouse he could not forget himself, his physical body moving, this point to that, his fingers and hands too conscious, too aware of themselves. He worked well enough, saw to technicality and line, watched over the work of others.

But more and more now the place was like the maw of a giant beast, a great mouth stretching, and he a shrunken figure. Cowering. The new glasswork was well underway; he had worked day and night, sometimes without sleeping. Now, more and more he left the final tasks to the local glass men. They had been with him for most of the year now, through the execution of its lines and curves and points, the exactitude demanded by its scale. They had not let him down. Still: the terror that assailed him when he thought of it. The responsibil-ity. But this dissipated as he left Woolloomooloo and when he finally reached the security fence of the Opera House. Then all else fell away, he was merely a vessel and, once inside the shed by the water, an invisible one. Hidden. Even to himself.

Here he worked alone once more, drawing and experi-menting with the shape of the last pieces that would form part of the larger form. A doll, eyeless. A corner torn from a map. And something that might be a human in repose. In repose or sleep or death, how could he know? It would be up to others to read them now. At odd times, in moments of joy or clarity, he knew that was precisely the nature of the work. A voyage, not so much to understanding but to posing the right questions. It was nothing as certain as knowledge; nothing as closed or unmanageable. When he stepped outside the shed and surveyed a structure that was in itself just that, a voyage, a quest, it was confirmed in him. The government might want the definitive, everything reduced to its baseline, a rule. But Axel knew that, in art, there was no such thing as certainty.

—

Flowers were rampant in the crab apple tree, dusk settling slowly among them. They sat at the wrought iron table and watched night absorb day, darkness eat light. A plate of cheese and pears and dark bread between them. Into the quiet Axel said: *It's what Vallien says about glass.* Pearl lifted her eyes to him. Time felt slowed, faulty; whole minutes passed before he turned his gaze from the horizon, or so it seemed.

A cool wind had come up, spiking skin and air. Pearl pressed a blade through pear flesh. *Yes, you've mentioned it. But what does he mean?* She took the finest slice, almost transparent, between thumb and forefinger, held it momentarily against the sky. Lay it on her tongue.

He means that light is captured within the glass. In his own work at least, it is re-directed, held there. He lifted his head. *Like a pearl.*

They passed cautious glances one to another. Pearl was wary of the quiet in his eyes, his hands. But she turned a wine glass between her fingers and began. *I met a woman the other day,* she said, feeling her way, gentle, *who lived in Sweden years ago.*

Oh? Axel was staring past her to where the last of the sun knifed through the overgrown garden.

Pearl followed his gaze. Spoke towards the grasses, the rioting weeds. *Her husband was a Swede. He'd worked in the resistance, with the White Buses.*

His head came slowly around; he met her eye. Picked up his own wine.

A good man, by the sound of it, but badly affected by the war. The camps, what he saw. The shock of it.

She let the words settle between them. *We talked for a while. I thought he might have known Utzon, or even your father. Might be able to help with your search.*

His hands tight around the glass. His face pale. Two birds, lapwings, cried out in the yard next door.

Pearl waited. Her skin needled in the cooling air. Finally, in a voice she might use for a child: *He didn't disappear, did he, Axel?* She watched his eyes, unblinking. Fixed now on the wall, the paint peeling from gutters, like fingers beckoning.

Axel?

Yes. His voice when it came was calm, quiet, but his eyes were glassy with tears. *Yes,* he said. *He did.*

Her hand on his forearm. Her own tears hard to control now, because of course he was right. The refuge of water. She wiped her eyes: the sudden inkling of why he was here. The water had closed over him too like the answer to a question.

You won't find your father in Sydney, she said. *But there's a reason you are here, Axel.* She spoke gently, as if to a person just waking. The light moved around them, inching backward like a tide. Pearl could feel her own heart, its work timeless and blind.

Axel looked from the garden to his hands. The wine in the glass. He wondered not how to calculate the weight of water but of misery. Emptiness. The tears on her face. America, the thought automatic, comforting. Argentina. Australia. Åfors. Axel – Anders – America.

⁓

This is what the boy should not remember, what is disallowed: the light, the silence. All his senses shut down except this:

what he sees. So that feeling and sound, everything, became visual. Trepidation is a long grey plank he must walk along. The silence a cloth, soaked in ether, a rag for amputation. His sight is avian, whole worlds within its scope. Somewhere in the layers of sky air cloud mist tree roofs lake earth: his father. He is gone but utterly there, with him. There, there.

Everything is reduced to a sightline. He concentrates his eyes. Walks.

The light, the silence. A kind of white, or white-out, the colour of chalk on pale slate. Or smoke in a cloud. Even the lake, small trees crumbling at its edge, is the colour of milk. This is what he is trying to understand, to place, when he sees the men.

Four of them. They seem to emanate from water. They step through the shallows but their legs don't disturb it. The quality of their movement is grey. And slow. He doesn't know it, but his own pace has slowed to theirs, though they are still mid-distance, still part of a landscape stitched from dreams. He watches their dull movement, sluggish as the tide. Still, one falters, and at this moment sound returns, and touch: a bird crying, his own hands at his sides. Heavy, empty. As tired as his eyes. Suddenly.

Suddenly, now. His eyes. They refuse to see. Refuse. Because the man, faltering, has moved his arms, adjusted his grip on the form they carry. Boat-shaped, man-sized, grey like the water and their faces. He stops. Everything. Stops. So he sees but doesn't see: the ankles, the one boot and its laces lolling, the flash of colour, obscene, that might be father flesh and might be a sound rather than a colour, the sound of a shout, his own throat, and then nothing. Except white. Sky and ground and sheets pulled up, his mother's face white against his.

⁓

There is no memory of after, save shards of things, something unseen, something refused. Life mixed up his senses again, so for a while he tasted numbers and felt flavours, heard colours. Even when this was righted – he remembered doctors, talking – there was nothing where his voice used to be. *Have you used up all your words, Axel?* His mother would ask. Not angry. *Are there none left?* He looked at her face and wondered what she meant.

There were afternoons, days, with his grandmother or his uncles. In his grandmother's kitchen he rolled out dough for cinnamon buns, stirred the soup. One day a thought turned round and round with the spoon: his father had gone and was it his fault? Had he, Axel, wished him away? Was he somehow deficient, as a boy, as his father's son? Perhaps that was why he had been sent away. Away from his mother, from the house they had lived in. He stood in the silent garden where his grandmother's poppies flamed like questions. He felt punished, exiled. He stood alone, looking out: there were cows in the field beyond the fence, their bodies of brown velvet. They dipped their heads to the grass, calm, as people dipped their heads in prayer. The pine trees whispered psalms into the stillness. He looked to the sky. Not wanting answers. Wanting his mother.

—

It was in the glass shed that sound returned, rolling through his mouth like soft wind in grass. *It has a secret,* he said to Lars. There in front of him, his uncle was coaxing mystery from fire and light, or so it seemed. Out of the elements of the earth, sand and minerals and water and heat: something hard that could yet be broken. Impossible but it happened here, a metamorphosis, those elements blazing into a globe of glass, a drop made solid, a wish, a hope, materialised there in front of him in the dim shed where the blowers shone with sweat, even in December.

He was aware of his uncle's eyes on him. Flickering up from the maver, the bench where he rolled out his magic, pure, transparent.

Yes, Lars said. He looked at Axel, curious. *You're quite right. You have to find it. Its beauty has to be located, worked for.*

Shell

The glass inside you. Axel stared at the shape. *You can't let it break.* He could sense its power, its consolation. That this might be his life, might save him: the making of a watery reality, a solidity, turning the inchoate into something to hold in his hand. Not long afterwards, he made his first piece of glass. Even then he was making something solid from a vacuum: the rain, the melted snow, the lake. His liquid world. The small, rough cylinder he produced could hold something, he told his mother. Water, flowers, schnapps. *Or it could just be,* she said, setting it on the kitchen bench.

Gradually he saw that everything was mediated by water. As if he looked through it to or at the world, making it more substantial, more able to be apprehended. That, he thought, is what he wanted from this: to find and hold the memory of water.

So he began to go more and more to the glass shed. He was happy there. He entered not just the room but the feeling of the glass. The qualities of it a comfort to him, the glass itself a place to enter, an atmosphere, a room. Here no one spoke of his father. As if the mention of him might disturb the thin membrane they survived beneath, all of them. The caul of safety and silence they had made or submitted to, he didn't know. Or couldn't remember.

His memory had been cleaved in two.

Summer, January 1966

She stepped into the new year as if it was a dark new country, full of unfamiliar scenes and air. Time stretched out, week after week, each one a trapdoor to fall through. Potentially. She wanted to see her brothers.

There'd been one phone call, both of them exhausted, vague. The training was hard, day and night, in all weather. Yes, they'd let her know. Yes, they'd ring their father. And they did call Patrick at Christmas, their voices manly through the phone according to the young nurse who held it to Patrick's ear. They didn't call her and she wasn't surprised. The things Patrick did not know, could not ask.

Two pieces of her 'Affront' series were scheduled for the summer break. Tennant and Dark. Judith had given her the news as she would a surprise Christmas present. *People have more time to read in the holidays,* she'd beamed.

No one will read them in the holidays. Pearl smiled as she walked away. *Have you noticed circulation numbers in January?* She was meant to feel grateful they were even getting a run.

349

Back at her desk she pulled out the file and knew she would not write the others.

⌒

When she finally heard Jamie's voice down the line her blood ran hot and cold. Joy and trepidation, and in the end it was just that: he'd be out soon on a Skippy flight to join the 1RAR. But Will wouldn't. *Same wrist he broke up north,* Jamie said. *Came down hard on a training run.* He was unlikely to go at all.

When will you? she asked.

No date, he said. And paused. *Strange now to go without him.*

When he rang off, she called Suze. Unable to face an empty flat after work. *My last art students have graduated,* Suze said, *come and celebrate.* She gave Pearl an address in Surry Hills. *They're young, but they're interesting.*

⌒

It was close to midnight. He looked at his watch, startled by the numbers, the minute hand relentless. Time had detached itself from the room, from him, the hours atomised. He looked around, walked to the windows, saw the compacted hours of stillness outside the glass. Perhaps it was he, Axel, who had detached himself. What was it that Pearl had said? *It seems like you're there, but are you?* He looked again at the watch face. It was meaningless. The second hand drifted between numbers, began again. He raised his eyes to the room and knew his mind had been temporarily lost.

But no, there were no visions, no ghouls sweeping in from the harbour, no tremors. He slumped in a chair, held up his palms; steady, dry, familiar, brushed by grains of sand and colour. Blue, from the work he'd been at so blindly and for so long. That was it; he'd been blinded by his own vision, his own eyes. Hadn't noticed time gather itself in the room and bolt. But now his body felt it, all the hours and minutes he'd spent, in his fingers and hands, in his back, in his eyes. He angled his glasses from his face and propped them on his knee; rubbed his eyes with the heels of his hands. Took up his glasses again and circled the lenses with his handkerchief, felt his breathing slow with the rhythm. Then stood, walked around the table with its small, hard-worked pieces, covering them with sheets. Triple-locked the door on his way out.

No night shift tonight. Was there a strike? He walked quickly around the shells, checking. They glowed ethereal in the darkness. He'd been sure, since the night he'd seen the architect, that he would see him there again. If he only knew his schedule, his timing. He stepped around the cranes and glanced beneath the podium. No one. Loped towards the gate. Behind him the building hunched in the thick dark like a tired animal, slumped in sleep. He skirted around lengths of plywood boxing. The air from the harbour was clean and cool and encouraging, and though his limbs were tired he set off towards home as if he'd just woken from restful sleep. As if he was happy.

He walked around the quay to Cadman's Cottage. Had made the top of the stairs behind it, one foot lifted to the next step onto the street. His body in motion, so he felt, later, that the explosion had lifted him off the ground. A solitary lamp lit his way, and the beam of light itself seemed to move, splintering like a firework and then re-forming itself. Initially he thought: a collision. Bus or tram, something big. But the street was nearly empty. A constellation of thoughts ignited around him. If it wasn't a vehicle. If there was no ship at anchor. If it was behind him then ... Panic hurled itself up across the steps and through his body; he turned like a clockwork figure and leapt back down, running before he knew he was, back down the quay.

～

Pearl left the party in Surry Hills without any clear idea of the time. Late. That was what her eyes registered: the streets empty, the houses quiet. Christ. She'd have to walk halfway home before she found a cab. Stars smeared the sky above the terraces. Milky Way: it looked different in the quiet. More obvious. But there were faint flares of lightning above the horizon and the air felt electric. Unless it was the home-made wine. The Italian boy had pressed her to taste it, topped up her glass when she turned her back. The wine was rich, lovely, and the boy good-looking. She'd laughed off his approaches; he was only seventeen. That's what she'd said. Or eighteen? I'm the age of consent, he'd smirked in a broad Australian accent.

She was aware of her stilettos, chiming on bitumen like an invitation. Tried to step softly. Unsuccessful. Felt in her bag then for her mother's hatpin, buried in a side pocket. It was a sentiment, not a precaution, that's what she'd told herself, but now she fingered it as she entered another darkened street. Stepped up her pace.

Later, she would be uncertain of what came first: sound or feeling. Or if both swelled together into the sudden heat that rose in her body, a flash of danger she felt first as the street, the ominous dark, before the stars shattered around the impact of thunder. Only it wasn't. She stood still, not falling. This confused her too, that the impulse to drop, to minimise herself, had failed her. The sky reassembled itself. It was not thunder. And it emanated from somewhere around the harbour. She was suddenly sober. Pulling off ridiculous shoes. Running at full pelt towards Hyde Park.

A knot of people at the fountain. She stopped, caught her breath. Tugged someone's sleeve. *Some kind of explosion.* The boy had a Beatles haircut and bad teeth. *A big one. Could be the Opera House.*

She turned and yelled, waved her hands. Whistled as a cab slid into view, leapt into its front seat. *Opera House*, she breathed, *close as you can get.* All the way down Elizabeth Street and into Phillip she prayed to the god she didn't believe in. *Axel Axel Axel.* Past the courts and she could see: fire engines and police screaming towards the Point. *Here!* she snapped as the cab neared Customs House, opening the door before it stopped. She pulled pound notes from her purse. And ran.

~

He rounded the quay with no notion of how he'd got there. No longer himself but an assembly of muscle and bone. The first sirens screamed and he ran faster. Trying to see the source of the sinister orange glow, the flames. A fire truck behind and another coming. They screamed over and over: *the glass the glass the glass.* It might have been inside him.

He reached the Point and police already gathering. He breathed, smiled: the Opera House was as still and quiet as a chapel. He laughed then, bent over his knees, sick with relief. It wasn't the building. When a police officer approached, Axel said, *I work here.* The officer shrugged and walked away. *Well you can't tonight.* Then looked back, cocked his head towards the south. *Could be more, we're closing it off.*

~

On the road around the quay, blue uniforms, fire engines, people running against her. She pushed past them. And there, two hundred yards away, crouched in the glare of search beams and street lights, the shells of the Opera House, their clean lines untouched by disaster.

Sirens cut into the air; their screams relieved her. She was not imagining, then. Couldn't be: somewhere to her right, another, softer blast of sound. Thunder growled. A bright flash that might have been lightning, or might have been in her head, her ears.

Now a wall of blue uniforms. She dug around for her press pass, slipped past the police. *Telegraph*, she said to one. *What is it?* He glanced at her and said: *Explosion on a vessel, round past Mrs Macquarie's Chair.* And turned away. Over his shoulder: *Stay behind the lines.*

But relief gave way to a new terror now. The danger was not only in the explosion itself, in shrapnel and debris; it was in rolling waves of sound. This had happened in the war, she knew, and more rarely and precisely in places like the one on the Point: where a voice might erupt and pierce the air on the ecstatic, high points of a single note. A note that soared endless, gripping air and breath – until the splinter and starburst of a glass, symmetrical, perfect.

She ran on until metal reared, a fence, a barricade. As she reached it, a hand on her shoulder. Axel. His breath short from running, his face strange. He was staring past her; she turned to more police, some of them undercover, they were easy to pick. Among the white shirts and brown trousers, Ray. Murmuring to a cop next to him. They were all straight-faced, expressionless. Ray looked just like they did.

She spun back to Axel. This made her dizzy; the world tipped. When she opened her eyes he was gone: running past the containment line towards the gate of the Opera House. There was a shout from the police. She watched as Axel angled away from the blue uniforms, moving faster now, a lone figure against the rearing building. This transfixed her, his ghostly image, so she didn't notice, not at first, his track towards the water. Not until he was there, at the edge, until he lifted his body into a perfect curve, a line to match the shells glowing silver above the mayhem, and speared into the harbour.

Her hand jerked from her ear to her mouth.

⌐

He emerged to light, brighter than it should be, in splinters and shards. His body heavy in the water, dragging. But that was all it was, a sensory effect, transitory. A feeling like any other; it could be expunged with movement. The thing was: not to stop. He must reach his glasswork, use his hands to stop the shattering. It was Utzon's glass now. Axel paused, caught his breath. The water was dark, but the sky glowed orange. He lifted his arms, over and up. Kicked.

He'd discarded his shoes but not his watch. Flung them away as he pushed towards the end of the point. Unbuckled his trousers with one hand while the other beat against water and his legs kicked them free. He swam more easily then, a labouring stroke that was somewhere between breaststroke and the crawl the locals had made their own. His breaths came hard.

⌐

Pearl's legs moved before her brain caught up. Sudden thunder, knives of lightning and the trees in the Gardens turned livid. She ran towards them and into the sharp arms of police. *Fuck off!* Later, she will say that fist met eye socket without her volition. That a man had gone into the water without his own. She had to get to him. But now her head was locked in a vice of hard muscle, and there was Ray, hands in pockets, calmly watching as they cuffed her. Their eyes met as she was dragged away. Kicking. She was surprised at the first word that came to her: *Quisling*.

⁓

There was a moment when the rain came and the whole world was water. A confirmation. Or a baptism, it didn't matter. He stopped stroking and felt it; the pull, the surrender. More lightning and it would be easy, in that fluorescence, to concede. The harbour lit from within. And he was tired. But then the deep percussion of thunder. His mother's face. He kicked. Arms pushed away, pushed away water. He scrambled up and onto the rocks at Mrs Macquarie's Chair. Ran.

Rain had turned the surrounding gardens silver, leaves indistinct. The glint of water, grass, trees. A collision of joy and terror; he could save him, couldn't he? If the glass was intact. If it had survived, so would Utzon. The trees in shadow, flick, flick, flickering, his legs pneumatic now, they pump over moss and leaf, barely touch the ground. He is above, he is flying. And all the time the dull flames on the edge of his vision. Don't look around, keep to the course.

The sky lowering. Faster. In his head now the story

of Utzon's children. Running, like him, through a forest of trees to meet the train, to meet their father, to tell him the good news. He had won the competition. He would build the Opera House. Their legs flying over the forest floor.

Leaf. Dark water. Sky. The harbour not the harbour but a huge animate thing, black. It spoke to him and listened to him in turn. The dark folding in, but he is almost there, he feels the nearness of it in his feet and his hands, in his mouth, where the words wait, swelling out of him, thickening on his tongue. *Here I am!* He will let them fall into his father's face, lighting it with triumph. With joy.

Woolloomooloo Bay in peopled darkness. All eyes on the fire dying in the water, on the outline of a vessel, smouldering not so far from the wharf. He slipped into the shadows of the shed. No key. None was needed; a side window had cracked and shattered. His stomach turned. He cleared the glass and crawled inside.

The storm had passed, and remnants of moonlight cut through the dark. Axel stood, hands useless at his side. The glasswork was whole, its shape intact. Still he could not breathe, waited for light to glance over its curves. And there, along its shimmering flank, its textured surface so clean, so hard won, a crack like a whip mark, a scar. Fine as a fresh knife wound.

The world split open. He opened his mouth and didn't hear himself cry.

—

They were all wise in retrospect. Ray and ASIO, the set-up: they'd all suspected. But didn't say. Pearl knew: they felt the same way she did, naïve, ashamed. *Blown out of the water,* she said to Bridget and tried to laugh. They sat on benches in a cell that smelled of vomit and Phenyle. So much for instinct. Now she was more unsure than ever: who could be relied on, who was real. Suspicious of everyone, chiefly herself.

They weren't surprised to find themselves in the lock-up. Though Brian couldn't account for Axel, who had been brought in before them and discharged, they were told. *What was Sweden doing here?* he said. *Broke the police lines,* Pearl shrugged. *They thought he was one of us.*

It took twenty-four hours for their bail to be posted. *Some elderly woman,* the sergeant said. He peered at the charge sheet. *Name of Olive Jarratt.*

Outside they turned to Pearl as if she, like Ray, had been in disguise. *What do you mean, his landlady?* But Pearl was already turning away. Her wrists tender from the cuffs, the smell of sweat and disinfectant on her. She caught a cab to The Rocks.

February 1966

In his memory there is just this: the fire, the water. His body in its hold. The darkness.

There was nothing in the water, was there Axel? Pearl had held his hand, his arm, as she sat by his bed in the Mercantile. Words had left him again; she spoke to him, for him. *Only you. And you came out.*

—

Pearl had expected an older version of Axel but the man she met at the door of the shed was brown-haired, grey-eyed, his face pale after two days of flying. He shook her hand formally and she saw the resemblance then, in the way he held himself, the tilt of his head. Together, she and Lars stepped into the glass shed.

The sun had moved to the windowless side, so she flicked on the light.

And stood without moving. Before her, a vision: a crystalline boat, and it shimmered in the air as it might in water, suspended low from the ceiling on fine steel wire.

As long as a lifeboat, or more, but tapered at each end, part canoe, part longship. It was shot through with the colours of the harbour but at different angles it seemed transparent, so the observer looked through a spectrum of blue, or saw a blue of their own making. Pearl stood still, a breath caught in her throat. The beauty of it. The astounding lines, the surface so tactile she had reached her hand out to rest on its curve without realising. The warmth a surprise. She looked to Lars to find him weeping.

To rescue, he said. *To reclaim.*

At eye level, the shapes within the cavity might be floating, submerged by flood or tide. A ragged piece from a celestial map. A clock face undulating in brine. Two figures, arms outstretched, reaching or floating in embryonic fluid. Sleeping. Drowned. Other shapes, indecipherable as sea wrack, weightless as dreams. Each altered with perspective, with the angle of sight, each more than the sum of their parts.

Above them, across the body of the boat, a pair of broken oars. Made not from glass but some fragile wood, petrified. Or was it? Pearl wasn't sure. They might be fossilised, ancient. Broken oars. Their shape, the jagged surfaces where they were torn apart, suggested a journey interrupted, a violent elision. Or some potential unmet, a promise not kept. Loss.

But the blue: cobalt? Pearl couldn't say. It was piercing or soft, glowing, depending on the angle of light and where the observer stood. How it was seen. Ethereal, perhaps. Otherworldly one minute, and in the next – a step this way or that, eyes open or squinting – utterly of this place. In its ambiguity, part transparent, part reflective, part shimmer and translucence, Pearl could hear their conversations, hers and Axel's. The uncertainty of glass, of its substance, how it destabilised perception and truth. The boat was at once a vessel and an element in itself, born of fire and water and ash, of salt. As humans were.

Lars walked slowly around the suspended shape, bending this way and that, looking from all angles. The split ran from end to end, an unstitched wound. He lifted his hand to it, ran his fingers along the edge. Turned his head slowly from side to side. *Yes,* he said quietly, *it can be fixed.* The words heavily accented. *But it will be up to him. When he is better. When he is himself, again.* He looked at her. *I will take him home until he is. His mother is waiting.*

~

She walked along the quay towards the ferry. The city quiet, unmarked by the turmoil of the past weeks and her own life. This town! She stopped at a news stand to buy flowers and cigarettes. Its posters still blared the aftermath of the bombing, the charges against members of some protest group. 'Bludgers and cowards!' one poster blared. *But we all know it was ASIO,* she said to the attendant, a small smile on her lips. *Don't we?*

He handed over her change. *Old news now,* he said evenly. *They've just sacked the bloke who did the Opera House.*

It took a long time to settle herself. Utzon was gone, and she was glad Axel was not here to know. But as she stepped aboard the ferry she realised that of course, he had antici-pated it. The evidence was hung in the jagged air of the glass shed by the harbour at Woolloomooloo.

The ferry tacked towards Bennelong Point. She pulled three stems from the bunch she'd carried. The callistemon had already begun to shed its crimson and gold, but the rough bouquet would still please him, she knew. He'd loved these ordinary flowers. As he'd loved Utzon and the unordinary building that soared beside her now. Its shells partly tiled and shining, pearlescent. She went to the rail of the ferry, leaned over glass-blue water, and cast the flowers to the wind.

Author's Note

This book had its genesis in a handful of small incidents, pre-occupations and alignments that gradually coalesced, bringing together two blood lines, two hemispheres, two landscapes: Scandinavia and Australia. The physical and cultural legacies of my Swedish father and Australian mother, questions and ways of thinking that grew, rather than diminished, through my writing life.

It might have begun the day when, like Axel, I stood in a rain storm and watched raindrops smack onto bitumen and form the exact shape of some of my Swedish candleholders. Or the day I drove through the glass province of Småland, north of my father's country, and found myself on roads that seemed to run over lakes. Or the moment in a newsroom when I realised I could no longer live with my journalistic objectivity.

But it was truly born, I think, when one of my Norwegian nieces came to Australia and couldn't leave until she'd seen the Opera House. We flew south, her family and me, and crawled over and around the building in a way I never had before. The children ran their hands over white tiles made in Sweden. Their thoughts vaulted with the arc of the shells imagined by a Dane. This, I saw, was their building too, its concept and lines miraculous but not strange to them. It was something to do with the grandeur and humility implicit in its shapes. Scandinavians have no trouble holding two opposing ideas in their heads at the same time. The Opera House, with its massive base and steps and soaring shells, encapsulates this.

Later that morning, on a ferry across the harbour, I watched the Opera House recede and knew I was seeing it through their eyes, their Scandinavian way of looking, their sensibility. From that moment I developed a kind of double vision of the building, of this city, of this country. Or realised I'd always had it. That, I knew, was where I wanted to write from: a place where there were no hard certainties, no one way of looking. Only *a* way of seeing.

My fixation with glass was, of course, part of that. As a substance it prohibits certainty, prohibits one interpretation. I am magnetised by its Janus face: hard and yet fragile, something created from the minerals of earth and sea. Its expressive and utilitarian potential. It has always been around me: in my parents' home and the homes of my Swedish relatives, candles burned from glass cups in window alcoves and on tables and sideboards; akvavit is drunk from tiny thimbles of crystal and sweets or jewellery are dropped into transparent bowls on ledges and shelves. Each time I visit them, I leave with one or two pieces wrapped in scarves in my luggage.

But it wasn't until a summer some years ago that I became magnetised by the art and meaning of the substance, its metaphorical underpinnings in the country. Driving north from Skåne with my cousin through the glass country, I noticed for the first time how the road ribboned between lakes. They were plates of water, glass-like. The whole province was more water than land. Of course glass would be made in such a place, I thought. The vague outline of Axel Lindquist was born. The character shares the name, the gentle persistence and quiet humour of both my Swedish grandfather and my Australian grandson.

~

The mid-sixties were watershed years in Australia. The old was giving way to the new, the young. Our eyes finally moved away from Britain and glanced elsewhere, mainly to the United States, and the idea of social change, of minority uprisings, began to travel like a rumour. The young began to question the fusty complacency of established orders in politics, gender, sex, race and art. On other continents and in Asia, the scent of war and revolution was in the air, and by 1965 it had begun to waft towards Australia. For a writer infatuated with the notion of neutrality, the peace movement and conscription, that year was like a bright beacon.

It brought together two seemingly disparate events: the Australian government's decision to send conscripts to the war in Vietnam and the dramatic decline in political and media favour of Jørn Utzon, the Danish architect of the Opera House. Another character strode onto my mind's stage: a spirited journalist named Pearl Keogh, whose own notions of political neutrality and personal objectivity might be challenged by the events of that year. As a journalist struggling with notions of injustice, as a woman fighting her own female preoccupations with guilt and honour, she *might* share a particular emotional makeup with me.

I made my first trip to Sweden with my family in my mid-teens. I was named for my Swedish grandmother, and perhaps that contributed to the strong connection I felt for the place long before I saw it. In my childhood the *idea* of it was all around me: there were frequent visits by friends of my father's from the ships he'd worked on; Swedish names seemed to dominate those of the companies he dealt with as an electrical engineer, and there were my grandmother's letters and postcards and the stories my father told. Despite his determination to make a new life away from the old, my own Australian sense of the world was always mediated by the push of my Swedish blood, my growing awareness of Sweden's otherness. Looking back, I can see I learned early to size one country up against the other.

The idea that a nation could actively choose not to take part in armed conflict was very attractive to a thin-skinned child sensitive to every hurt and slight. It wasn't until my own politicisation years later that I understood the complexities of it, the enduring resentments against Sweden around the globe. What neutrality gives a country, what it takes away. What people will do within its confines. Its personal nature came home to me as a journalist when I realised that, on some issues like injustice, like racism, I could no longer remain outside, no longer *not* take a side.

But these seeds were sewn when I was a child. It was my mother who, very early, opened my eyes to these issues with her strong notions of fairness and equality, her compassion for those who suffered. And it was my mother who was responsible for my vehemence around conscription. Not true national service, in which men and women commit to defending their country with the assurance they won't be sent to overseas wars, a system which the Scandinavians have used for years. This was about Australia forcing young men to leave to fight wars which were not theirs. Federal governments tried it in World War I (and failed at two referenda to enforce it) and got away with it partially in World War II, when the concept of 'overseas' was dropped for service in New Guinea. And again in Korea.

But Menzies was triumphant in Vietnam. It was after the tragedy of that war that my mother began to talk about conscription and war more often, in language I've never forgotten and gave to the character of Amy Keogh, Pearl's mother. One morning my then young son was helping my mother and me clean out my bookshelves, dislodging the sticky nests left in books by wasps in Queensland summers. I don't recall how the subject came up, but I do remember the look in my son's eyes when his grandmother said to him: *You know, if there's ever a war like that again, you won't be going. I'll hide you in an attic somewhere. Or shoot off one of your toes.*

My gentle mother. She smiled at him then and he smiled back, understanding it for what it was. An expression of love. He would not be lost, under any circumstances.

It took me years to understood it properly myself. By then, we'd been reunited with my brother Peter, the child stolen from my mother's arms when he was just a year old. It accounted for the indecipherable grief that burned in her all our childhoods, her tight grip on us and our safety. After Peter returned I did the calculation: during the years of Vietnam, this is what my mother knew and we didn't: she had a son of conscriptable age. In those long years, she had no idea where he was. The knowledge lodged in me like a stone, and it has never left.

But as with all my books, *Shell* was not written because I knew something. I write, always, compulsively, because I *don't* know something. It is always about a question. Or several. Ideas and notions and doubts coalesce into a long and intricate conversation with myself, or with an invisible other. In this case the conversation lasted five years. At the end of that process I find I have no solid answers, no certainties. Only possibilities, a whole new set of questions. The more I write, and read, and the older I get, the more comfortable I am with *un*certainty. With being the humble servant of the questions, the story.

Kristina Olsson 2018

Acknowledgements

My thanks and gratitude to:

Bertil Vallien, master glass artist, for the pivotal conversation in Småland, the generosity of time and ideas.

My sister, Sharon, as ever: for your steadfast love and support, and for getting me on the plane to Sweden.

The many friends who have held and reassured me through the past five years, have championed this book's potential and reassured me when I couldn't. In no particular order: Marg O'Donnell, Jill Rowbotham, Debbie Kilroy, Donna Hancox, Cathy Sinclair, Jo Clifford, Sandra Hogan, Jennifer Batts, Emma Felton, Alex and Stephanie Miller, Kaylene Smith, Sally Piper, Charlotte Wood and her Sydney writers' group, Paula Peeters and Raymond Carpenter and everyone at Sisters Inside.

Most especially: Krissy Kneen, Ashley Hay and Anthony Mullins for support above and beyond. My family in Sweden and in Norway. And in Yorkshire, Sarah Moor and Keith Mott, for many things but especially time in The Roost, where the last paragraphs of *Shell* were (finally) written.

My friend Raymond Evans for historical facts at odd times of the day and night. Bev Fitzgerald for the precious copy of *A Vision Takes Form,* by the artist Robert Emerson Curtis. *A Vision* is one of several books I've had at my side for the past five years including the superb *Building a Masterpiece: the Sydney Opera House,* edited by Anne Watson, and *Vallien,* by Gunnar Lindqvist.

Shell

The staff at Kosta Boda-Orrefors in Småland, and those at the Sydney Opera House and the Mitchell Library for vital assistance.

As always, my family, for holding me up along this lengthy path: Tony, Zoe, Justine, Dane and Anita, my brothers Peter, Ashley, Andrew (especially for crucial advice in physics), Allie Olsson and Mary Venning, and the extended Chambers and de Goey tribe. And for the light and joy they bring me, the children: Amber, Axel, Oskar and Charlie.

A thousand thanks to Jane Novak, for your insight and energy and all you've given this book, and to Fiona Henderson and Dan Ruffino at Simon & Schuster Australia for the depth of your vision, your boundless enthusiasm and commitment to me and to *Shell*. Thanks also to the rest of the wonderful S&S family at Cammeray, especially Michelle Swainson and Anna O'Grady, and to my other S&S publishing families at Atria in New York – with special thanks to Sarah Cantin – and to Ian Chapman and Suzanne Baboneau at Scribner UK in London. I'd also like to thank designer Christa Moffit for her superb cover and photographer jp Bratanoff-Firgoff for allowing us to use his spectacular image.

This book has been supported by a grant from the Literature Board of the Australia Council, a fellowship from Griffith Review and residencies at Varuna, the Writers House. An extract of *Shell* appeared in *Griffith Review 58: Storied Lives*.